QUICKSILVER ECSTASY

"Do you love me?" Jordan asked at last.

Kathleen turned her head away. "Yes," she answered calmly, her heart beating so fast she could almost hear it. "But it doesn't change anything. I want to share more than just the physical side of love with you." His hand touched her cheek and she jerked away. "Please, I don't have much strength where you're concerned. Don't tempt me. I know now how much you want me, and I want you, too, but—"

"Want you!" The harsh exclamation indicated that Kathleen had understated his need.

Her movement away from him was roughly checked. His hand captured her face, lifting it to meet his descending mouth. Her resistance lasted only for an instant as his hard, demanding kiss aroused the response she had known it would.

Circling her arms around his waist, she allowed herself to be swept away by pure desire. His hands slid down, molding her pliant flesh against the hard contours of his male body. His mouth parted her willing lips, sending quicksilver fires of ecstasy through her veins . . .

from "The Matchmakers"

Books by Janet Dailey

CALDER PROMISE

SHIFTING CALDER WIND

GREEN CALDER GRASS

MAYBE THIS CHRISTMAS

SCROOGE WORE SPURS

A CAPITAL HOLIDAY

ALWAYS WITH LOVE

BECAUSE OF YOU

CAN'T SAY GOODBYE

DANCE WITH ME

EVERYTHING

FOREVER

"The Devil and Mr. Chocolate"
in the anthology
THE ONLY THING BETTER THAN
CHOCOLATE

DANCE WITH ME

Janet Dailey

ZEBRA BOOKS
KENSINGTON PUBLISHING CORP.
http://www.kensingtonbooks.com

ZEBRA BOOKS are published by

Kensington Publishing Corp.
850 Third Avenue
New York, NY 10022

All Kensington titles, imprints and distributed lines are
available at special quantity discounts for bulk purchases for
sales promotion, premiums, fund-raising, educational or in-
stitutional use.

Special book excerpts or customized printings can also be
created to fit specific needs. For details, write or phone the
office of the Kensington Special Sales Manager: Kensington
Publishing Corp., 850 Third Avenue, New York, NY 10022.
Attn. Special Sales Department. Phone: 1-800-221-2647.

First Printing: July 2004
10 9 8 7 6 5 4 3 2 1

Printed in the United States of America

CONTENTS

FIRE AND ICE

CHAPTER ONE

"With your face and figure, it should be easy to get a husband. Too bad you were born with an ice-cold personality." The young man leaned back in the chaise set beside the Las Vegas hotel pool. He took a deep drag on his cigarette while studying the golden, tanned body of the young woman sun-bathing beside him.

"You forgot to add 'and my money,' Michael." Her eyes remained closed, shutting out the glare of the Nevada sun midway down in the afternoon sky. "And I wasn't born with an ice-cold personality. It took years of hard work before I successfully discovered its benefits."

His gaze traveled over her slim ankles and the slender long legs, the lime-green bikini that showed off her narrow waist and the gentle swell of her breasts, before stopping at her face to admire her perfect profile and the pale gold color of her naturally blond hair. An amused chuckle escaped his lips. She opened her eyes and stared at him quizzically.

"Poor Alisa." Michael stared at his cigarette rather than meet her clear blue eyes. "You hate men and yet you have to marry one!"

"There's nothing amusing about that!" Alisa Franklin said angrily, reaching for her gold cigarette case lying on the table beside Michael. She had given up trying to quit for another week, considering the stress she was under.

"Oh, come now." A cynical gleam brightened his eyes as he leaned over to light her cigarette. "Surely you see the irony of the situation, especially since you think it's all your mother's doing."

"My mother happened to believe that a woman wasn't complete without a man."

"And managed to marry five times to prove it!" Michael laughed. His lean body, clad only in black trunks, leaned back against the chair.

"She was a fool!" Alisa exclaimed. "Anyone could push her around. She knew how I loathed those summers I spent with Roy and Marguerite—and she was stupid enough to be taken in by their lies and state in her will that they were to have custody of Christine!"

"Not to mention all that money that goes with her," Michael added.

"I don't care about the money and you know it." She ground the half-smoked cigarette out in the ashtray. "Mother knew my father's trust fund left me amply provided for, which was the reason Christine was the main beneficiary of her will. The poor kid will never enjoy any of it with Marguerite and Roy in control. You should have seen the way she looked at me when I left her there yesterday. Damn it! What am I going to do?''

"I don't see what you're getting so excited about," he mocked. "Your mother stated very clearly in her will that *if* you were married, the custody of Christine would be yours. You merely have to marry someone. Kind of a strange arrangement in this day and age, but stranger things happen all the time. You aren't going to leave your sister with your aunt and uncle. I know you.''

Michael was right. She would never abandon Christine. Never.

"You forgot the other provision—I must live with whoever I marry for at least one year." Alisa lit another cigarette and puffed on it in angry frustration. "I wish you weren't my cousin, because you could solve all my problems. As it is, I can't think of one man I'd like to spend an evening with, let alone twelve months.''

"The only reason you tolerate me is because I don't stroke your ego the way everyone else does." Michael's mouth curled sardonically. "I knew you when you had braces on your teeth and were as skinny as a reed, tagging along after me like a puppy. I suppose your cynicism amuses me, as well as your money.''

"Don't sneer at me, Michael," Alisa said in a dangerously cold and quiet voice. "You're only twenty-six, just two years older than me. You're an adequate escort, very occasionally amusing company, but more importantly, you don't subject me to any degrading pawing.''

"Oh, my. The ice maiden has no cousinly affection for me at all? Then go ahead and buy a husband. He might be more satisfactory. I'd love to see you married to some domineering tyrant.''

"You can wipe that smug smile off your face, because I'll never marry anyone that I can't control and that's that!'' Alisa rose from her chair, sweeping her long white-gold locks away from her face before slipping on the lacy beach robe. "You did reserve a table for the Parisian revue this evening as I told you to do, didn't you? Or did you blow all the money I gave you on the dice tables?''

"No, I obeyed your imperial command and slipped an extra tip to the reservation clerk to get us a great table." He got to his feet, his lanky tall frame giving him only a three-inch advantage as he stood facing her. "I'll pick you up at eight-thirty. We'll have time for dinner before the eleven o'clock show." As Alisa turned to leave, Michael asked quietly, "What are you going to do about Christine?''

"Find a husband." Her voice was sharp and contemptuous. But as she continued, Michael heard the ringing pride creep through. "He'll be someone worthwhile, from an important family. I won't marry some fortune hunter and be laughed at. Not even for my sister!''

Alisa didn't wait for Michael to comment on her statement. She traversed the full length of the pool area, disdainful of the ogling male eyes and suggestive remarks that followed her. Her total disregard served to goad them to more attempts to get her attention, but Alisa's disinterest was genuine. Her only reaction was one of revulsion that left an unclean feeling when she finally reached her suite.

Only after she settled down in the marble bath filled with bubbling suds did she feel free of the disgusting traces of leering eyes. Once out, with an enormous white bath towel draped around her, she sat down in front of the vanity, gazing silently and absently at her composed reflection in the mirror. She had become accustomed to the perfection that stared back. Only once had Alisa wished she had been born a plain Jane, but that had quickly passed. Her own love of beauty would have rejected the lack of it in her own appearance. She realized that, had she been plain, she would quite likely have been ridiculously romantic—and foolish, mooning and sighing over men like so many women did.

But those silly notions were behind her, gone with the braces and the endless waiting until her body had matured enough to catch up with her gangling long legs. With an amused and bitter smile, Alisa realized how much she owed her mother. Her mother had divorced Alisa's father, her first husband, only three years after the birth of their only child. Two years later, when she was nearly five, he was killed in a car crash. She had clung childishly to his image, bestowing on him all the positive attributes that she dreamed a father would have. But the parade of men through her mother's life had quickly tarnished her faith. It had seemed to Alisa that she was forever being shuttled off to her aunt Marguerite and uncle Roy's to make way for another honeymoon or another divorce.

The summer of her fifteenth birthday had been the most traumatic of all.

Her third stepfather, wealthy as all her mother's husbands were, had taken an intense interest in Alisa. The soft curves of womanhood had just begun to show on her slender, boyish frame. Her teeth had been straightened by braces and the unsightly wires were gone. For a month Alisa had basked in the warm glow of his attention. They had gone sailing together nearly every day. Her mother, who was a terrible sailor, had remained ashore. It was on one of those expeditions that Alisa had become aware of a change in his behavior.

It was a gorgeously sunny day, perfect for lazy sunbathing on the deck. The slight breeze had died, leaving the sails slack underneath the warm rays of the sun. Alisa had lain stretched out on the sailboat's deck, her swimsuit of the summer before not quite fitting her newly formed curves. She remembered her stepfather walking towards her, stopping to stare down at her; remembered being puzzled by his gaze and the curious light in his eyes. A strange fear had swept over her when Alisa remembered they were alone on the boat and at least two miles from shore. She had shaded her eyes from the brilliant sun to gaze up at him, noticing for the first time the dissipated lines around his mouth, the paunch that hung over his swimming trunks, and the can of beer in his hand, one of a constant supply.

He had knelt down beside her, his eyes resting on the slight cleavage of her swimsuit top before moving to the pale gold topknot of hair on her head.

"Take your hair down, Alisa," he had commanded thickly.

Her fingers had fumbled to obey as a shiver of fear raced through her. As her hair had cascaded down on to her shoulders, her stepfather's hand had reached out to capture the spun gold in his hands. Aware that what was happening wasn't right, Alisa had attempted to stand, but he quickly pinned her to the deck, his heavy breathing sending waves of alcoholic odor over her face as she tried to turn away.

"How about a kiss for your old stepdad?" he had muttered.

It was utterly sordid, the kind of story that provided material for talk shows and income for psychiatrists. Alisa had done her best to forget the ugly details, but they had haunted her ever since.

Kicking, scratching, and screaming, Alisa had tried to ward him off, but without much success as he at last had covered her mouth with his. The disgustingly repulsive memory of his mouth practically slobbering over her face was as fresh today as it was that afternoon when she had finally broken free and dived over the side. Luckily she had managed to flag down a passing boat which took her to shore, where she had sobbed out the story to her horrified mother.

Not even her mother's divorce and subsequent successful marriage to Dale Patterson had managed to erase or blot out the events of that afternoon. Her cool reserve had begun. As she moved through her teens, Alisa was aware her looks were the envy of girlfriends and that any of the more popular boys were hers for the asking. But few boys interested her enough, and those that did had always met the same fate.

Alisa had realized with growing disgust that once she accepted a date with a boy, it wasn't the pleasure of her company that he was interested in. At first she had tried to endure the good-night kisses, but they always expected more the next time. Gradually she refused all dates, hating the sense of obligation that came with the acceptance. She shunned nearly every social gathering, and those she couldn't, she was escorted to by her cousin Michael.

There were only two things she enjoyed in life anymore, her precious half-sister Christine and the gaming tables in Las Vegas. Alisa's gambling wasn't an obsession; if she won, she stopped. If she was getting behind, she stopped too, always knowing that as long as her inheritance held out, there was always another day. But Christine? Alisa sighed deeply, removing a brush from the table, and began brushing her hair. There was no question about whether or not she wanted Christine.

Dear, darling little Christine whom Alisa had taken care of since her babyhood. To keep Christine, Alisa had to have a husband, a seemingly simple acquisition for someone so beautiful and wealthy, but a galling one at the same time. Even as names and faces danced in her head, Alisa was rejecting them. Never once did she doubt that if she chose one, she would fail somehow to get him to the altar. She loathed the more acceptable ones who were quick to cater to her just as she feared the ones who would attempt to force themselves on her. If only she *could* go out and buy herself a husband, Alisa thought with a sad little smile.

Although the entire revue had been well staged from the dazzling routines of the scantily clad dancers to the individual acts of the entertainers, Alisa hadn't been able to enjoy the show. Her mind was centered on finding a solution to her problem. When Michael had picked her up earlier in the evening, Alisa had been determined to put her thoughts behind her, taking forever to choose her dress before finally settling on a new silver lamé evening gown, sleeveless with a mandarin collar. With it she had worn a black lace shawl with silver threads running through the rose design. Her pale blond hair was swept back into a sophisticated chignon at the nape of her neck.

As they entered the casino area, Michael paused near the dice tables, a feverish gleam lighting his eyes as he watched the dice bounce across the green felt. Poor Michael, Alisa thought without much sympathy. He had run through his inheritance in less than a year, but still he was anxious to lose more at the tables. She touched his elbow lightly and reluctantly he followed her as she continued wandering through the crowds.

The din of ecstatic winners and disgruntled losers mingled with the jangling bells of the slot machines and the casual voices of croupiers and dealers. People in expensive evening clothes rubbed elbows with others in sportswear. It was an incongruous mixture amidst the plush carpeting and dazzling chandeliers. There seemed to be only one place where the élite were separated from the average Joes and Josephines, and Alisa knew that her casual pace would eventually bring her to the secluded baccarat table.

Stopping at the ornate railing that isolated the players from the crowded casino floor, Alisa felt the nervous thrill she always experienced when she was about to take part in this aristocratic game of chance. Michael stood silently by her side, watching the coolness of her expression with the same amazement he felt every time they went through this routine. In a moment she would turn to him and discreetly pass him some money so that he could go off to his own game at the dice tables.

Through large, unexpressive blue eyes, Alisa studied the play in progress and the players. As her gaze drifted around to each person, she ignored the younger women at the table, employed by the casino to add color and attract legitimate players. Her pulse quickened as her eyes rested on the last player at the table.

His black hair gleamed under the soft glow of the chandelier. Under the dark eyebrows, thick dark lashes outlined his eyes, so dark brown that they appeared black. Even now, at this distance, Alisa could see the burning intensity of his gaze as he studied the cards before him. His cheekbones were well-defined, suggesting leanness that wasn't there. The long, narrow nose looked as uncompromising as the rest of him. Finally her eyes rested on the cruel line of his mouth.

Her left eyebrow lifted with her mounting excitement. There couldn't be two people who looked so much alike. A cool wave of resolution washed over her as Alisa turned slightly towards her cousin.

"That man sitting to the left of the croupier, what do you know about him?"

Michael glanced at her in surprise. Alisa was usually unconcerned about who she played with and rarely showed any interest in her fellow players, but his gaze went obediently to the man in question. As he recognized the man, Michael inhaled deeply to conceal his surprise. When he turned to Alisa he was equally surprised to see a glittering light in her eyes.

"That's Zachary Stuart. I haven't seen him in Vegas since before his father died. He's a ruthless gambler, or at least he was. He had the most uncanny luck at the tables, especially when you consider that he never seemed to care one way or the other. You'd do well to follow his lead in betting, Alisa.''

"I don't care how he gambles." Her gaze returned to the man at the table with a chilling calculation in her expression. "I want to know everything you know about him.''

"What for?" But at the freezing flash of her blue eyes, Michael shrugged resignedly. "You probably know as much as I do. I'm sure you've seen him at a couple of Elizabeth's parties in San Francisco. His father was a big import-export tycoon in San Francisco, dabbling in real estate and land developments. He went under about seven years ago when he invested a little too heavily in a development that was wiped out by mudslides. Rumor had it that the accident that killed him was really suicide, but it was never proved. Zachary—he was about twenty-five at the time—inherited all the debts, which is about the time he stopped coming to Vegas. I've heard that the only thing that he was able to keep, outside of his mother's house in San Francisco, was a small vineyard in Napa Valley. The winery and the vineyards had been abandoned for several years, so I understand, which means whatever profits he's made these last few years have been poured back into the property.''

Alisa permitted herself a smug smile when Michael finished. *So the arrogant Mr. Zachary Stuart is in need of money,* she thought with jubilant bitterness. "He looks like a man who would do anything for money," she said aloud.

"I don't know if I would put it quite that way.

Let's just say he would be pretty ruthless in getting what he wanted.''

"Is he married?"

"Him? No. Does he look like the marrying kind? Though a lot of women have tried." Michael laughed softly as he withdrew a cigarette from his pocket. "He views women the way you do men, with one exception. He believes women were put on earth for the purpose of providing a sexual outlet for men. I'm sure it's quite rare for him to find a woman who would deny him his pleasure." He glanced at Alisa with mocking amusement until he saw the grim expression on her face. "Oh, no, Alisa, if you're thinking what I think you're thinking, you'd better just forget it. There's one man that you couldn't make toe the line."

For half a second, Alisa felt a twinge of fear that Michael just might be right, but she quickly pushed such a thought aside. "He meets all the requirements: an important family name though a little impoverished, and first-class social credentials. It's all a matter of price, Michael dear."

"Think about how much you'll have to pay," Michael said, but Alisa ignored him. She walked forward to the roped gate, nodding serenely to one of the men when he escorted her in and seated her at the baccarat table beside Zachary Stuart.

Although Alisa received several appreciative glances from other male players, there was no such recognition coming from Zachary Stuart. She sensed his indifference and set about subtly drawing his attention to her. At first she waited to place her bet until he had done so, then deliberately bet opposite him. He played skillfully, as if Lady Luck were sitting on his lap. Still, he seemed unmoved by the growing stack of money in front of him and totally oblivious to Alisa's bets. Finally she removed a cigarette from her case, tapped it lightly on the table, and let it dangle in front of him absently as she watched the play. But when he courteously offered her a light, she declined and placed the cigarette back in its case. A few minutes later Alisa removed the cigarette again and just as Zachary's hand came out of his jacket pocket with a lighter, she turned to an older man on her other side and asked for a light. The deliberate snub got to him.

When Zachary refused his turn to deal the cards from the shoe, Alisa did likewise. The small stake that she had started with was nearly depleted, so she abstained from placing any bet. As she leaned against the back of the chair, she felt his dark gaze studying her. Now she turned to meet it, her own eyes sparkling with the excitement of this new game she was playing.

"Would you like to have a drink with me?" he asked in a low, carefully modulated voice that had a condescending ring to it, even as his dark gaze mocked her.

"I don't know you," Alisa replied coolly, reaching forward to stub her cigarette out in one graceful movement.

"I'm Zachary Stuart." He indicated to the banker that they would be cashing in.

"Alisa . . . Alisa Franklin," she said calmly, despite the quivering elation of triumph racing through her as he rose to pull out her chair for her.

Without asking her what she wanted to do next, Zachary Stuart proceeded to guide her towards one of the more secluded, dimly lit lounges on the edge of the casino floor. She discovered that he was even taller than she had thought. When Alisa was wearing heels, she was nearly five foot ten, which usually put any of her dates at eye level. But with Zachary Stuart, she just reached his chin. His height also gave the illusion of lankiness that was misleading, for his shoulders were wide and broad. Alisa was glad when they were finally seated at a small table and she no longer had to look at him.

He ordered two dry martinis, again without asking her, which she found irritating. With anyone else and in any other circumstances, Alisa would have refused the drink when it arrived at the table, merely to assert her authority though she probably would have ordered the same drink on her own. In this case, she managed to accept it graciously and quelled the tiny rebellion inside. As Alisa took a cigarette from her case and placed the filter-tipped end to her lips, a lighter snapped open and touched its yellow-orange flame to the cigarette.

"Tell me," Zachary Stuart said, "are you always like that?"

"I beg your pardon?" Alisa nearly choked on the smoke.

"That bit about who lights your cigarettes was an ingenious and insulting way to get my attention. You succeeded completely." His face was shadowed, but his voice left no doubt that he was amused by her ploy. "Alisa Franklin. I believe I've heard your name before."

"It's quite possible. My mother, Eleanor Patterson, was killed in a plane crash a few weeks ago."

"I can see you're in deep mourning for her." His sarcasm brought a coldness to her face, which she quickly tried to hide.

"I believe I've heard of you before, too, Mr. Stuart. Wasn't your father a very important person in San Francisco before his . . ." Alisa paused so that her words would carry the full implication, ". . . untimely death? You have a small vineyard now in Napa Valley or so they say."

"You seem to know a great deal about me."

"Oh, this and that," Alisa replied with biting softness. "How's business?"

Zachary leaned forward, the small candle on the table illuminating his expression. There was a sardonic curl to his lips.

"I have the strange feeling that if I said it was good you'd be disappointed." He regarded her with malicious amusement as a fleeting expression of discomfort flashed across her face. "I don't think you want the key to my hotel room, so . . . tell me exactly why you agreed to have a drink with me."

"Why waste time, right? I have a proposition for you, Mr. Stuart." At his disbelieving look, Alisa added hastily, "A business proposition."

When she paused for his reaction, Zachary moved back into the shadows of the lounge. Alisa tried to stifle her growing irritation, but some sharpness crept through.

"I understand that you're financially strapped right now and that you could use some money to make improvements on your vineyard and winery. I'm prepared to give you that money."

"That's very interesting. I can't help wondering why you should choose my business to invest in. There must be something you hope I'll give you in return."

The barest hint of a blush touched her cheeks

as Alisa straightened her shoulders and lifted her chin and spoke with as much dignity as she could.

"I need a husband."

A short, derisive laugh came from the man across the table. "There must be any number of marriage-minded men who would jump at the chance to marry a beautiful woman like you. I recall hearing your name linked with Paul Andrews. Why don't you marry him?"

"Paul?" For a brief moment, Alisa tried to put a face to the name, before the image of a strong, gentle man with light brown, almost blond hair came to mind. "Oh, him. Always panting at my heels like a puppy dog. I wasn't interested." Alisa's voice made her distaste clear, although her expression remained composed and indifferent.

"Did you hear he attempted suicide when you ordered him to leave you alone? It was about a year ago, I think."

"That was a gutless thing to do. And he couldn't succeed at that either." Alisa wasn't about to be distracted from the business at hand. "My marriage would only be temporary. That's why I'd prefer it to be to a stranger."

"Are you pregnant?"

"Of course not!" Alisa said angrily.

"Well, it used to be the usual reason why women had to get married," Zachary mocked, his dark eyes twinkling at her in amusement. "What do you have to gain by marriage?"

"My half-sister Christine, who's seven years old," Alisa retorted in cold defiance, wishing she could slap that derisive expression off his face. "My mother's will stated that I could have permanent custody of Christine only if I were married and lived with my husband for one entire year. Otherwise her guardianship would go to my aunt and uncle.''

"Do you care for this little girl, or do you just hate your aunt and uncle?''

''My feelings for both are equally intense—if it's any of your business.'' She lifted the martini glass to her mouth and sipped it calmly.

''If I were to agree to your ridiculous proposal, what would you be prepared to pay me?'' The lighter flared again in the dimly lit room as Zachary inhaled on his cigarette. The brief, flickering flame revealed black fires in his eyes as he watched her reaction.

''It would depend on what you required.''

''Around half a million. Maybe more. Modernizing is expensive.''

''That's a very high price.'' The words were spoken through tightly clenched teeth. Alisa wished she could tell him exactly what she thought of him.

''You get what you pay for, Alisa. My freedom's worth a great deal to me.'' He studied her face. ''What made you decide to put your proposition to me?''

It had been at one of Elizabeth's parties, just as Michael had said, when Alisa had first seen Zachary Stuart. Paul Andrews had been making a nuisance of himself. Perhaps that was why when he had left her side to greet the tall, dark-haired man just arriving, Alisa had spared the time to look. It had been Zachary Stuart, Alisa realized now. Paul had attempted to bring Zachary over to introduce him to Alisa, but Zachary had declined.

Later that evening, when Alisa was just leaving the ladies' room, she had overheard Zachary talking. It had been a case of accidental eavesdropping, with only his profile against a backdrop of greenery to identify him. But he wasn't the kind of man she would forget.

Some woman had been teasing him about his reluctance to meet Paul's new love. Zachary Stuart's cutting reply had remained with Alisa.

"From what Paul's told me," Zachary had said, "she isn't my type of woman." He had spoken with the cool arrogance of a man who always got what he wanted. "I wouldn't waste my time on a cold, dumb blonde who's afraid of men. I want someone with a little more heart and fire, and less ice and vanity."

"I picked you, Mr. Stuart," Alisa chose her words carefully, "because you come from an important family. Despite your lack of a personal fortune, you're considered a catch by the people I associate with. You're not some overgrown trust fund brat who can't make his own decisions. You strike me as a mercenary type who would go to great lengths to get what he wanted. Right now, you want money."

There was a long silence following Alisa's statement. When Zachary did reply, his voice was light and somewhat amused.

"You don't have a very high opinion of me, do you?"

"I don't have a very high opinion of any man, Mr. Stuart," Alisa answered contemptuously.

"And how do you feel about love?"

"The act or the emotion?" She glanced at him with frigid coldness. "Not that it matters, since my opinion of both is equally low. The first is disgusting and degrading and the second is a trap invented by men to ensnare women."

"Maybe in the twelve months that you live with me, I might teach you a different understanding of love." His dark eyes raked over her tense face and body. "But," he shrugged, "you probably wouldn't even listen."

"I'm glad you feel that way, because this arrangement is strictly business!" Alisa emphasized harshly. "I take it you're accepting my offer."

"With a few conditions."

"Which are?"

"First of all, the money's mine to do with as I please. Whether our marriage lasts a week or a year, that's my price for allowing you to take my name." Zachary smiled at Alisa's reaction to his condescending attitude. "Secondly, while we're married, you will live where I live and off my own earnings. I can assure you, my home is quite comfortable. Finally, I'm sure your rigid pride will allow you to agree with me that no one besides us should know that this is a business arrangement for our own mutual benefit. And I hope that in the company of our friends and family you'll make some effort to display affection towards me."

"Is that all?" She made no effort to hide her indignation or her growing anger. "Has your male ego been satisfied?"

"For the time being. When are we getting married?"

Alisa stared at the almost satanic pleasure in his expression, silently wishing that the freezing scorn in her own eyes would get to him, but he seemed impervious to it.

"The sooner the better." She gathered the black lace shawl around her shoulders and rose from her chair as he simultaneously joined her.

"I'll make the necessary arrangements," Zachary announced, extending his hand to her.

Reluctantly, Alisa placed her hand in his, wondering if this symbolic act of shaking hands to seal an agreement was really an act of putting her future in the hands of the uncaring fates.

"Hmm. That's strange," Zachary murmured, glancing down at their clasped hands. "Your hand is cool."

"So?" She attempted to withdraw it, but he held it firmly.

"Haven't you heard the saying, 'Cold hands, warm heart'?" He was laughing at her again behind those fiery bright eyes.

"That's just a phrase." Finally managing to free her hand, she turned away from him and began to walk towards the casino area.

"I'd be careful if I were you." Zachary was at her side almost immediately, his large hand imprisoning her elbow. "You already have one warm spot in your ice-encrusted heart for your sister. Some day a fire might come along and melt the rest away."

"I don't know what you're talking about." She turned her frosty blue eyes towards his jeering smile.

"Which brings up another point. I'm not cold-blooded, unlike you. Since this is to be a marriage in name only, I sincerely hope that you don't expect me to be celibate for an entire year."

"Go ahead and have affairs," Alisa said calmly, while allowing her distaste to show. "Just have the decency, if you can, to keep them discreet. Now, if you'll excuse me, I see a friend waiting for me."

"Certainly," Zachary agreed smoothly. "I'll call

you at ten to let you know the time and place of our wedding. What room are you in?''

Alisa gave him the information, disliking the imperious look on his face. He seemed to think he was doing her a favor. As quickly as she could and with as much composure as she could summon, she left his side to join her cousin, who, as usual, was completely engrossed at the dice tables.

When Alisa finally dragged him away from the tables, and told him about her coming marriage to Zachary Stuart, Michael was shocked and outspokenly against it. He knew a great deal more about Zachary Stuart than he had told his cousin, mostly because he never dreamed that the man would even consider a proposition like Alisa's, let alone agree to it. His words of warning were wasted when he tried to explain to her that Stuart was merciless when it came to getting what he wanted, that he could be extraordinarily cruel to those who had incurred his displeasure, and that he had no qualms about making advances towards his friends; women, unmarried or not, willing or not, though it was seldom that the women weren't willing.

But Alisa turned a deaf ear to it all, confident that she could handle any situation. In her twenty-four years she had learned a lot. Zachary Stuart might prove to be a more formidable opponent, she declared, but he was still just a man, not some all-powerful demon as Michael was trying to make her believe. As a matter of fact, she had found him to be reasonable enough during their discussion. His occasional jibes and several references to crude subjects had been irritating and disgusting, but certainly nothing that couldn't be handled as long as she didn't let her irritation give way to anger and remained cool and composed. Besides, she was getting Christine, and that was the whole point.

No matter how deeply Alisa buried her head under the silk-encased pillow the persistent knocking wouldn't stop. Drowsily she realized that she had dozed off to sleep after her wake-up call. Bleary-eyed, she stared at her wristwatch on the bedside table—nine-forty-five! It must be room service, she decided, with her breakfast. Fighting sleepiness, Alisa crawled out of bed, grabbing the robe that matched her pale blue nightgown from the chair before walking over to unlatch the door and hold it open.

She stared in blinking disbelief at the tall, dark man standing in her doorway. Self-consciously her hand reached up to the lace ribbons that held the yoked neck of her robe together.

"Good morning." Zachary moved easily past her into the room.

"You said you would call . . . at ten." She tried to inject a cold censure in her voice, but it ended up sounding like what it was, a surprised and embarrassed protest.

"I changed my mind and decided to stop by instead," he answered, settling himself in one of the plush blue velvet chairs before returning his attention to her to stare with uncomfortable thoroughness.

"Did you change your mind about the wedding?" Alisa managed to ask calmly as if his answer didn't matter to her at all.

"No." His gaze drifted over the pale blue robe that curled around her ankles, its soft material clinging to her legs, hips, and waist before stopping at the high yoked neckline with petite capped sleeves. "I wanted to see what my prospective bride looked like in the morning. I like the robe. It's like you, prudish but provocatively sensuous." She glared at him coldly before seating herself in the chair opposite him, taking great care to gather the robe around her tightly. "It's a comfort to discover that you can look as disheveled as any other normal woman in the morning."

Alisa turned quickly to glance at her reflection in the gilt-framed mirror on the wall. A pale face stared back at her, scrubbed clean of make-up from the night before. Her hair was all tousled, and there was a red welt on her cheek where she had lain on her arm.

Damn! Why did he have to come when I'm looking like this? she thought angrily.

One corner of his mouth lifted in mocking amusement which only made Alisa angrier, although she took pains not to let it show.

"Why are you here, Stuart?"

"I'm your future husband. Call me Zachary," he replied with a cynical smile. "I thought we'd get the marriage license this morning. I've made arrangements for the ceremony to take place this afternoon at two, which gives us time to catch a flight out of Vegas any time after three."

For a moment the speed with which he was arranging things surprised her, until Alisa realized his motive.

"You're awfully anxious to get your hands on the money, aren't you?" she snapped bitterly.

"You could change your mind." His dark brows raised in challenge. Then, as if he was tired of playing games, he sighed and rose from the chair. "I'll meet you in the lobby in half an hour. From there we can get the license, have lunch, and then go to the church."

Alisa stiffened at the commanding tone of his voice. She had hoped that everything would be done as quickly as possible, but he might as well know now that she was equally capable of snapping out orders.

"OK," she said, "you can book us on a flight to San Francisco this afternoon. Tomorrow morning we'll go to the bank and arrange to transfer the money into your account. Then we can stop in Oakland to pick up Christine."

Zachary smiled lazily at her clipped words, seeming amused by her attempt to exert authority over him, but he nodded and repeated that he would meet her in the lobby in half an hour.

CHAPTER TWO

Alisa studied the stern but handsome profile of the man behind the wheel. Amid the razzle-dazzle world of Las Vegas with its myriad neon lights and dancing fountains, her actions had seemed reasonable, even practical. The difference between winning and losing before had depended on the throw of the dice or the turn of the card, but now it had been ironically decided by her signature on a marriage certificate. She had won custody of Christine, but what had she lost?

Would she ever shake off the misgivings that had possessed her when the taxi stopped outside the church the day before? The driver's snickering looks and sexual innuendoes had sickened Alisa as Zachary had tipped him generously and sent him on. She had tried to hide the trembling of her hands as she smoothed the white lace of her dress over its underlining of pale blue. The matching cloth hat had a tiny bouquet of orange blossoms fastened on the wide floppy brim. Her pale gold hair was smoothly coiled in its austere chignon.

This was a silly, ritualistic ceremony, she had told herself, nothing to warrant this sudden attack of nerves. These vows they were going to take had no meaning. After attending three of her mother's weddings, she was an authority on that. Once inside the church, her poise had still been rattled. She had tried to refuse the woman witness who had quickly shoved a handkerchief in Alisa's hand, whispering "something borrowed."

Zachary's voice had been calm and clear as he said the vows, but Alisa's had been low and tense, revealing her rigid control. That control had almost broken when she stumbled over some of the words and glanced up into Zachary's mocking eyes. Those eyes had laughed at her twice more. Once when he slipped the plain gold band on her finger and again when she had perfunctorily brushed his lips with her own.

His goading had continued, whether directly or indirectly. Yesterday at the airport and later at the hotel when he had booked separate rooms, Zachary had identified her only as his wife, Mrs. Stuart. Even this morning at the bank, it had turned out that her banker was a close friend of his family and she was once again pushed into the background. Her identity had been lost. Now she was just Zachary Stuart's wife. And he was taking pleasure in making sure she understood that fact. She hated him even more, if that was possible.

"Is this the house?" Zachary slowed the car down in front of a plain white two-story house, the lawn immaculate, the hedges meticulously trimmed.

"Yes," Alisa answered breathlessly, her blue eyes searching eagerly for any sign of her sister. But the closed doors and blank windows stared back unwelcomingly.

Alisa waited impatiently as Zachary maneuvered the car into the driveway and walked around to open her door. Her sparkling eyes and quickened steps betrayed her excitement.

"You really do care about this kid." Zachary courteously took her arm as they reached the porch steps.

"Of course I do," Alisa asserted, hurrying past the elegant white lawn furniture that looked as if it belonged in a Victorian garden.

In response to the chiming bells, the door was opened by an elderly woman, her iron-gray hair braided into a coronet on top of her head, her posture rigidly erect.

"Alisa!" Her false smile of welcome was mirrored by the irritation showing in her small dark eyes. "I was so surprised when you called me this morning and said you were married." The woman's gaze turned briefly on Zachary. "This is your husband?" The sarcastic intonation wasn't lost on Alisa.

"Zachary Stuart," Alisa introduced him impatiently. "My mother's sister-in-law, Marguerite Denton. Where is Christine?"

"Please come in and have some coffee." The woman opened the door wider, completely ignoring Alisa's question as she led them through a dark, paneled hallway into an equally somber room. A table was already set with a silver coffee service.

"You two got married in quite a hurry, didn't you?" Marguerite drawled. She seated herself immediately and began pouring the coffee.

"Once Alisa agreed, I didn't want to give her an opportunity to change her mind." Zachary glanced down at his already seated wife with a show of fondness that bordered on mockery.

"Did you say you were only married yesterday?" Marguerite's malicious gaze lighted accusingly on Alisa as she handed her a fragile china cup. "You two haven't even had a honeymoon. I'll be glad to take care of Christine if you want to go away for a few weeks."

"That won't be necessary," said Alisa.

"Not that we don't appreciate your offer," Zachary said quickly, a charming smile enhancing the softness of his words. "We're more interested in making sure Christine understands that Alisa hasn't deserted her. We want her to know that she's a very important member of our family. You see how it is?"

"Yes, I do." Marguerite's mouth trembled with ill-concealed anger, as she stared from one to the other.

"Where is Christine?" Alisa asked again.

"She was terribly upset this morning when I told her you were married." A smug smile brought a bright gleam to the woman's eyes. "She had settled down nicely here. I don't think taking her away is a good—"

"Where is she, Aunt Marguerite?"

"In her room. I made her lie down for a while."

"Please get her—or I will," Alisa threatened. Her eyes sparkled with a cold fury.

"I'll get her." The woman rose abruptly and left the room.

As Marguerite left the room, Alisa let out a long breath, angry with herself for allowing her aunt to rile her. Her gaze moved to Zachary, irritated that he had stepped in to offer an explanation of their speedy marriage. Marguerite hadn't been fooled.

As if reading her thoughts, Zachary said, "She can wonder all she wants to about why we got married, but there's no need for her to know for sure. It would only give her another weapon."

"I can handle her," Alisa asserted, inhaling slowly. "She has no weapon."

"Your fear of her and your love for Christine."

Her eyes flashed quickly over Zachary, uncomfortably aware that he was much too perceptive.

The sedate, even tread of Marguerite's footsteps in the hallway was accompanied by shuffling, reluctant, lighter steps. Alisa turned eagerly towards the doorway, her face brightening momentarily as a child appeared at her aunt's side. Although Alisa's arms opened, they remained empty as she stared at the lowered head of her sullen little sister.

"Chris?" she offered hesitantly, surprised at the complete lack of welcome.

The small brown head with its highlights of coppery red raised slightly, revealing a trembling chin and rebellious brown eyes. Christine's slender arms were tucked behind her back and the corners of her mouth were turned stubbornly down.

"I don't think Christine is very excited about seeing you." A triumphant smile flashed on Marguerite's face.

"That's not true!" Christine's head jerked up quickly, fixing a mutinous glare on her aunt before turning to look at her sister. "I'm supposed to tell you that I want to stay here, that I don't want to go with you." Tears began brimming in the brown eyes. "But I do, I really do!"

In the next instant, a small wiry body flung itself in Alisa's arms.

"Take her!" Marguerite called out shrilly, her malevolent eyes returning Alisa's accusing look. "She's nothing but a nuisance—and a spoiled brat. Just exactly what you'd expect of Eleanor's child!"

"Take Chris to the car, Alisa. I'll handle this." The smoldering anger in Zachary's eyes nearly took her breath away when Alisa turned a grateful look on him.

She clutched Christine to her tightly and hurried past her irate aunt, then down the hallway and out the door. Once in the car, Alisa disentangled the slender arms from around her neck, dried the tears from her sister's cheeks, and reassured her that she didn't have anything to worry about anymore. After the elfin face had finally managed a hesitant smile, Alisa glanced towards the house. Her eyes gleamed with anticipation of what was going on in there. Even she had been intimidated by Zachary's authoritative voice and she wished she could have witnessed his confrontation with Marguerite.

Through most of her life, Alisa had dealt with things on her own. Her mother had always been too involved with a boyfriend or husband when Alisa's childhood and teenage crises occurred. She had never known the security of a stable family. Dale Patterson had made her mother ecstatically happy and they had both attempted to draw Alisa into the circle of their love. But she had grown too cynical for her young years to believe in any of it. Alisa had been appalled when her mother had informed her that she was going to have a baby at the age of thirty-seven. Although Alisa had loved her new sister dearly, she was never quite a part of the new family, always standing back, increasing her reserve unless she was alone with Christine. She had poured out all the love that she couldn't safely give to anyone else on her sister.

The knowledge that Zachary was in that house doing battle with the aunt she despised was a new sensation to Alisa. The glow of gratitude was still on her face when Zachary came striding out of the house carrying a small suitcase in one hand. Not that she had needed him to fight for her, she told herself quickly. After all, she was capable of handling Marguerite herself. But, as much as she hated his mocking arrogance, Alisa knew she would never forget his show of kindness.

As he slid into the driver's seat, Alisa studied the stern lines of repressed anger still in his face. A shiver of fear scared away the softness she had felt earlier while she shuddered at the thought of ever facing that anger herself.

Sliding the key into the ignition, Zachary glanced at the pair, Alisa watching him with an outward calm and Christine peeping at him from the security of her sister's shoulder. His hands rested on the steering wheel as the banked fire of his gaze swept over them.

"I picked up a few things for Christine. The rest will be sent on to our home."

Alisa's jaw tightened at the word *our*. He didn't seem to notice or care.

There was a trace of animosity in Christine's brown eyes as she studied Zachary. "She said you didn't like little girls." Although her chin trembled, Christine spoke forcefully. "She said you wouldn't want me around and that you'd send me back if I did anything bad."

Zachary's eyes flared briefly at Alisa.

"Christine's referring to Marguerite," Alisa smiled, coolly dismissing his accusing look with a hint of contempt.

"Your aunt was wrong, Chris." He met Alisa's disdainful stare with an amused smile. "I like little girls very much. And I'm sure your sister will do everything she can, regardless of what you do or how bad you are, to make sure you never go back to your aunt." His eyes traveled over Alisa, taking in the creamy perfection of her face and neck and the sexy way her beige plaid jacket clung to her curves. As if satisfied with what he saw, Zachary turned away, started the car, and began backing it out of the driveway.

"She said you would want Lisa all to yourself, that you wouldn't want me hanging around her," Christine persisted, needing all her fears to be soothed away.

"Tell you what we'll do." His eyes never left the street ahead of them as he replied in a gentle, though amused voice. "I work during the day so you can have Alisa all to yourself then. At nighttime when you have to go to bed, then Alisa will be with me. How's that?"

"Fine." But there was a hesitancy in the child's voice that made Zachary glance at her curiously. At the compelling question in his eyes, Christine added, "My daddy had to work, too, but sometimes he did things with Mommy and me. We had a lot of fun." Her unasked question brought a slow smile to his face.

"I think the three of us could have a lot of fun, too. Don't you, Alisa?"

A cold, burning anger was welling up inside Alisa.

The new feeling of softness towards the dark-haired man who was her husband had rapidly disappeared. She could see through his reassuring words to her baby sister and understood him only too well: despite any claims by her to the contrary, she was dependent on him, and she needed him for the sake of the child. But that wasn't the way she had planned it. He should be under obligation to her. He should feel subjugated to her.

"Won't it be fun, Lisa?" Christine's plaintive voice broke into her musing.

Alisa glanced down at the earnest little face, forcing a smile that she was far from feeling.

"Zachary will be very busy, so we can't expect him to spend very much time with us. In fact, very little at all, but when he does, I'm sure it will be fun."

The jeering chuckle was like the scrape of chalk against a blackboard. "This is only the summer. Harvest season, the busy time, begins in August. There'll be plenty of time for all of us to do things together before then." Zachary flashed his mocking smile at her.

Christine clapped her hands together in delight, her happiness too important to Alisa for her to dampen it so soon.

"Where are we going now?" Christine asked. Her brown eyes, still lit with joy, gazed out the car window at the whirl of traffic around them.

"To our home in Napa Valley," Zachary told her.

"Where's that?" she persisted.

"About an hour and a half's drive from San Francisco." He smiled gently at the soft brown, inquiring eyes.

Satisfied, Christine settled down in the seat between Alisa and Zachary, contentment etched on her face, in the pertness of her nose and the glow on her face.

The car turned off the Silverado Trail between two winged brick pillars connected by a wrought-iron arch enscrolled with the name Stuart Vineyards. A cordon of massive oak trees hovered protectively over the narrow lane. Their trunks and limbs were gnarled and weathered by the years they had stood as sentinels over the gravel road. Gaping holes studded with rotted stumps marked the places where age had thinned their ranks. Beyond the thick foliage of their branches lay the vineyards where the dark green leaves of the vines were like the waves of the sea rolling over the sloping hills.

Alisa shielded her eyes from the brilliant midday sun when Zachary slowed the car down, as the corridor of trees opened to reveal a circular drive. Nestled on the far side of the circle amidst more giant oak trees was a two-and-a-half-story brick house, its turrets and cupolas and gables daring an ordinary roof to compete with its uniqueness. Around the arched, white-trimmed windows and doors clung tenacious Boston ivy, its green leaves hiding the dark red brick exterior. Another narrow lane branched off the circular drive and led towards the rear of the house before breaking away to go up the hill behind it to another set of buildings. Alisa was stunned by the magnificence of the estate. She had somehow expected to be taken to a modest winery with one of those unexceptional houses that always seemed dwarfed by the winery buildings themselves. The lawns were immaculate. There was a small flower garden on the south side of the house, surrounding a patio with plushly cushioned white rattan lawn furniture.

Christine was chattering at Zachary, who had stopped the car and was already opening the door on Alisa's side. His dark eyes mocked her silently as she tried to take in the old-world elegance of his home. A horrible thought struck her. This was not the home of a poor man.

"The plumbing is kind of temperamental, but I think you'll find everything else to your satisfaction, Mrs. Stuart," Zachary said solemnly while taking her hand as she stepped out of the car.

"It's very impressive." Although she attempted to put an air of nonchalance in her voice, it mixed rather falsely with genuine wonder. "Hardly what I was led to believe."

"But then you never asked me for much information." Apprehension crept into her eyes as he forced her to meet his compelling look. "What I needed money for was the expansion of my winery."

Alisa breathed a silent sigh of relief. For a moment, she'd thought he was going to drop some bombshell of information on her. She glanced around for Christine, who was already racing towards the steps of the house, calling them to hurry so that she could explore her new home. With a sardonically amused smile, Zachary took Alisa's arm and led her to the big white door with its large brass knocker where Christine stood impatiently hopping from one foot to the other.

"I want to see you carry Alisa through the door!"

she cried, a wide smile beaming expectantly to each as they reached her side.

"That's a silly custom," Alisa admonished, "and you know I don't believe in that kind of thing, Christine."

"Well, your husband does," Zachary laughed, sweeping her up easily in his arms and nodding to Chris to open the door.

"Put me down!" Alisa whispered sharply, her hands pushing stiffly at his broad chest.

"Why don't you relax and enjoy it?" He merely laughed at her weak protest.

"Because I don't like being held by you or any other man," Alisa answered. Her voice was still lowered, yet implicitly expressing her distaste of his touch.

"I could teach you to like it," he murmured, giving her a sly look while he crushed her tighter against him.

Giggling, Christine called from inside the door, "Aren't you going to come in?"

Ignoring the rigidity with which Alisa tried to hold herself away from him, Zachary carried her over the threshold and into the foyer of the house. Once inside, he stopped, but still didn't put her down, smiling with amusement at the cold contempt in her face. At the sound of footsteps approaching from another room, he turned, letting her down only when a woman came into view. As the woman drew nearer, Christine hurried to Alisa, taking her hand for comfort. Zachary's arm was still around her waist, and Alisa knew she had to endure his touch for a few minutes longer.

"Zach!" The gray-haired woman reached out to clasp his hand with both of hers, her pale blue eyes beaming up at him in happiness before she glanced curiously at Alisa and Christine. "We didn't expect you back for another two days."

"You know I couldn't stay away from my second best girl for a whole week," Zachary teased, touching his lips to her cheek in an affectionate kiss.

The woman looked again at Alisa. Her eyes anxiously surveyed the coolness in Alisa's gaze as well as the pale gold coiffure and the perfection of her beauty.

"Nora, I want you to meet my wife, Mrs. Alisa Franklin Stuart." There was the barest trace of mockery in his eyes as he gently nudged Alisa closer. "And her little sister, Christine Patterson. Alisa, Chris, this is my housekeeper, Nora Castillo."

Alisa didn't care for the way the housekeeper studied her now that she knew Alisa was Mrs. Zachary Stuart. She had the peculiar feeling that she was a pound of meat in a butcher's shop that had been weighed and come up short. The woman was evidently unaware of her place. Their mutual exchange of greetings was cool, each disapproving of the other in their own silent way.

"Just a light lunch will do us, Nora." Zachary broke into the hostile silence. "We'll take it on the patio in about an hour. In the meantime, I'm going to check in with George. I'm sure Alisa would like to freshen up and Christine needs it." He ruffled the brown head on the other side of Alisa briskly. "Take Mrs. Stuart up to the lavender room."

"The lavender room?" Nora repeated, casting a pointed look at Alisa.

"Yes." His tone definitely dismissed any further questioning. "Is there anything you need from the car?"

Alisa shook her head. "I'll bring the case up later, then," Zachary finished.

His hand left her waist and came up to brush her cheek in a feathery caress before he walked away. It was all Alisa could do not to flinch away from his touch. His mocking glance had told her he knew it and so did the sharp eyes of the house-keeper.

"Where am I going to stay?" Christine pulled impatiently on Alisa's hand.

"Is there a room near mine?" asked Alisa, meeting the disapproving eyes of the gray-haired woman.

"Yes, down the hall. The green room. Please follow me." The heels of the housekeeper's shoes clicked across the marble tiled floor of the foyer as she led them towards the ornately carved open staircase.

The pale yellow walls blended smoothly with the oak woodwork and the traces of gold in the mar-bled floor. The steps of the staircase were overlaid with matching marble tiles, their width adding to the aura of wealth and elegance. At the top of the stairs, there was a rich carpet of gold to silence the sound of their feet. The wide hallway with its high ceiling and pale walls consisted of two branches from the stair landing, one leading to the left and the other to the right. Nora Castillo led Alisa and Christine to the right, where she paused at the first door on the left side.

"This is the green room," she announced, open-ing the door and stepping inside.

Alisa walked on past the housekeeper into the room, with Christine following shyly behind her. The walls were a cool spring green with the wood-work painted white to match the gilded white

French Provincial bedroom set. The single bed had a draped canopy with a myriad of floral bouquets printed on chintz, which matched the bedspread and curtains.

"It's like a bed for a princess!" Christine stared at the canopy, her eyes filled with the magic of the thought. She turned to Alisa. "Is it really my room?"

Alisa nodded, her face glowing with the happiness reflected in her little sister's eyes.

"The bath is through this door," Nora said as she opened a white-enameled door, "with a connecting door to your room, Mrs. Stuart."

A note of reproof in the housekeeper's voice made the smile on Alisa's face fade. She asked Mrs. Castillo to show her the lavender room, which turned out to be as charming as Christine's airy boudoir. As before, she saw pale walls and white woodwork, but this room had been done in Italian Provincial. The deep purple velvet bedspread was set off by the palest lavender sheets. Underfoot was a plush ivory carpet.

"The master bedroom is next door—where Zach sleeps." Nora Castillo made her displeasure with the separate bedroom arrangement clear.

"Is there a connecting door?" Alisa asked quickly, glancing at the wall that separated them.

"No." The housekeeper looked challengingly at Alisa. "Would you care to see the master bedroom?"

"No, thank you. I don't believe I'll need you for anything else." Alisa dismissed her sharply, not liking the woman's attitude.

For a moment Alisa stared at the door that had closed behind the retreating woman before Chris-

tine came bursting through the connecting bathroom door.

"Isn't it wonderful? Your room is pretty like
mine, too. Oh, can I go exploring?"

Alisa smiled broadly and hugged the dancing
girl to her. The warmth of her love for her sister
brought a faint misting of tears to Alisa's eyes as
she released her. She shooed Christine out of the
room, reminding her that lunch was in a little less
than an hour and telling her not to stray out of
the garden. When silence once more permeated
the room, Alisa sank into the velvet-cushioned
chair in front of the dressing table, her fingers
reaching up to rub her temples.

The woman looking back at her from the mirror
looked somehow alien with her smooth skin, pale
gold hair, and her clear, untroubled eyes. No matter how many times Alisa looked in the mirror and
no matter how pleased she was with her reflection,
she was always a little surprised by what she saw.
She wanted to see someone as free and as happy
as Christine, as full of life and love, but always the
same cool eyes stared back at her, reminding her
that she had gone through a great deal of pain to
acquire this total composure—and that she was
still vulnerable.

Life was not the wildly happy thing that the fairy
tales she loved had once led her to believe. She
was better off accepting reality and not looking at
it through rose-colored glasses, she told herself. All
those romantic stories were designed to encourage
false hope. The love of a child, of Christine, was
the only safe thing she could cling to, the only
thing she could trust.

Alisa rose abruptly, removed the beige plaid

jacket, tossed it on the bed, and hugged her arms around herself as she walked to the window. She knew what kind of a woman the housekeeper was: one that believed in an old-fashioned concept of marriage, the traditional wife subservient to her husband, willing to be mistress, mother, and maid to him.

"Do you like the room?" Zachary stood inside the doorway, her suitcase at his feet.

"It's a lovely room. Who wouldn't be satisfied with it?" Alisa answered indifferently, the startled light at his unexpected appearance now gone from her eyes.

"You." His dark eyes studied her thoroughly. "I thought you would have found something about my home you don't like by now."

"I'll only be living here one year," she rose to his sarcasm. "It would hardly be worthwhile to do any redecorating for that short time."

"And Nora? What do you think of her?"

"I think she's much too familiar for a servant, regardless of how good she might be." Alisa met his intense, questioning gaze, bolstered by her own bitterness at any supposed depth of feeling between two adults.

"What would you suggest? That I get rid of her . . . for the duration?" Zachary seemed to bristle in anger, although his voice was calm, almost amused.

"That's an excellent suggestion," Alisa returned, "but kind of drastic, don't you think? The best thing to do is to have a talk with her and make sure she knows that she's a servant."

"So you're a snob as well as a bitch! What a surprise." His eyes gleamed with a satanic fire as he stepped closer. "If anyone goes, it will be you,

Mrs. Stuart.'' Zachary laughed without amusement at the frustration in her face. ''But then you can't leave and still keep Christine, can you?''

''Don't you dare bully me.'' Alisa spoke calmly, refusing to display the anger that was raging inside. To do so would be a show of weakness. ''Looks like you feel insecure. You demanded a high price to marry me, but the fact that I was able to pay is humiliating. You'll do or say anything to have the upper hand, won't you? Well, tough luck, my dear husband,'' she added with cool sarcasm, ''because I have what I want and you can't make me give up.''

Her head turned so her eyes could meet his gaze, their haughty coolness emphasizing the conviction of her voice. But Zachary was unmoved by it.

''You're right—I am interested in making you give up.''

Alisa felt a tremor at his words.

''But I don't think we're talking about the same thing, Alisa.''

''Well, I don't want to have any cryptic conversation with you,'' she retorted sharply. ''You did say lunch was to be ready in an hour. Let's go down now.''

''Is that an invitation or an order?'' Zachary asked as Alisa walked past him to the door. She stopped at the door, her head turning slightly back towards him at the almost ominous softness of his voice.

''Whichever you please.''

''I don't take orders, especially from my wife.'' A lazy smile played about the hard lines of his mouth as she turned at his reply.

"How quaint!" Her voice was deliberately frosty. "Perhaps you could learn."

"If there's any learning to be done, it will be by you and I'll be the teacher." His gaze locked challengingly with hers.

Alisa read the powerful intimidation in his eyes, the unspoken dare to fight on. Unwillingly she remembered Michael's statement that Zachary Stuart could be ruthless and unrelenting. But then he'd never met anyone like her before.

"You have nothing to teach me. And I don't care if you have lunch with me or not. I have no desire to sit at a table with you. As far as I'm concerned you can crawl back under the woodwork where you came from!" With complete poise, Alisa stepped out of the room into the hallway.

"You really would like me to vanish into thin air." His mocking voice told her Zachary was only a step behind her as she walked to the stair landing. "You can't walk through me as if I weren't here. And I'll never allow you to walk over me."

"Whatever," she smiled back at him with brittle sweetness, "I can still walk around you."

His eyebrows lifted in amused disbelief while his callused hand gripped her elbow as they started down the marble inlaid stairs. "Just try," he replied.

Christine's slight shyness in her strange new home had disappeared by lunch. And it was her chattering that covered the frosty silence of her older sister. Zachary was indulgent with Christine, but totally indifferent to Alisa. By the time the dessert of fresh fruit was eaten, she was seething with rage at his lack of interest. She had expected that he wouldn't attempt to coax her into the conversation, but she thought he would at least make some pointed remark about her continuing silence. He didn't. Zachary excused himself only to Christine, saying that he had work to do at the vineyard office on the hill.

The black German shepherd, which had been waiting patiently at the edge of the patio, padded over to Zachary's side and followed him as Zachary made his way through the trees towards the building further up the hill from the house. Alisa listened to Christine's exclamations about the dog, named Baron, and how they had made friends before lunch. At last Alisa broke through her sister's prattle and announced that they would unpack their clothes, then tour the house and grounds the rest of the afternoon.

Since most of their clothes hadn't arrived yet, it didn't take much time to unpack and put away their things. Christine immediately insisted on being Alisa's guide, taking her by the hand as they stepped out of Alisa's bedroom into the hall and pointing out that the rooms on the opposite end of the hall were only guest bedrooms.

Chris skipped down the stairs ahead of her sister, opened the double doors on the left, and in her most authoritative voice announced that this was the formal living room. Alisa took a moment to admire the comfortable furniture in the airy room before she was whisked into the dining room. Again, allowed only the shortest pause, Alisa could easily see that the large yet intimate room could be used by a small group or a very large one. Another set of double doors were opened.

"This is my favorite room!" Christine danced around a plush yellow flowered sofa that matched the bright yellow walls and white-trimmed woodwork. In front of the large latticed windows sat a small dropleaf table painted white. A large recliner chair took up one corner. "Nora said this is the morning room. Do you know why it's named that?" Chris asked, and immediately began to explain, "Because this is where we have breakfast. She said nobody likes to go into the dining room because it's so elegant, and nobody feels elegant in the morning!"

Alisa couldn't help agreeing. It was the perfect room to enter in the morning, bright and spacious, yet filled with cozy, snuggly furniture where sleepy people could relax and wake up slowly.

"The kitchen's through that door," Chris went on, continuing her hectic pace back into the hall. "But Nora said the cook doesn't like people messing around in her kitchen."

The pair had arrived back at the entrance foyer where Chris paused in front of a set of double doors opposite the living room.

"This is the 'lion's room,' " she giggled.

"The 'lion's room'?" Alisa repeated.

"That's what Mommy and I used to call the one at home." A wistful expression appeared in her brown eyes. "Daddy called it his den, but he used to roar so if anyone disturbed him that we called it the 'lion's room.' Nora said that this was Zachary's room where he works sometimes and that I wasn't supposed to go in there."

"Yes, Zachary might roar at you, too." Alisa compressed her lips in a firm line, although her voice was light. "But you shouldn't call the housekeeper Nora. Her name is Mrs. Castillo."

"I told her to call me Chris and she said I could call her Nora," the little girl shrugged. "Besides, that's what Zach calls her, so it's all right."

"That's true, he does call her Nora. But a young girl should call grown-ups by their last names. It shows respect," Alisa insisted, irritated by Chris's sudden reference to Zachary as if he were the authority.

"But then I'd have to call you Mrs. Stuart." The brown eyes widened with innocence.

"I'm your sister, so it's different. I'm a member of your family."

"So's Nora. She said so and Zach did, too." Christine's stubbornness was beginning to set in.

"We'll discuss it later." Alisa knew that until she had an opportunity to talk to Zachary and straighten him out, it was useless to argue with Christine. "I think we should go upstairs and change into some shorts before we explore outside."

Her auburn hair bounced wildly as Christine's slender young body tried to keep up with her ever-whirling skipping rope. The late afternoon sun cast an odd shadow of the girl, making her all legs and arms as she counted the number of times she hopped over the spinning rope until at last it tangled in her feet and she collapsed in the chair beside Alisa.

"How many was that?" she asked, gasping for breath.

"Sixty-two," Alisa replied. Her blue eyes smiled brightly at her red-faced sister.

"It was not! It was forty-nine times," she corrected crossly.

"How do you know?" Alisa teased.

"Because I counted."

"If you were counting, then why did you ask me to count?"

"If I make you count for me, I know you'll watch me." Christine grinned impishly.

"You silly goose, I always watch you." The aloofness that usually marred Alisa's perfect features had been erased by the laughter and love she felt for her little sister.

Christine stirred restlessly. "Let's go up to those buildings on the hill and find out what Zach's doing."

"I told you we weren't going up there." Alisa meant it. That had been a repeated request that she had denied practically the entire afternoon. The last thing she wanted to do was show an interest in what he was doing.

"Supper's at seven o'clock. Don't you think we should tell him?"

"You mean dinner," Alisa corrected.

"Dinner, supper, it's almost time to eat." A mutinous scowl clouded the girl's face at her sister's evasion.

"I'm sure he knows what time we eat without being told."

"I'm going up there whether you do or not," Christine rose, putting as much adult indignation into her words and manner as she could.

"Christine, don't be difficult."

"I'm not being difficult. You're being difficult!" The lashes of her brown eyes fluttered widely as Christine gave her a defiant glare.

"You're being rude!" Alisa retorted sharply. "I told you not to go up there. If you're so interested in seeing Zachary then you can walk up to that big tree and wait for him. But you are not going to the winery, and that's final!" Christine's temper flared brightly as she stalked off towards the distant tree while Alisa sighed in exasperation. Her sister had been so spoiled by her mother that she resented not getting her own way. Alisa had been just as guilty before, allowed by her love for the child to be wheedled and coaxed into anything that would bring a happy smile to Christine's face. It was just as well that Chris learned now that she couldn't have everything her own way.

Uncrossing her legs, Alisa slowly rose to her feet, her hand reaching up to adjust her soft blouse and smooth the scooped neck. From a nearby chair, she gathered her long wraparound skirt and fastened it around her waist over her shorts, then buttoned it halfway down the front, leaving the rest open so that the light golden tan of her legs would be set off by the white linen skirt. She had rearranged her hair earlier in the afternoon into a romantic Gibson Girl style that lent a delicate air to her face.

Tires crunching on the gravel drive drew her attention. The car came to a stop near the front entrance and the driver stepped out of the car to stand by his door, staring at Alisa on the patio. Slowly, as if his feet refused to obey, the man walked towards her.

"Alisa?" his questioning voice called, speaking her name almost reverently.

The stunned face and the familiar blond-brown hair grew clearer as he walked towards her. Long hands reached out to capture hers while earnest blue eyes searched her face. Numbed by the realization that it was Paul Andrews—the man she had dismissed so scathingly to Zachary—Alisa didn't even attempt to withdraw her hands from his.

"I thought you were a ghost. I couldn't believe my eyes when I saw you standing here when I drove in." His voice was hardly more than a hoarse whisper as he gazed at her in undisguised adoration. "What are you doing here?" As Alisa opened her mouth to explain, he shook his head to silence her. "You don't have to tell me. I've already guessed. Zachary brought you, didn't he?"

She nodded and tried again to speak, but he began to laugh with relieved pleasure. "I've never had a friend like him before. Alisa—you wouldn't believe all he's done for me. When you told me you didn't want to ever see me again, I went to pieces. I hated the whole world! But Zach was there to put me together again. He must have guessed, though, that I still love you. That's it, isn't it? He brought you here so you could be with me."

"Paul, stop!" Alisa protested. She felt pity and embarrassment growing inside her for this attractive but misguided man, where once he had only aroused disgust and indifference.

"I can't. I'm so happy!" When he tried to draw her into an embrace, Alisa pushed away.

"You don't understand!" she cried. "It's not the way you're thinking!"

"What do you mean?" The almost pained look on Alisa's face brought Paul to a stop. His brow knitted into a frown as he suddenly noticed her unease.

"I didn't know you were going to be here," she

explained, regaining her poise and calming her voice.

"Figure it out! Zach meant to surprise us both!" Paul laughed, then stopped short to stare at her again. "You're more beautiful than I remembered."

"Paul, I don't think Zachary is as much of a friend as you think he is," Alisa tried to explain, and at the same time stay the hands that were trying to draw her nearer.

"Nice way for my wife to act behind my back." Both Paul and Alisa whirled sharply at Zachary's contemptuous words. The dark eyes glowed with triumphant amusement as they captured Alisa's glance.

Paul had moved hastily away from Alisa and was now staring from her to Zachary in numbed disbelief. Without even a glance towards Paul, Zachary walked over and put an arm around Alisa's shoulders and crushed her to his side. He ignored her rigidness as he stared down into her eyes with mock affection.

"She's everything you said she was, Paul, and a lot more." Alisa knew Paul was too stricken to hear the sarcasm in Zachary's voice. "I was going to call to tell you the good news. We were married yesterday in Las Vegas."

The tanned face grew ghostly pale as Paul swallowed and managed a mumbled "Congratulations." But Zachary ignored the lack of enthusiasm and continued to allow his gaze to rest on Alisa's accusing face.

"I have to thank you, Paul. I knew a lot about Alisa before I even met her. Talk about a whirlwind courtship! I never gave her an opportunity to think about what she was doing until I was safely escorting her out of the church.''

"Marry in haste, repent in leisure," Alisa drawled, and was rewarded for her spiteful teasing by the slowly intensifying pressure of Zachary's hand around her arm.

"That's not the kind of comment a new bride is supposed to make, honey," Zachary reprimanded. He would have kissed her, but Alisa turned her head so that his lips found her cheek instead. His eyes flashed fire briefly before he released her in the general direction of the house. "Go and get us some sherry, woman. High time our wedding was toasted by someone other than ourselves."

Alisa glanced hesitantly back at Paul and was sickened by the blank look on his face and the bitterness and pain in the depths of his sea-blue eyes. She knew the slight pity she felt was wasted, thanks to her husband. What irritated her as she walked towards the house was the callously cruel way that Zachary was dangling their marriage in front of Paul. Stepping through the French doors into the dining room, Alisa knew that this mean-spirited display was in keeping with Zachary's character.

When she returned with a small silver tray holding three crystal wineglasses and a decanter of dry sherry, Alisa found Zachary and Paul seated at the patio table. A bit of color had returned to Paul's cheeks, although the haunted look was still in his blue eyes when he looked at her. After the wine had been poured and the glasses raised, Paul made a poignantly sincere wish for their happiness.

"Does Renée know yet?" Paul asked just as Zachary poured himself more sherry.

"No." Zachary studied the tawny brown liquid in his glass before meeting Alisa's curious gaze. Paul glanced nervously at her.

"I really think you should call her, let her know," he suggested.

"Let her find out on her own. Or better yet, you tell her." Zach's dark eyes stayed on Alisa's face.

"I take it Renée is one of Zachary's former girl-friends?" Alisa directed her cool inquiry to Paul.

"You have no reason to be jealous, Alisa." His slow, lazy smile obviously irked her. "She's dark and petite and quite passionate. Not at all like the Snow Queen I married."

"Sorry. I didn't mean to start an argument," Paul apologized.

"Don't bother," Zachary laughed, reaching out from his chair at the table to grasp Alisa's hand and pull her over to stand beside him. His hand released her long enough for his arm to encircle her waist and to hold her there despite her attempts to wriggle away. "For some reason, my wife is reluctant to show her love for me. I like to tease her about it—"

"Stop it!" Alisa hissed as his free hand moved to rest his spread fingers on her stomach. When her own hand would have taken his and flung it away from her, he captured it instead, drawing it, despite her struggles, to his lips where he kissed the palm. His eyes danced with amusement at her frigid expression, not releasing her hand even when the caress was finished, knowing how much she longed to smack his face.

"Hey, Paul why don't you stay to dinner?" Zachary asked. It sounded like an impulsive invitation, but Alisa felt sure that it had been carefully thought out.

"I couldn't. It's your first night here. Two's company, three's a crowd," Paul reminded them.

"We already have a seven-year-old chaperone." Zachary nodded towards Christine, who was busy throwing sticks for the dog to chase out on the lawn. "One more and we'll have a party. We want you to stay, don't we, Alisa?"

"Maybe Paul has other plans," she prompted.

"Then, as his employer, I order him to cancel them." Zachary's eyes glittered at her with threatening fierceness before he turned a more amicable glance to Paul.

"Well, I . . ." Paul ran a hand through his blond hair while attempting to meet the intimidating sureness of Zachary's gaze.

"OK. Go tell Nora there'll be four for dinner," Zachary ordered Alisa. The corners of his mouth turned up into a grim smile that challenged her to refuse.

Whether it was because of his arrogant certainty that she would attempt to defy him, or because she herself had been intimidated by his air of dominance, Alisa calmly smiled at his command and excused herself to enter the house.

Having informed the houskeeper that Mr. Stuart had invited Paul Andrews to join them for dinner that evening, Alisa remained in the house, mentally refusing to go out on the patio and be baited any further by Zachary. A quarter of an hour later Zachary entered the living room where Alisa was idly flipping through a fashion magazine.

"So this is where you disappeared to," he remarked before explaining that Paul and Christine had gone to wash up. "Wasn't it rather rude not to rejoin us?"

"Not any more rude and insensitive than you've been," she retorted, flipping the magazine shut and tossing it on the table in front of the blue sofa. "How could you invite him to dinner?"

With panther-like ease, Zachary lowered his tall frame into the matching chair, his head leaning against the back, watching her every move.

"It's time he stopped thinking of you as some virginal goddess on a pedestal. The shock of discovering you're married to me will do him good. He has to get used to it and face facts before he goes off on his own to brood some more." He paused to study her. "The dinner will also give you a chance to show me just how well you intend to fulfill the conditions of our marriage."

"What are you talking about?" Alisa gazed at him contemptuously.

"We agreed to act as if we actually like each other in front of other people. And if that's what you've been attempting to do so far this evening, then you're a terrible actress."

"If you think I'm going to allow you to caress or hug me every time someone comes into this house, forget it!" Alisa exclaimed, rising to her feet in anger.

"You're exciting to look at, Alisa, but you're cold to the touch. An arm around your shoulder isn't a hug, and I have yet to caress you. I doubt you have the experience to tell the difference." His tone was nonchalant. "I'd be satisfied with a smile from you, even if it does damage that mask you wear."

"I smile quite often, thank you," she retorted

sarcastically. "And if a smile will keep you from touching me, I'll smile all the time. Caresses, hugs, whatever—it's still touching."

"Where did you learn that?" Zachary mocked.

"From a man." Alisa's chin tilted up with indignation.

"You've never known one."

"My cousin Michael has been my constant companion for nearly five years."

"Oh, him. The creepy guy who followed you around in Vegas picking up any change you left behind!" Zachary rose to his feet, his jeering chuckle leaving no doubt as to his opinion of Michael. "Like I said, you've never known a man."

"I suppose you think you are." Her eyes shone with scorn as she looked up at him when he stopped in front of her.

"Some day I may decide to prove it to you." He seemed almost bored as he scanned her face and pale blond hair.

"Don't waste your time!"

"I never do," Zachary replied, shrugging his shoulders. Glancing over her shoulder, he waved his hand. "Here we are, Paul. Have you seen Christine?"

"She was heading down the hall towards the dining room as I was coming down the stairs," Paul replied.

"Guess we're all ready to go in, then." Zachary moved around so that Alisa was on one side and Paul on the other as he ushered them into the dining room.

Christine was leaning against one of the chairs, one foot resting on the other while she glumly surveyed the elegant table setting with its candelabra and flower centerpiece. The white bone china glistened, surrounded by polished silver and an array of sparkling crystal glasses. The little girl turned her gloomy expression on them as they stepped to the table.

"What's the matter?" Alisa asked in a low voice as she held the chair for her sulky half-sister before pushing it up to the table.

"I bet I never get to have hamburgers and french fries here!" Christine made no attempt to lower her voice and it rang out with embarrassing clarity.

Zachary's laughter drowned out Alisa's attempt to reprimand Chris. "Don't scold her. She's just being honest," he told Alisa. "I think we can arrange something with the cook so that you can have your hamburgers and french fries occasionally. How's that, Chris?"

"Fine!" Her brown eyes glowed to match the shimmering highlights of her auburn hair.

"But this is our first dinner together in your new home and I think Mrs. March wanted to impress you both," Zachary explained, astounding Alisa with his patience and ability to appeal to Christine's understanding.

There was no gentleness in his face. There was no room for gentleness in the hard features. Alisa decided it was the authority in his tone that had reached Christine—and again she experienced the growing irritation at his ability to dominate all who came in contact with Zachary Stuart. All except herself; she would remain unmoved by him. He could command anyone else that he wished, be the lord of the manor to whoever was willing to kneel at his feet, but she would never do it.

Alisa immediately took charge of the conversation, focusing her attention on Paul Andrews, questioning him about his position with Stuart Vineyards, showing no surprise when she discovered he handled sales and public relations. For all his gentleness, Paul had an appealing personality, as well as a wealthy family that still had a lot of influence in this part of California. His weakness was his obsession with Alisa, the first thing that neither his money nor his name had been able to buy. Still, he could be charming when he wanted to be. And tonight, under Alisa's attentive regard, his bitterness gradually fell away as he responded eagerly to her interest.

From the soup to the salad, through the fish course and the meat course and finally the dessert, Alisa could feel the displeasure emanating from Zachary when she talked to Paul. A few times she had smiled rather sweetly at him, asking if he agreed with a statement, then continued without giving Zachary an opportunity to comment. At last Zachary broke in to suggest that they move to the living room to sample the latest bottle of muscat produced by his winery. When Paul would have escorted Alisa in, Zachary moved to her elbow, his sardonic eyes compelling Paul to precede them.

Once in the living room, Christine hurried to where the big dog lay on the blue Persian rug near the fireplace, sitting down beside him. Alisa, hoping to thwart any attempt at intimacy by Zachary, seated herself in the large cushioned chair near the couch where Paul was seated. But after passing out the small crystal glasses filled with the pale golden wine, Zachary moved to Alisa's chair and rested his lanky frame on the armrest, his arm trailing along the back of the chair so that his hand was in easy reach of the escaping tendrils of hair. They were inseparably joined in Paul's vision. Any remark he made had to be addressed to them both.

Subtly, with Alisa hardly aware of what was happening, Zachary took charge of the conversation, steering the subject to the winery and the harvest a month away. Even as she turned her cool gaze up to him, meeting the brooding anger of his black eyes, she couldn't be sure of his emotion. In that moment, as she looked up at him and his two fingers captured a wispy strand of hair in an intimate gesture she knew she hated him, violently and totally. But Zachary only smiled at her when she pulled her head away from his caress, as if openly mocking her attempt to escape him.

"I think your sister has had a pretty long day. It's time you put her to bed, Alisa," Zachary said.

Alisa glanced guiltily towards the hearth and the yawning child who was nodding drowsily beside the sleeping German shepherd. Her concern for her sister kept her from reacting to the commanding tone of his voice. She quickly excused herself to Paul, adding pleasantly that they would see each other often, which brought her another severe look from her husband.

"After Christine falls asleep, come down and join us." Again there was no invitation, only an order in Zachary's voice.

But Alisa just smiled, feigning sincere affection while prompting Chris to say good night, happy to leave the room and her husband's suffocating presence.

An hour later, Alisa had bathed Christine, finally persuaded her to change into her pajamas, and listened patiently to her endless jabberings about

Baron, Zachary's dog. When the last burst of energy abated, Alisa tucked her into bed, smiling that she would be in the next room and that she would leave the connecting bathroom doors open in case Chris needed her. She had no intention of obeying Zachary and going back downstairs.

If she had to look up once more and see that black hair over those equally dark eyes and that aristocratic nose and hard mouth, Alisa felt she would scream. So instead she undressed, before busying herself with washing off the light makeup she used. Seated at her lighted dressing table, she applied a night cream, which gave her lightly tanned skin a golden glow. Then Alisa unpinned her hair and began brushing it with strong, vigorous strokes.

The electricity crackled through her hair as she bristled inwardly with hatred for the man who was now her husband. He was so arrogantly confident, the epitome of the superior male, that the thought of him sickened her. Even now in the sanctity of her room, Alisa could feel the masculine vitality of his presence surrounding her and stifling her with the force of his will. She tilted her head to the opposite side, her brush attacking her long hair as her eyes strayed to the mirror in front of her, meeting the reflection of a pair of dark, insolent eyes belonging to the tall figure standing just inside her door.

"What are you doing here?" Alisa turned to face Zachary for a fraction of a second, then looked back into the mirror.

"You didn't come back downstairs."

He had a smooth way of putting her on the defensive, she had to give him that.

"I didn't want to," Alisa replied, resuming the rhythmic strokes of her brush. At his failure to answer, she set the brush down, pivoting on her bench to face him once more. "This is my room. Will you please get out!"

"It's a shame you weren't downstairs," Zachary said calmly. "I gave an excellent performance for Paul about my anxious bride waiting upstairs for me. Kind of funny the way he up and left."

"I'm not amused; I'm disgusted." Alisa retorted viciously. "Do you steal candy from children, too?"

"What is this?" Zachary laughed. "A touch of conscience at such a late date? I wasn't the one that drove Paul to attempt suicide. Are you trying to tell me that you would've treated him differently if you'd known he'd try to kill himself, all for the love of you?"

Alisa looked away to hide the blush of shame on her cheeks, remembering her own callousness.

"I don't know," she murmured, then more positively, "No, I wouldn't have treated him differently. But you were just plain cruel. Do you know that he actually thought you'd brought me here for him, persuaded me somehow to give him another chance. And then you informed him that I was married to you. You could have had the grace to break it to him gently, but instead you flaunted me in his face as if I was some kind of trophy."

"You're not a trophy, you're a booby prize," Zachary drawled, deep amusement in his voice. "Pampering and pity are wasted on Paul. If you'd cooperated with me this evening, instead of fighting me, we could have accomplished more."

"And how would allowing you to paw me accomplish anything for Paul?'' Her beautiful eyes reproved him.

"I already answered that question and I don't intend to repeat myself!" Zachary blazed at her, his gaze narrowing threateningly. "At least you've told me the real reason you didn't come down. You were afraid of me—or more specifically of my touching you, no matter how innocent it was."

"That's a lie!" Alisa spat. "You disgust me, true enough, but I'm not afraid of you or your adolescent displays of virility in front of others. We've made a business arrangement. Any ideas that it will become anything other than that are totally wrong. I loathe the entire male race—and especially you!"

"We've been leading up to this discussion since yesterday." Zachary shrugged. "Are you challenging me deliberately, or is it possible that you secretly want me to make love to you?"

Her tightly controlled temper snapped at his revolting statement. Grabbing her brush as a weapon, Alisa rose from the dressing table to fling herself at him. Zachary caught the arm brandishing the brush, twisting it until Alisa dropped it with a cry of pain. She struggled, clawing with her free hand at the arm that held hers. He captured that one easily, drawing both behind her back where he held them with one hand. At the same time he crushed her to his body.

"I hate you!" she hissed, her words muffled against his chest.

"Do you expect me to believe that?" Zachary chuckled, twisting her chin up so that she was forced to look into his face. "You knew this would happen when you made that pathetically feminine attack. You knew you'd end up a prisoner in my arms.''

A shiver raced through Alisa. She knew there was truth in his words, but the idea was too preposterous. Anger at his egotism had made her attack him, forgetting his superior strength at the height of her temper.

"You're incredibly vain.'' Most of her composure returned and her words were uttered with her customary coolness.

"Am I?'' At the small sound of contempt that Alisa made, Zachary added, "I could make you fall in love with me.'' With a gesture of disdain, he released her, pushing her away from him. "But that wasn't part of our bargain. You paid me to marry you in name only. There was no provision that we had to sleep together.''

"Of course not,'' Alisa retorted, incensed by his tone of voice. "I didn't want you and I still don't.''

"Let's get one thing straight, Alisa.'' Zachary was angry now, his eyes blazing with dark fires. "I don't want you either. I can't imagine why any man would.''

Alisa stiffened at his arrogant assertion. Her mouth opened to emit a cutting reply, only to close at the sound of a small voice on the other side of the room saying accusingly, "You woke me up!''

"Chris,'' Alisa murmured, turning at once to the sleepy pajama-clad child as Zachary gave her one last, long look and left the room.

It was nearly twenty minutes later when Christine was soothed enough to put her head on her pillow and sleep, and Alisa returned to her own bedroom. Sitting on the edge of the purple velvet bedspread, she rubbed her wrists, the soreness brought on by their imprisonment in Zachary's strong hands bringing fresh tremblings of anger to her. With it came the logical and jarring realization that physically he could master her. And though she thanked God that he didn't want her, Alisa knew that her only two weapons were useless against him. The first was her money, of which Zachary had plenty—why had he wanted hers? The second was her beauty and desirability, which usually induced men to do her bidding. But Zachary had made it quite clear that she didn't sway him in the slightest.

It was a restless, troublesome night for Alisa.

CHAPTER THREE

Both Christine and Alisa arose late the next morning with Chris bouncing and eager for the new day and impatient at having to wait while Alisa dusted her face with cornsilk powder and applied light eyeshadow and mascara. In the morning room, they were informed by the housekeeper that Zachary had gotten up in a tone which indicated her disapproval of their late rising. But cereal, juice, and fruit were quickly placed before Christine while Alisa settled for toast and coffee.

The July sun had climbed high when Christine finally pursuaded Alisa to go outside. Her long-sleeved dress protected her from overexposure to the sun. She had learned some time ago that she looked best with only a light golden tan but Christine never tanned at all, acquiring more freckles with each outing in the sun. Every time Alisa tried to slather on sunblock, the little girl squirmed and protested—but Alisa prevailed in the end.

The pair wandered amid the tall oak trees that encircled the house, pausing near the fence that separated them from the vineyards and their endless rows of grapevines. But Alisa was too preoccupied to pay much attention to Christine's numerous questions. And at last Christine turned to her own imagination for entertainment, taking twigs and grass to build a tiny house for the little people that lived in the oak grove. Alisa watched her solemn sister as she carefully constructed the walls and roofs.

With Christine absorbed in her task, Alisa's thoughts were free to wander. Inexorably, they were drawn to Zachary. Alisa knew she was attractive. There was no vanity in the knowledge, just common sense. Her beauty should appeal to him. Yet he seemed to admire it and simultaneously to shrug it off. Her wealth and beauty had always lured a long string of admirers—none of whom she wanted, it was true, but they were there, all under her control. But this sensual, unpredictable man she had married was not.

Last night Alisa had attempted to take a stand, to let him know that she had no intention of obeying his orders. But she had been fool enough to lose her poise and her temper. Zachary had been quick to take advantage of both. Remembering the leashed violence with which he had so easily dismissed her attack, Alisa was also forced to recall the effortless way he crushed her against his chest. Any such intimate contact with a man she had shunned in the past. The few instances when it had occurred could be numbered on one hand.

That was why, she told herself, she had weakened against the firm rock wall of his body.

Her senses had been heightened, making her totally aware of the arms imprisoning her, the masculine scent of his cologne engulfing her, and the way his breath had warmed her hair. But the haunting, seductive softness of his voice when he had said that he could make Alisa fall in love with him had disturbed her the most. At the time Alisa had felt only contempt. Yet the memory drifted back.

Zachary had released her immediately after saying that, repeating that their marriage was a mockery and would remain that way as long as he chose. Despite her bold protests to the contrary, Alisa was forced to acknowledge that it was true. And, although she hadn't shown it, she had been frightened. Part of her had longed to cower in the face of his anger. But she had fought for herself too long. Alisa couldn't help wondering what would have happened if Christine hadn't woken and the argument had continued.

She had definitely underestimated Zachary. The marriage had been her solution to the conditions of her mother's will, a sacrifice of her own principles for the sake of her sister. She had chosen Zachary, thinking to bring him under her thumb. But Alisa had failed, miserably. Her wealth was no longer a thing to be held over his head. Her coldness was an easy target for his taunts. Although she had once considered her desirability a weapon, now she was grateful that it held no allure for Zachary. For once she felt lucky that he didn't want her—even though one feminine part of her yearned to know why.

Since her coolness couldn't keep him at arm's length and losing her temper only amused him, the only path left for her to take was to avoid him as much as possible. She and Christine would make their own little world, excluding Zachary Stuart. After all, Alisa thought, without fuel, a fire can't burn—or scorch those who come too close.

Relieved by her decision, Alisa turned to watch Chris's fascinating imagination working as she continued building a series of miniature grass homes. A drumming sound carried through the trees, its staccato beat turning Alisa's head in its direction. The sight of a horse and rider looked incongruous through her window of trees and vines. The petite figure astride the chestnut horse was clearly female, dressed in dark pants and a sleeveless red top. Someone must have called out to her, because Alisa saw the girl rein her horse in viciously, forcing him to turn at the same time.

Off to the side of one of the buildings housing the winery, Alisa saw Zachary looking cool and composed in shirt sleeves and khaki pants. The horse danced to a halt in front of him as his rider sat stiffly in the saddle. They were too far away for Alisa to hear their conversation, but it was evident that the dark-haired girl was angry, although the arrogant set of Zachary's shoulders indicated that he was unmoved by her. Without warning the girl's hand raised and the quirt in her hand came down with sudden swiftness. Zachary raised an arm to block the blow and with the other grabbed the girl and pulled her out of the saddle. Alisa could see Zachary laugh as his captive struggled uselessly in his arms.

Then there was a moment of stillness. His mouth

was moving in speech. Whatever it was that was said Alisa didn't know, but the girl's arms suddenly entwined around his neck as she pulled his head down to hers. Her stomach churned with sickening nausea, yet she was unable to look away from the obviously growing passion of their embrace. At last she shut her eyes, no longer able to stand the abandonment with which the girl gave herself to Zachary.

She hated and despised the man. Her body trembled with the violence of her feelings. He was an animal, a beast—she wished only she would never see him again. How could they carry on like that out here in the open where anyone could see them? Alisa glanced quickly at Christine who was still engrossed with her little world. At least she hadn't seen them.

CHAPTER FOUR

At lunchtime, Nora informed Christine and Alisa that Zachary would not be joining them. Sandwiches were being sent up to him at the winery. Although Christine was disappointed, Alisa could barely hide her relief at not being forced to sit at the same table with him. Her vow to avoid him was renewed with vigor.

By dinnertime that evening, her barriers were firmly in place, only to have the satisfaction taken away by the paper wall of the *San Francisco Chronicle* that Zachary erected between them. Rising from the table after dessert had been served, Zachary excused himself, saying that he had paperwork to catch up on, then sarcastically adding that he was sure Alisa didn't object to entertaining herself. She had no alternative but to agree, much as it annoyed her that he was the one to do the suggesting and not herself.

The pattern continued for five days, with Zachary always making sure that Alisa was the one who was left alone. Never once did Zachary use the den for his work, leaving the house instead to walk towards the winery. Alisa couldn't help assuming that he was keeping an assignation with the rider of the horse.

The fifth night it began raining shortly after Zachary had left. The entire day had been threatening with heavy clouds, which had finally released their burden. Alisa was curled up on the couch trying to convince herself that the book she was reading was interesting. But after four previous nights of only a book for company, she was becoming bored. And the steady beat of the rain outside made her restless. She set the book down and wondered if there was anything on television.

The phone rang sharply in the still room, momentarily startling Alisa with its harshness. She waited, expecting Nora to answer the hallway phone before she remembered that the housekeeper had already returned to her home on the grounds, formerly a coach house. Alisa picked up the living room extension just before the third ring. Just as she started to speak she heard Zachary's voice announce, "Stuart Vineyards."

"Did you order this rain, Zach?" The woman's voice was teasing with a sensuous huskiness to it.

"No, I didn't," Zachary replied. There was a slight pause. "Excuse me, Renée, I think someone else is on the line. I got it. You can hang up now."

Alisa inhaled sharply at his sarcastic tone and slammed the receiver down, hoping it would break their eardrums. He had to have known it was she on the other end. No one else was in the house except Christine, who was already in bed. There he was having an affair with another woman and he had the nerve to imply that she, Alisa, was behaving improperly! At least, she thought smugly, the rain dampened this evening's rendezvous.

The sun finally came out again late in the afternoon of the following day. The gentle breeze carried with it the salty tang of the Pacific Ocean. Alisa watched her half-sister contentedly ministering to the needs of her doll, which had arrived with the rest of her things the day before. A little sigh escaped her lips as Alisa wished for more happy days for the child.

It was a consolation to know that Chris was happy, since that had been the whole purpose of this marriage. Alisa loved Chris dearly and didn't begrudge the sacrifice she had made. But she had never felt so bored, restless and frustrated in all her life. Even more irritating was the fact that she was the only one that felt that way. As Alisa had found out last night, Zach had other diversions, while she sat alone in the house playing the part of a dutiful wife.

The housekeeper, Nora, was still barely civil towards her. And Alisa wasn't about to associate with the short-tempered cook, although she knew that Christine came and went from the kitchen whenever she pleased. Zachary rose and was gone from the house before Alisa awoke. Again Christine invariably breakfasted with him before she went to waken her sister. There was no one for Alisa to associate with, and as much as she loved her little sister, Chris couldn't provide the adult companionship that Alisa wanted.

"Nora said you were out here. May I join you?" a masculine voice asked from the veranda door of the house.

Alisa rose quickly at the voice. "Paul!" she cried, stretching out her hands in relief and welcome. "It's so good to see you again. Come on out."

In that brief second when she recognized him, two different emotions coursed through her. One, that she was glad she had worn the white jeans that hugged her hips, and the sky-blue crop top that matched her eyes. She knew the outfit was cute on her. The second feeling was that Paul had changed. Perhaps it was the air of confidence that enhanced his natural attractiveness.

Now, as he stepped forward to take one of her hands, Alisa noticed the beribboned gift in his other arm. She quickly drew him over to a chair near hers and sat down, offering him a glass of iced tea from the pitcher that sat on the glass-topped table beside her.

"I wasn't too sure how eager you'd be to see me," Paul said, accepting the frosted glass, a warm and endearing smile on his face. "Especially after I made a fool of myself the last time. I must have embarrassed you."

"I was only embarrassed for you and a little angry with Zachary for not letting me know you were here." A glitter appeared in her eyes in the memory of that evening.

"I brought you a wedding gift." Paul talked over Alisa's protest. "It was the least I could do. You can open it now or you can wait for Zachary, whichever you want."

A wedding gift—a chill went through Alisa at the thought that their mockery was going a step further. But she managed to smile and assert that she would open it now. When she unwrapped the gift and sifted through the protective packing, she found a most exquisite set of crystal wineglasses. They were beautiful and certainly appropriate for the newlyweds of Stuart Vineyard, but she just disliked the linking of Zachary and herself even by a wedding gift.

"I know this probably sounds strange to you," Paul said, "but since I couldn't have you, I'm glad you married Zachary. Our families have been friends for years. I don't know of anyone who doesn't admire and respect him." Alisa longed to correct Paul and say there was someone who didn't, but she kept her silence. "Looks like marriage agrees with you. You're not as aloof as you were. There's a warmness and compassion about you that wasn't there before."

Had she changed? Alisa wondered. Compassionate—yes, she was. Once she had been impervious to Paul's feelings, uncaring of whether he had been hurt or not. Now she did care. Part of her saw him as a child much like Christine. Why hadn't she noticed this unselfish side to Paul? She had been so quick to condemn him before, to laugh at his pathetic declarations of love. But now her conscience asked if it were his declarations that were pathetic or her reaction. Alisa refused to consider the question. For the moment it was enough to realize that Paul was a true friend, the first one who had ever wanted nothing more except her happiness.

With a sincerity that surprised even Alisa, she

asked about his home, his family, his life, noting the pride in his voice when he spoke lovingly about his parents and earnestly about his position at the vineyard. Chris was the one who finally broke into the discussion, tiring of playing by herself and with touching innocence enlisting Paul and Alisa into a game of keep-away with her big yellow ball.

Twice Alisa found herself laughing at Paul's exaggerated attempts to keep the ball from being tossed past him. She couldn't honestly remember the last time she had laughed in the company of an adult, not even Michael. At last Paul intercepted the ball and it was Christine's turn to be in the center. With a sense of elation, Alisa knew this was the way she had always imagined a family would be. As she took her turn in the center, Alisa managed a hesitant smile of gratitude at Paul, hardly knowing that the animated glow on her face was a breathtaking change from the supremely poised expression that Paul was accustomed to seeing. Chris tossed the ball high over Alisa's head, laughing delightedly when her older sister jumped in the air after it. Coming down, Alisa slipped on the wet grass. She would have fallen if Paul hadn't grabbed her by the waist and steadied her.

She had turned her ankle on landing and felt a flash of real pain when she tried to put her weight on it. Paul immediately insisted on helping her to a chair, then kneeling on the patio to inspect her foot.

"I only turned it, Paul," Alisa protested, but a warmth went through her at his worried frown. His solicitude was contagious and Christine hurried to bring Alisa her glass of iced tea—anything to make up for the unintentional injury to her sister.

As much as the fussing pleased her, Alisa finally insisted on standing, compelled to show them that she wasn't seriously injured. Paul's hand remained firmly on her arm as she walked without limping to the other side of the patio and back.

"You see, I'm fine. It only hurt for a minute or so," she said, arriving back at her starting point.

"Okay, okay." Paul shook his head in relief. "We'd better call off the games for a while, Chris. That grass is too slippery. The next time someone just might get really hurt."

Chris agreed, then went off bouncing the ball vigorously over the patio, announcing that she was going to count to see how long she could keep it bouncing. Paul and Alisa watched her silently for a time before Paul finally rose to his feet.

"I'd better be going, Alisa. I didn't intend to stay this long."

"I'm glad you came, and I hope you come often," Alisa returned, for the first time meaning every word she said.

"Not too often," Paul smiled. "I'd hate to make Zach jealous."

"Who cares what he thinks?" She covered her biting tone with a smile. "Chris and I would love to have you here any time. I'll walk you to your car so you can be sure I'm fine."

Paul protested, but Alisa could tell it was only halfhearted. At the edge of the drive, Paul took her hand as he said good-bye and held it longer than was really necessary, but Alisa didn't mind. Afterwards when he had driven off, waving to her and the distant Christine, she stood for several minutes by the drive watching the car as it drove down the tree-lined lane and disappeared from sight.

"That was a touching little scene."

The contented expression on her face froze as Alisa turned her head just far enough to see Zachary standing behind her. There was an underlying current of anger in his voice. Even though Paul's car was out of sight, Alisa returned her gaze to the road.

"You should have sent someone to let me know he was here," Zachary continued.

This time Alisa turned around, staring coldly up into his dark face. "I don't think he came to see you."

His eyes glittered. "Then what did he come for?"

"Oh, he wanted to apologize for embarrassing me the last time he was here," Alisa replied smoothly, enjoying the way Zachary's eyebrows raised in displeasure.

"How long did it take him to do that?"

"About an hour." Her blue eyes shimmered with defiance.

"I thought I'd made it clear that I didn't want you encouraging him. I thought you'd done enough damage the last time without leading him to believe that you want him around even now that you're married. Haven't you done enough harm to him?" Zachary stood tall, looming over her intimidatingly.

"I did absolutely nothing to encourage him to believe I wanted anything other than his friendship," Alisa replied sharply. "We spent an enjoyable afternoon together."

"You two can't be friends and you know it." Anger smoldered in his gaze while his barbed tongue lashed her unmercifully. "You may not be experienced enough yet to know that fact, but you'd better accept it as truth, because as long as you're my wife, I don't want your relationship with Paul to go any further."

"The mighty lord and master has spoken," Alisa announced scornfully. "And just how am I supposed to view your relationship with Renée? Are you just acquaintances, or lovers?"

"I wondered how long it would take before you brought that up." His anger was momentarily shelved to make way for his mocking amusement. "Surely you remember that I made it very clear that I had no intention of being faithful. I knew the ice maiden I married was chaste enough for both of us."

"You didn't think I would condone an affair being carried on right beneath my nose, did you? I knew what kind of man you were. The only thing I asked was that you would be discreet. But you can't even do that!"

"You don't know what you're talking about, Alisa. You'd better end this conversation now before you push me too far." His words were spoken concisely as if he were exercising the most extreme control.

"What do you think I am, some dumb blonde who can't see or hear or add up what she does see?" She ignored his warning look. "Don't deny that you were kissing Renée near the winery buildings. I understood that you usually do the books and paperwork at the house. What changed your routine?"

"That's enough, Alisa!"

"Is it? And just how do you propose to shut me up?"

The speculative gleam that danced within his fiery gaze frightened Alisa a little, but outwardly she remained calm.

"I think you'd like me to force myself on you so you can convince yourself all those horrible things you've been thinking about me are true." He took in her defiant stance with slightly cynical amusement. "You also know I'm not about to turn the other cheek. You're too proud and too self-important. What you need is to be taken down a peg or two."

Alisa swallowed nervously, trying to shake the feeling that she was watching a jungle cat just before it leaped for its prey. She started to turn to walk away so that he would be left with his threat dangling in the air. But her wrist was pinioned in his viselike grip. When her other hand tried to rescue the first, it too was captured. For a minute she allowed herself to be his captive, attempting to lull him into a sense of security. Even as she did so, she was bracing herself so that the moment he relaxed she could twist her wrists free.

The moment came. Alisa could feel the slight loosening of his hold. Immediately she tried to pull away, stumbling backward a step or two as she seemed to succeed. Then his grip tightened and she used all her strength to tear away from it. Just as she was beginning to think she wouldn't succeed, Zachary let go. Between the suddenness of his release and the strength with which she was trying to pull away, Alisa lost her balance and fell, white jeans, crop top and all, right into the largest mud puddle in the driveway.

"Damn you!" she cried in a helpless rage as she stared down at her mud-soaked jeans and at the same time tried to shake the goo off her hands. Zachary merely looked down at her with an infuriating smile of satisfaction.

She slipped twice trying to get to her feet, each time glaring at Zachary for his failure to help her out. By the time she got out of the puddle and had walked with mud squishing through her toes on to the lawn, Christine was standing beside Zachary, regarding her mud-drenched sister with open-mouthed surprise.

"There's a utility room with a shower at the rear of the house next to the kitchen. You can clean up there," Zachary told her with maddening amusement.

"What happened?" Christine whispered. But the furious look from her sister told her quite plainly that she wasn't going to get an answer.

Alisa stalked angrily to the house, aware of Zachary and Christine following her at a respectful distance. She could hear her younger sister giggling and Zachary's laughing voice admonishing her. Briefly she contemplated going through the front door and tracking mud across the polished tile floor, but she couldn't bring herself to do that, no matter how much she wanted to get back at Zachary for humiliating her. Instead she walked to the rear entrance. She was immediately met by Nora, who stared at her in horror.

"Which way to the utility room? I need to clean up." Alisa squared her shoulders with all the dignity she could. "And I need some towels, too. Please go up to my room and get my lavender caftan and some slippers."

Nora nodded silently, led her through the kitchen to the small room, then left, still staring at Alisa incredulously. Minutes later she was back, bringing snow white towels and a washcloth. Alisa had just decided that there was no way she could pull the mud-covered crop top off without getting the mud in her hair, too, when Christine walked into the room.

"Zach said you'd need some shampoo." She covered her mouth quickly to stifle the giggle that kept trying to bubble through her voice.

"Christine, so help me . . ." Alisa trailed off threateningly.

"I can't help it. You look so funny!" This time the little girl laughed in earnest.

Alisa looked down at her once-white jeans, the streaks of mud on her bare belly, and her splattered blue top. With a resigned smile, she had to admit that she probably did look pretty funny.

"All right—out, you little scamp!" She finally managed to speak in a more understanding voice. "I've got to get undressed before the mud hardens on me."

Christine succumbed to one more burst of giggles before she left the room. Alisa undressed swiftly, adjusted the water temperature, then stepped under the shower. She was busy toweling her long hair to a state of damp dryness when Chris reappeared in the room.

"I'm supposed to tell you that dinner is ready just as soon as you're through. Zachary said you didn't need to worry about how you're dressed because it would just be a simple meal."

Alisa said she would be out in a few minutes and that Christine should pass the information along.

The door had barely shut behind her sister when Alisa muttered a few choice descriptive words about Zachary Stuart.

Guess I shouldn't fuss over my appearance, she thought bitterly. *Not that he seems to care what I look like, anyway.*

She unwrapped the terry towel that had covered her and slipped on her underwear and the lavender print caftan. Hurriedly she combed out her golden hair, parting it in the center so that it fell freely to below her shoulders. Slipping on her white sandals, Alisa decided to forgo any lipstick or mascara or other cosmetics. After all, the great lord and master awaited.

Arriving in the dining room, Alisa was informed by the housekeeper that dinner would be served on the patio that evening. She was just about to open the patio door when she looked out to see Zachary bending beside Chris's doll carriage, attempting to fix a wobbly wheel. It was a curious thing to watch this arrogant man taking so much care with a child's toy. When it was fixed, he hoisted Christine on his shoulder and was rewarded with a kiss.

Alisa made a lot of noise rattling the doorknob, almost stamping across the cement patio, and shutting the door a little louder than was necessary. But if she hoped to break up the intimate scene she had just witnessed, she was mistaken. When she focused her attention again on the pair, Christine was still in Zachary's arms and they were both looking at her with obvious amusement. Alisa regarded Zachary coldly.

"Your sister's here. Looks like we're ready to eat,

peanut," he said teasingly to Chris, slowly setting her on the ground.

"Why do you call me peanut?" Chris demanded, bending her head way back so that she could look up into his face.

"Because you're about the size of one and you're as nutty as one." Zachary ruffled her hair affectionately. "Your menu is courtesy of little sister tonight," he said to Alisa. "Hamburgers, french fries, coleslaw, cokes, and ice cream for dessert. Not exactly gourmet fare, but it's tasty."

"And we have pickles, ketchup, mustard, onions, tomatoes, cheese, just everything to put on hamburgers. Come and see, Lisa!" Christine tugged Alisa's stiffened arm impatiently.

Alisa met Zachary's mocking gaze, which told her clearly that she looked unharmed by her unglamorous fall into the mud puddle. She longed to tell him how rude he was, except that she knew such a statement would be ignored or dismissed. Instead Alisa assumed an air of unconcern, allowing herself to be drawn to the patio table by Christine and her innocent cheerfulness. As long as her attention was focused on Chris instead of Zachary, Alisa found she could enjoy the meal. Eventually, once the little girl's appetite was satisfied, she hurried off to wheel her newly repaired doll carriage around the house. And Alisa was left with Zachary for company.

The evening sun cast long shadows. Those from the tall oaks gently stretched over the pair. The breeze had died until there was only a slight sensation of movement in the air. Birds sang somewhere far away, a distant trilling that soothed her. All the strain and anger that had filled Alisa was strangely whisked away by the hush of nightfall.

"I love these lazy summer evenings," Zachary said softly. His dark eyes glanced swiftly at Alisa as if apologizing for breaking the stillness. "It's when we rest up before the harvest season. Once you've been here at harvest time, it's hard to believe it was ever as serene as it is this evening."

"You're a strange man," Alisa murmured.

"Am I?" This time his reserved gaze settled on her face, studying her calmly, and yet somehow Alisa got the feeling that he was interested in her answer.

"You don't seem like the kind of man who would want to own a vineyard except as a hobby. Something you could fool around with now and then."

"What kind of man do you believe I am?" This time he studied the far horizon.

"Oh, an entrepreneur, a wheeler-dealer. Someone who's good at manipulating others to get your way. The image of you as a vintner doesn't fit. I just can't picture you being dictated to by the sun and the wind and the weather. Why didn't you follow in your father's footsteps, pick up where he left off?"

"Well, my father was an important, powerful man, because that's who my mother wanted him to be. His happiest times were spent here at Stuart Vineyard. It was a rundown, shabby place when he bought it. His dream was to make great wine and go national. There's no joy in dominating other people, but beating Mother Nature—now that's a challenge." Zachary smiled the wry smile of an adult to a child, of one who knows to one who is learning.

"Then why do you try to dominate me?" she asked, irritated by his knowing attitude.

"All I'm doing is seeing to it that you don't dominate me." He spoke smoothly, without any suggestion of rancor in his voice. "And you do try to, Alisa."

Seized by a restlessness brought on by his subtly probing gaze, Alisa rose and walked to a spreading oak tree at the edge of the patio. Yes, she was always testing, trying to see if he would allow her to dominate him. If he would be as weak as the others and cater to her needs. She stared at the purple sky infused with a brilliant fuchsia pink, aware that Zachary had risen, too, and halted a few steps away from her. She turned her troubled blue eyes toward him.

"You look so vulnerable right now," Zachary said. "Not much older than Christine, with your hair down and no makeup."

Alisa did feel vulnerable. She didn't know how to handle Zachary's sudden gentleness. It frightened her, the way some of her defenses were breaking down. She turned her back to him and stared into the sky at the silvery slip of moon that hung so precariously.

"You try so hard to be independent and strong." His hands slipped under her hair and began gently massaging the tense muscles in her neck. "You've taken the world on your shoulders." His voice was a soft, caressing whisper that was oddly soothing and hypnotic. "You've made Chris your sole responsibility, and you refuse help from everyone. Haven't you ever wanted anyone to take care of *you*?"

As much as she wanted to, Alisa couldn't admit

any such feeling to him. Instead she came as close as she could to saying the same thing. "I've often wondered what my father was like. If he was kind and gentle, or strong and powerful . . ." She paused. "I was only a child when he died, and my mother remarried so many times after that." She wasn't aware of the slight drooping of her shoulders or the fact that she was resting against Zachary's broad chest. His hands had moved to knead her upper arms.

The languid summer night, the tender massage of Zachary's hands, and the murmur of his voice combined to draw Alisa into a world softened by the warmth of his hands on her and the thought of security and safety once provided by a father she had never known. How wonderful it would be to have a father you belonged to, to know that he would always be there whenever you needed him, Alisa thought, and to be loved just for yourself, not because you were beautiful or talented or rich.

"Come out of your dream world, Alisa. Your father was no saint." His voice, though still soft, sounded harsh in the still air. "Every human being has flaws. Your father could have been one of the world's all-time losers."

"How can you say that?" Alisa cried, springing forward to be free of his hands while turning to see his face. "You didn't know him! You didn't know what he was like!"

"Neither did you." Zachary studied her with a hard and thoughtful gaze. "You're a beautiful and desirable woman. I just want to be sure you don't confuse male attention with fatherly affection. No man could look at you and have paternal concern on his mind, including myself."

"You're a pompous, arrogant . . . !" Alisa spluttered. "I didn't get to be twenty-four years old without learning that lesson!"

"I'm glad. I'd hate to see you get your dreams mixed up with reality."

"Zach, there's a phone call for you!" Nora called from the house.

"That must be Renée. Did you miss another rendezvous?" Alisa asked spitefully.

"I told you once that you didn't know what you're talking about. But since you don't choose to believe me, just keep your opinions to yourself!" His eyes flashed a fiery warning which she shrugged off. Zachary hesitated as if to argue the point with her, before finally turning sharply and heading for the house.

Zachary returned a few minutes later to tell Alisa that his mother had called. He added, sarcastically, that his mother would be driving from San Francisco to have dinner with them a week from Sunday and to meet his wife. After relaying all that, Zachary started to leave. Inadvertently Alisa asked where he was going.

He looked her up and down thoughtfully. "I'll be back later this evening," was his only reply.

It was nearly one o'clock in the morning before Alisa heard the car pull into the driveway and she knew that Zachary had returned. Sleep had escaped her. The books she had picked up couldn't hold her attention. Finally she had just lain in bed waiting subconsciously for her husband to return. Only after she had heard him come up the stairs, the sound of his bedroom door opening and closing, did she finally turn over in her bed and fall into a heavy, dreamless sleep.

That following week Christine had been cranky and out of sorts, demanding more and more from Alisa. Several times she slipped away, going up to the winery in spite of orders from Alisa to the contrary. But Christine had ignored the scoldings, regaling Alisa with tales of men taking the temperature of the wines, sipping out of different glasses and talking about what the wine tasted like. Alisa silently envied her sister's escapades, but she couldn't figure out how to halt her wanderings or curb Chris's headstrong ways.

One evening Zachary had finally stepped in and ordered Christine to bed. Alisa had stood silently by while Chris stomped up the stairs before Alisa flew at Zachary in a rage. But he had been adamant. If Alisa couldn't discipline the kid, then he would. And he had no intention of letting a seven-year-old child rule his house with her whining and tantrums.

Alisa knew he was right, although she absolutely refused to admit it. She had pampered Christine too much, trying to make sure she didn't miss her parents more than was necessary. Zachary had dismissed her concerns, saying that children were more resilient than adults and could adjust quicker to a change in their environment. What had been harder to take was Christine's attitude. Alisa had gone up to her bedroom when her argument with Zachary had reached a stalemate. Christine had gotten ready for bed and was busy saying her prayers. After her usual "God bless Mommy and Dad, who are in heaven, and tell them I love them," came "God bless Alisa and God bless Zach." It was the first time Alisa had ever heard her include Zachary's name in her prayers.

Gently, trying to hide her curiosity, Alisa had asked, "Aren't you angry with Zachary anymore?"

"No. I wasn't angry with him before. I just wondered if he put up with me because of you, or whether he really liked me," her little sister replied. "Now I know he likes me."

"How? Because he ordered you to your room?" Alisa frowned.

"Yes." The simple statement was accompanied by a wide smile as Chris crawled under the covers of her bed. "You only yell and get mad at the people you like."

Alisa had to be satisfied with that explanation. Although it was contradictory, it made sense. But it also made her wonder if she should delve into her own feelings on the subject, something she was reluctant to do.

Alisa had difficulty making up her mind what to wear to the dinner with Zachary's mother. After removing half the clothes from her closet, she finally decided on a featherlight suit in ivory with a paisley print blouse. As she was adjusting the collar, a knock came at her bedroom door. Impatiently she called to whoever it was to enter, thinking it was Christine again, who was not looking forward to the day at all. But it was Zachary.

"I just suggested to Chris that she eat in the kitchen with Nora," he said, looking very impressive in a casual light brown suit. "She isn't quite old enough to be included in an adult dinner."

"She'll be happy about that," Alisa replied, ignoring the gaze that sought hers in the mirror. He walked slowly across the room to lean against the wall beside Alisa's dressing table. Reaching into his coat pocket, he withdrew a small black box, flipped it open and removed the ring inside. He reached down and clasped her left hand, slipping the ring on her finger.

"They'll expect to see something other than the gold band," he said in answer to Alisa's surprised glance. A deep red ruby encircled with diamonds gleamed brilliantly at her from its setting. "A blue sapphire would have more suited your nature," there was sarcasm in his voice, "but I chose to include the fire you lack in the ring."

"It's very beautiful." Her eyes glimmered coolly. "But you didn't have to go to this extreme just to keep up appearances."

"You don't believe I spent my money for this?" he mocked.

Alisa ignored his taunt, her mind flitting back to his first statement that "they" would be expecting a ring.

"What did you mean when you said 'they' would be expecting me to wear a ring?"

"Didn't I tell you? My mother is staying with the Gautiers. I decided that we might as well have them over as well. They're our nearest neighbors. This dinner will stave off any need for a get-acquainted party in the future." His eyebrows raised as if he was surprised by her question. Then Zachary smiled. "I invited Paul and your cousin Michael, too, which should make you happy."

"It's so thoughtful of you to tell me of this ahead of time." With jerky, angry movements, Alisa picked up her lipstick case and reapplied the mocha tint to her lips. "I hope you don't intend to subject our guests to any of your tasteless scenes."

"Let's just say that as long as you appear the model wife, I'll be the model husband. Solicitous, but not overly affectionate."

Alisa glared coldly at his jeering expression as she rose from the dressing table and walked to the bed to slip on the matching jacket to her skirt.

"What time is everyone supposed to arrive?" she asked.

Zachary glanced at his wristwatch. "Oh, half an hour to an hour. Are you coming downstairs to welcome them with me, or are you planning a grand entrance after they've arrived?"

Stiffening momentarily at his biting sarcasm, Alisa finally turned to look at him. "I'll be at my husband's side, of course."

"I'm glad you said that," he replied smiling that lazy smile that reminded Alisa of a Cheshire cat. "I didn't want to insist."

Michael was the first to arrive, taking in the decor as if he was assessing the place. He seemed awed by Zachary, which didn't dim his curiosity any. It only gave him a faintly furtive air. Taking a glass of sherry from Alisa, he winked and whispered, "You're an old married lady now, huh? He's quite a handful, don't you think?"

Alisa laughed off his I-told-you-so smirk with ease, hoping to shatter Michael's assumption that the war was tilting in Zachary's favor. Zachary answered the door alone when the bell rang again to announce the arrival of Paul. He was escorted into the living room where Alisa and Michael were seated. By the time Zachary had given him a glass of sherry, the bell rang once more. This time it was several minutes before he returned to the room. Alisa hid her nervousness behind a bright smile as an older couple entered the room. The man was slim, neither tall nor short, with a distinguished touch of white at his temples and dark, curling hair. The plump woman on his arm wore a dark blue dress. Her hair, too, was very dark, but it was streaked throughout with gray which her hairdo didn't hide.

Behind them walked Zachary. The woman on his right was the first to come into Alisa's view. She was petite and slender, dressed in an elegant pink chiffon dress that went well with her chestnut hair. Only when she stepped closer could Alisa see the betraying lines of age around her eyes and neck. Zachary began to introduce Louis and Estelle Gautier when Alisa saw the girl on his other side. He drew her forward gently. "This is the Gautiers' daughter, Renée."

Alisa knew a chill had come over her features as she extended her hand. But it was mild in comparison to the glaring hatred in the brown eyes looking back at her. Alisa couldn't help studying this girl who met secretly with her husband. Her hair was long and black; she was easily four inches shorter than Alisa, with provocative curves displayed to advantage in a tangerine silk dress. Her lashes were naturally long and thick and framed eyes that were lovely despite the hostility in them. Her heart-shaped face was equally lovely with a smooth forehead, a button nose to match her petiteness, and full, sensuous lips outlined in a trendy orange-red to match her dress. At last, after Renée had murmured with false enthusiasm how pleased she was to meet Zachary's new wife, Zachary stepped forward with his mother.

His eyes traveled mockingly over Alisa's frozen expression even as he introduced his mother. There was interest but no friendliness in Mrs. Stuart's face as she greeted Alisa. In fact, Alisa got the impression that the woman didn't like what she saw.

"I've looked forward to meeting you, Mrs. Stuart," Alisa managed to say politely. She was intensely aware that Michael had picked up on the hostility between her and Renée and was amused. He also seemed very anxious to find a place beside Renée.

"And I've wanted to meet you, the woman who managed to spirit my son away without any advance notice." Mrs. Stuart laughed a tinkling, teasing laugh that made Alisa feel uncomfortable. "Of course, he knew I always hoped he would have a big wedding. But you know how men are about such functions—always so anxious to get them over with. Zachary, bring me some of your sherry. Then run along and talk about your winery with Louis like you usually do."

Zachary nodded and moved away. Alisa knew where her husband had acquired his dominating personality, especially when Mrs. Stuart insisted that they sit down and get to know one another. Zachary returned with the sherry and waited while his mother sipped it, commenting, "It's very good, darling." Then he seated himself in a chair next to Louis Gautier and Paul. Alisa was quick to note that Renée had draped herself on the arm of her father's chair nearest to Zachary. Her blue eyes glanced at Zachary, who smiled wickedly back before turning to speak to Louis. Michael was busy trying to get Renée's attention, without much success.

"I understand you have a daughter," Mrs. Stuart said brightly.

"A daughter? No, my little sister, Christine, is living with us," Alisa corrected. "Our parents are both dead."

"Oh, how unfortunate for Zachary." She smiled with solicitous sweetness at Alisa. "And for you, too, dear. I just meant that it was too bad that you two had to start out with family responsibilities immediately."

"Christine has a trust fund, so she's really not a financial liability to us," Alisa retorted, a little more sharply than she intended.

"Who has control of this trust fund?"

"I do," Alisa replied coolly.

"That's good. Sometimes lawyers and bankers can be so insensitive to the needs of a child, if you know what I mean." Zachary's mother's smile was so ingratiatingly coy that Alisa had to grit her teeth to keep from making a sarcastic remark. "It was such a shock to me when Zachary called to tell me he was married. I wasn't even aware he knew you. Now that I've met you I can see why. You're very beautiful."

"Thank you. That's a very nice compliment for a mother-in-law to make." The words practically choked her even as Alisa said them.

"You're not exactly Zachary's type. I always imagined that he would pick someone with dark hair and eyes, like himself. Now you and Paul would look so good together, with you both being so fair." The raised voice brought Zachary's gaze to Alisa.

The conversation was growing increasingly unbearable for Alisa and a severe strain on her patience. Mrs. Stuart smiled at her in a confiding yet apologetic way. "Oh, the Gautiers and I always felt that Renée and Zachary would marry. It would have been ideal, you know. The vineyards join up to the north. And the Gautiers are such a respected name in California. Poor Louis is getting so much older and he only has Renée to inherit his holdings. For a while, she and Zachary seemed awfully fond of each another—and a marriage would have pleased both our families. But of course, that was before he met you, dear."

Alisa wondered what Mrs. Stuart's reaction would be if she learned that her son and Renée were still "fond" of each other, and what she would think if she found out that Zachary had married Alisa for money. It would probably make no difference, Alisa decided, since she had the impression that Mrs. Stuart was a social climber and not all that impressed by mere money."

"I think I've made Zachary quite happy in the few weeks we've been married," Alisa commented, not knowing what else to say in the face of Mrs. Stuart's obvious preference for a different daughter-in-law.

"I'm sure you have." The woman patted Alisa's hand insincerely. "I just wish I could have met you sooner, but my son was insistent that you two should have time together alone before you met his dragon of a mother." Again there was tinkling laughter.

Unconsciously Alisa pulled her hand back a little. Her ruby ring flashed the bright reflection of the flame.

"Oh, is that your ring?" Mrs. Stuart exclaimed. "My son has such exquisite taste."

"Let me see it!" Renée rose from the arm of her father's chair, moving gracefully across the small space to where Alisa and Mrs. Stuart were seated. Her delicate hand caught hold of Alisa's as she raised it higher to see the ring more clearly. "A ruby!" she cried, casting the amused Zachary a teasing glance. "My favorite gem!"

Alisa fought an unaccountable urge to tear the ring off her finger and hand it to the girl. Instead she smiled and thanked Renée politely, meeting Zachary's eyes for a moment before he turned his gaze to Paul who was talking to him.

"How strange that Zach would pick a ruby for your engagement ring," Renée was saying with lilting huskiness to her voice. "It doesn't really suit you. Diamonds or sapphires would look better." The malevolent gleam was back in her dark eyes.

"I don't let other people decide what suits me. They're invariably wrong." Alisa held back none of the sarcasm in her tone as she met the brown eyes with a frosty glare of her own. If Renée wanted to do battle, Alisa decided that she might as well know she had a formidable opponent.

"Mother, Alisa," Zachary interrupted. "Dinner is ready." He offered an arm to each, smiling down at Alisa in what probably seemed to most an amiable smile, but Alisa saw the warning look that was meant strictly for her.

Zachary was seated at the head of the table with Alisa at the opposite end. Alisa was happy to see his mother seated to his left. Now she wouldn't have to tolerate any more of Mrs. Stuart's barbed remarks. She was already upset by the fact that Renée was on Zachary's right, batting her big brown eyes, flirting outrageously with him. Michael was to Renée's right, trying to compete with Zachary as the center of her attention. Alisa was able to quell a flash of anger by turning to Louis Gautier and his wife, who were sitting on each side of her. Mrs. Gautier was a self-effacing type, referring any opinions to her husband. Her politeness and soothing manner eased Alisa's tension. Paul was between the two older women, charming both of them, as usual.

As the meal progressed, Alisa became more and more conscious of deliberately avoiding any glances towards the opposite end of the table. But she couldn't stop hearing Zachary's voice, so low and so musical as he replied to Renée's questioning. There was no mockery, no amusement in his tone, only charm and interest—so different from their own conversations.

When the main course of roast rack of lamb arrived, Zachary poured a glass of rosé wine for each guest. Louis held his up to the light, studied it, smelled it, sipped it, then nodded approvingly to Zachary.

"Light, fruity—yes, it is good." Louis Gautier smiled widely as he turned to cock his head towards Alisa. "What do you think?"

"I'm not really a wine connoisseur," Alisa apologized, noting the reverent way he had inspected it.

"Ah, but you'll learn. Zachary will teach you what qualities we look for in our wines. Has he shown you around the vineyards yet, and the winery?" At

Alisa's negative shake of her head, Louis looked reprovingly at Zachary. "The harvest season is almost here. Soon you won't have time to take her around."

"When Alisa and I are together, we don't think or talk about grapes." Zachary smiled wickedly across the table at Alisa.

"Aha. The mind of our new *vigneron* has been dwelling on his golden-haired wife and not on his golden-green grapes," Louis laughed. "That's what these lazy summer nights are for, while our succulent grapes grow heavy on their vines, yes, Estelle?" Passing his plate to be served, Louis turned to Alisa and sighed. "You must learn about the grapes and the wines so you will know why your husband is so busy all the time. And you should learn the history and tradition of the Napa Valley. My papa came here in 1896 with his papa all the way by ship from Bordeaux. They brought with them cuttings from the finest vines to hybridize with the American vines. The conditions were right but still they had to protect their vines from mildew, black rot and disease. Their wines were good. Yet when I was twenty-five they sent me back to France for five years that I could learn at my cousin's winery and become a good *vigneron*. I met Estelle there." He gazed fondly at his wife, who gave him a pleased yet shy look from behind her dark lashes. "My papa and grandpapa started with forty acres and we now own over five hundred. I would have bought this vineyard, too, but I'm getting old, and my daughter has not provided me with a son-in-law."

"Papa, now that Zachary has been stolen away from me, who is left?" Renée laughed enchantingly at her father while eyeing Zachary with mock remorse. Alisa's mouth was set as she met her husband's penetrating gaze.

"I've often wished that Zachary were—never mind," Louis said. "But it is not so. He is going to have a splendid vineyard one day. In a few years he won't have to sell his grapes to other wineries, and can bottle them all himself."

"I won't be selling many this year," Zachary told them. "I bought more cooperage. It arrived last week."

"What kind?" Louis's eyes lit up with interest.

"Stainless steel," Zachary replied.

"After dinner you must take me to see them," Louis ordered, lifting his glass towards his host before bringing it to his mouth.

Zachary returned his smile before his gaze slid to Alisa's knowing look. At last she knew where the money she had given him had been spent. She had wondered about it ever since she arrived at his handsome house. His dark eyes danced with mockery at her nearly evident relief. To avoid him Alisa turned to Mrs. Gautier and struggled to carry on a conversation with the gentle, quiet woman.

The men paused politely with the women at the end of the meal. Her cousin Michael cornered Alisa privately for a moment, tossing in a few jibes about the ruby that "her" money had bought.

"You're really trying to make this marriage look real," he jeered. "I don't think that ring is going to hold back Renée. Not if she wants Zachary."

"Michael, you know this never was a love match," Alisa reminded him, her irritation growing.

"Well, you still didn't seem too happy about the way they carried on at the table," he pointed out.

"Neither did you," she retorted, trying to keep her voice low so the rest of the guests couldn't hear. "Is the competition too stiff?"

"Maybe. I'll let you know." Michael lifted his glass of wine before sauntering off in Renée's direction.

The men exchanged a few more pleasantries with the women before Zachary led the way towards the winery to show off his new winemaking equipment to Louis. Once they had gone, the conversation was controlled by Mrs. Stuart and Renée. Alisa sat quietly on the couch beside Mrs. Gautier, wondering how she could tolerate being so obviously left out of the conversation. But Mrs. Gautier's attention was on her daughter as if she was amazed that anything so vivacious and volatile could have come from her. Alisa wondered, too.

She found her eyes wandering to the clock, wishing the time would pass more swiftly so that this tedious afternoon would come to an end. Alisa even caught herself wishing that Zachary would return from the winery so that his vitality would fill the room and rescue her from these two boring women. But the pendulum of the mantel clock swung slowly and the faint ticking couldn't drown out their voices. When she discovered her fingernails were making marks in the palm of her hand, Alisa decided she had had enough. With the excuse that she wanted to freshen up, she left the room.

Upstairs in the seclusion of her room, her pose of cool sophistication fell away. She glared into the mirror, suddenly angry at Zachary for ever having the dinner in the first place. He obviously knew what kind of woman his mother was. And springing Renée on her without any warning had been a choking humiliation. Alisa stared at the bottle of Chanel No. 5 on her dressing table. She picked it up, carried it into the bathroom, and poured it down the sink. That was the fragrance that Renée had been wearing. Alisa realized that she hated it. A short, hollow laugh escaped her lips as it occurred to her that the perfume was probably the most expensive drain freshener ever.

Reentering her bedroom, Alisa wondered how long she could stay up here before her absence would be considered a breach of etiquette for a hostess. If it wouldn't be conceding victory to Mrs. Stuart and Renée, she wouldn't bother returning. Her pride wouldn't allow her to acknowledge defeat. She reapplied her lipstick, remembering how Michael had referred to it as putting on war-paint. In this case, that was exactly what it was.

"Oh, here you are," Renée drawled from the doorway, poised in its frame like a model making an entrance, before swishing into the room. "I decided I'd better freshen up, too, before the men get back."

Alisa hid her surprise quickly, smiling coolly as she welcomed Renée into her private room. "I doubt that the men, being what they are, will even notice that we've done anything," she murmured, watching Renée fussing with her hair in front of the mirror.

"Zachary will notice. He always does, you know." There was an intimacy in her reply that threatened to curl the hair on the back of Alisa's neck.

"Really? Oh, I'm sure you could tell me a lot about Zachary," Alisa said, hoping her shaft of cold sarcasm had found its mark.

"Yes, I could." The light of battle was in Renée's

eyes as she turned to face Alisa. "Zach and I have been close, very close, for a long time. As he has often said, we're two of a kind."

"Maybe that's why he got tired of you," Alisa retorted sharply.

Renée's face paled slightly before it was flooded with color. "Is this your room?" With deadly calm, she changed the subject, or so Alisa thought when she replied that it was. "That's strange. I expected you to be in the master bedroom next door to where Zach sleeps. Why do you have separate rooms? Is he tired of you?"

"I can answer that one," a bright voice rang out from the door.

"Christine!" Alisa exclaimed. "What are you doing here?"

"I thought I'd find out how the party was going and the dark-haired lady in the blue dress said you were up here." After answering Alisa's question, the child turned towards Renée. "I know why they don't sleep in the same room."

"Chris, you shouldn't be talking about such things," Alisa interrupted quickly.

"Let her talk," Renée smiled. "This ought to be interesting."

"I asked Zach one morning why you two didn't sleep together like Mommy and Daddy did." Chris's voice rang with authority before a smile tugged at the corners of her mouth. "You know what he told me? He said that Alisa snores so loud that he can't sleep!"

Alisa met the triumphant glance from the dark-haired girl as she grasped Christine by the shoulders to usher her out of the room.

"Can I sleep with you sometime, Lisa, so I can hear you snore?" Chris asked plaintively.

"No. Now run along outside and play." Alisa's voice was firm.

"Looks like I'm not the only one who's commented on your sleeping arrangements," Renée laughed. "Not what one would expect for a newly married couple."

"That's between Zachary and myself." Alisa turned away, unable to combat the frontal attack.

"Do you expect to hang onto him if you keep him at arm's length?" Renée jeered. "Maybe that's how you got him to marry you, but, honey, you'd better come across with the goods or you're going to lose him."

"And you'll be right there to catch him, won't you?" Alisa pushed back her hair, hoping her hand wouldn't tremble and reveal how thoroughly Renée's jabs were getting to her.

"You bet I will! Zach's a passionate man and I know how to satisfy him." The long dark locks were tossed over her shoulder in a positive gesture. "You noticed the way he looked at me today. You can bet he's got a lot to remember about what went on between us. And he'll have a lot more."

"Isn't it dangerous, giving away your plans like this to the enemy?" Alisa asked coldly.

"Not with you it isn't." Smug sarcasm rang harshly in Renée's voice. "You're like a very lovely but cold work of art. You may have the equipment to keep him, but you don't know how to use it."

"I may not know how to tease him like you do, or exactly how to stroke his ego. But I won't tolerate you mooning over him in my presence, making eyes or whatever you call it. If you think that I'm going to just let you throw yourself at my husband without doing a thing about it, you're wrong!" Her voice shook with enraged anger as Alisa faced Renée. "There will be no more secret meetings or intimate phone conversation. From now on, you're not allowed into this house—"

"Alisa!" Zachary's harsh, commanding voice startled her.

Almost unwillingly, she turned to him, the sharp edge of her anger dulling slightly upon meeting the shimmering brilliance of his. Zach's fiery black eyes held hers for what seemed like an eternity before they moved to Renée. There was a shade of softness in his gaze as it rested on her. Alisa glanced back and was stunned to see two small tears trickling down Renée's cheeks. With a raised eyebrow, Alisa realized that she had underestimated Renée's ability as an actress.

"Would you excuse us, Renée?" Zachary asked with deadly quietness.

"I'm sorry, Zach. I never dreamed this would happen," she whispered in return.

Alisa's anger once again rose to its former peak as she watched Renée leave the room, knowing that little speech was for Zachary's benefit and he had fallen for it completely. As the door closed behind the tangerine silk dress, Alisa drew herself up arrogantly to face him.

"You have a headache, Alisa."

The strange statement momentarily stunned her with its tightly controlled tone. "What are you talking about?"

"I said you aren't feeling well, so you'd better stay in your room," he repeated, his voice raising slightly in emphasis.

"You're partially right." Her brilliant blue eyes flashed angrily. "I am sick! Sick of listening to your mother's tactless comments, of hearing what a more perfect couple you and Renée would make, of answering Renée's questions about our sleeping habits! I'm sick of it all!" She wanted to scream.

"I can understand how my mother can grate on you," he allowed. "But you had no business inviting Renée up here to your room. You brought that on yourself." There was no relenting in the fire of his gaze.

"I didn't invite her up here!" Alisa corrected him. "She barged in on her own. She acts like the mistress of this house as well as the mistress of its owner!"

"Don't you dare talk about Renée like that!"

"Ooh, how chivalrous of you," she retorted sarcastically. "Defend your mistress and not your wife. What about me? Look how you just humiliated me in front of her! Am I supposed to stand by while you ask Renée to leave the room so you can scold me in private for speaking the truth?"

"I expected you to be civil towards my guests. The Gautiers have been my friends for years."

"And how was Renée supposed to treat me— or are there rules for mistresses to follow?" Alisa jeered.

His jaw clenched tightly. At the side of his face, a muscle twitched to reveal the depth of his anger. "I want you to stay here in this room while I go down and explain that you're not feeling well."

"I will not stay here and let her win. No way!" Alisa said vehemently.

In one stride, she was imprisoned in his arms,

his angry face only inches from hers. "Who do you think you are?"

"Your wife, damn it!"

He crushed her to his chest, imprisoning her arms between their two bodies as his lips covered hers. Wildly she struggled to be free of his touch, but his hand clasped her hair and twisted her into stillness. The pressure of his kiss increased until the sensuality of it overwhelmed her. Still, mercilessly, it went on. At last, when she thought her very breath would be denied her, Zachary released her. Her hand went to her swollen lips, attempting to wipe away the erotic power of his kiss.

"You stay here," he muttered hoarsely, wiping the lipstick from his mouth with a handkerchief, "or I'll make you my wife in more ways than one."

Alisa found her hand closing around the empty perfume bottle on the dressing table. In the next instant, she had hurled it at the closing door, taking spiteful pleasure out of the explosive sound of it smashing against the wood.

CHAPTER FIVE

"Are you ready, Chris?" Alisa called.

There was a flash of white-shoed feet accompanied by a whirling strawberry-colored skirt as Chris danced into the room in excitement. "I'm ready!" she cried shrilly. "Hurry, Lisa!"

"You're not starting to school yet," Alisa laughed. "We're only registering you today so that you can go."

But her hand was quickly taken by a smaller one that insistently led her out of the bedroom towards the staircase. At the base of the stairs Zachary stood silently watching their approach. Alisa stared at him, the surprise at seeing him at this time of day evident on her face.

"Zach, are you ready, too?" Christine released Alisa's hand and raced down the steps ahead of her.

"Are you going with us?" Alisa asked, reaching

the bottom step and gazing into his inscrutable face with a combination of distrust and disbelief.

"We're going as a family today," Chris announced, now taking Zachary's hand and tugging towards the door. "Is everything ready?"

His pace was too slow for her, so Chris dashed ahead, out the door towards the waiting car. Alisa glanced puzzledly at him.

"Is what ready?" she asked.

"After the registration is over, we're going on a picnic," he said calmly, pointedly ignoring Alisa's reaction. "Harvesting begins next week when school starts. Christine pointed out that this will be the only time we can do anything as a family."

"You didn't have to say yes," Alisa retorted.

"I don't mind. She's a happy kid, nothing like her sister," Zachary said. "After all you've sacrificed for her already, surely an afternoon in my company can be tolerated."

She glared at him coldly. If only she could be sure this afternoon was for the benefit of Christine. There was no doubt in her mind that it was Chris's idea, but she wondered why had Zachary consented to it after ignoring Alisa's existence since the disastrous dinner party.

They had reached the car when his questioning "Well?" demanded a response. She sighed heavily.

"You've left everything until the last minute. I don't have any choice in the matter, do I?" she asked sharply.

"Does that irritate you?" Zachary opened the car door for her.

"Yes, it does," she hissed so that Christine, who was already in the backseat of the wagon, wouldn't hear.

Zachary smiled down at her as he closed the door for her, a wickedly smug expression that made her edgy. Before sliding into the driver's seat, Zachary removed his blazer and tossed it on the back of the seat. The late August sun beat warmly into the windows of the car. Christine bobbed happily behind them as the car pulled out on the lane. Her chattering, interspersed with replies from either Alisa or Zachary depending on who she was talking to, dotted the journey into St. Helena. Arriving at the school, she skipped ahead of them to the entrance.

"What do you say we leave our personal feelings out of it," Zachary said in a low voice, "and make this a pleasant afternoon for Christine's sake?"

"I'll do it for her," Alisa replied. "If you can keep your remarks to yourself."

"Deal." Zachary held the school door open for her with an amiable smile. "We may even surprise ourselves and have a good time."

Alisa's glance made it clear that she doubted it, but she didn't reply.

Transferring Christine's records from her previous school and enrolling her in the third grade went smoothly enough and the three were back in the car driving north of town. Their short journey took them past several vineyards welcoming visitors to tour their facilities before Zachary turned the car into a small park. Christine bounded out of the car almost the minute it came to a halt, racing over towards an old wooden structure that dominated the grounds.

"It's called the Old Bale Mill," Zachary explained as he and Alisa caught up with her. "It was built by a Dr. Edward Bale to grind grain for early Napa Valley pioneers. It's been restored recently."

Alisa walked over to stand beside the huge undershot waterwheel that had once powered the grindstones. The branches of a nearby tree rested against the towering wooden wheel, emphasizing its lack of use.

"It's really quite impressive, isn't it?" Alisa commented as Zachary joined her, his tie removed and thrown over his shoulder and the top two buttons of his shirt unbuttoned.

"A necessity in its day," he agreed.

"I'm going to find a good place for our picnic," Chris called before scampering away to investigate the rest of the park.

Following her, they made their way over a stony path, Zachary leading the way a half step ahead of Alisa. Her white sandals had a small heel that made negotiating the tricky rocks difficult. As she stepped off the flat surface on to another, the first rock slipped, sending Alisa falling forward. Two tanned arms reached forward, and her fall was arrested by Zachary's broad chest.

"Are you all right?" His hands went around her waist, supporting her firmly.

"Yes," she gulped. Her own hands were gripping his forearms tightly to stay upright. Beneath her fingers she could feel the erratic race of his pulse. "I think your heart is beating as fast as mine," Alisa said with a weak laugh.

"Probably because you're hanging onto me so tightly." Her gaze flew up to his face at the amused yet completely serious tone of Zachary's voice. The ardent fire in his dark eyes mesmerized her. "Do you know, you're a very beautiful and desirable woman . . . not cold at all.''

Her fingers immediately relaxed their hold on his arm.

"And you," her voice was husky and soft, with the barest tremble in it, "can show surprising concern when it suits you."

The soft curve of his lips broadened into a wide smile. "I think you just put me down," he said, releasing his own hold on her until only a hand rested lightly against her side. "Which means we'd better catch up with Christine."

This time they walked side by side, Alisa knowing no way to shake off his hand without arousing his mockery. The day was too peaceful and the park was too serene to let it be disturbed by their bickering. Besides there was Chris to be considered.

"You care about Christine more than anyone, don't you?" Zachary said. "I can't imagine any other woman with your looks and wealth who would have done what you have, especially for a half-sister who's so much younger. Have you considered what the future will be like for you?"

"Are you trying to tell me what a liability she is?" Alisa smiled. "I'm not really making any great sacrifice. It can't be considered a sacrifice when you're doing it for someone you love." She glanced up at him, expecting to see the usual cynicism on his face, only to find him regarding her with serious interest. "I just want her to grow up differently from the way I did. I want her to know a sense of security, that I'll always be there if she needs me because I love her."

"And what was your childhood like?"

"One long string of my mother's boyfriends and

husbands. I think the day she died she couldn't have even told you what my father's name was." Alisa laughed, trying to be funny, but a little of the bitterness peeped through.

"I assumed it was something like that," Zachary nodded. "Is that why you don't trust men?"

"Well, that has more to do with my not believing in love. There's like. There's lust. But I don't know about love."

Zachary gazed down at her with quizzical thoughtfulness. "There is love, Alisa. I hope someday you'll discover it for yourself."

"You're speaking as if you know it for a fact," she replied after a short pause, touched by the soft earnestness of his statement.

"Do you find it hard to believe that *I* could be in love?" Zachary teased.

Alisa stared up at him, her head tilted, trying to discover why he seemed so suddenly different. His hair was just as ebony black as his eyes beneath their lazily curling black lashes. She went back to looking at the ground in front of them.

"I don't find it hard to believe that you want Renée, and that you think she's a beautiful woman."

"There you go again," Zachary laughed, "inserting 'want' for love."

"It's practically the same thing."

"When you need someone because you love them, that's love. You're talking about the reverse when you love someone because you need them. They're two very different things, Alisa." He was staring off when she looked up to see if she could read the expression on his face. She had a feeling that he truly believed what he was saying. Aware that she was studying him, Zachary turned to meet her gaze with a sympathetic smile. "Hmm. That questioning look in your big blue eyes tells me that you're about to argue, so let's change the subject. This afternoon is for Christine, remember?"

Reluctantly Alisa agreed. But she found herself thinking about what he'd said uncomfortably often. Not even the exuberant Christine could completely pull her out of her reverie as she gave in readily to her younger sister's demands that the picnic be held on the grass and not on the tables. The hamper from the car was filled with food—cold roast chicken with carrot sticks, cherry tomatoes, and celery were in one box. In another there were buttered slices of egg twist bread. For dessert, there were fresh pears and cheese. As Alisa spread the food out on the checkered cloth, Zachary produced wineglasses and a bottle of wine.

"Unfortunately, this isn't my wine," he said as he uncorked it, pouring the ruby red liquid into the two glasses. "It's cabernet sauvignon from the Gautier winery. I promise you it's the very best of the California red wines."

"Can I have some grape juice, too, Zachary?" Christine piped up.

"You aren't old enough to drink wine," Alisa smiled.

"Let her try it. One tiny sip won't hurt. She's been at the winery often enough, she deserves to have a taste," declared Zachary, holding out his own glass for Chris to sip.

The red liquid had barely touched her lips when Christine pulled away, her mouth curling in an expression of distaste. "It's rotten!" she exclaimed, staring at Zachary as if he had attempted to poison her. "It doesn't taste like grape juice at all!"

"No, but wine is made from grapes. It just doesn't taste like grape juice," Zachary laughed heartily.

"How can you drink that stuff?" Her small shoulders shuddered.

This time it was Alisa who laughed. "You grow accustomed to it, Chris."

"Not me, I never will!"

"Nora must have read your mind,"—Zachary reached into a second hamper and took out a thermos bottle—"because she also sent along some lemonade, if I'm not mistaken."

"Oh, goody!" Chris's sudden burst of elation halted as she turned her head to Zachary. "Hey, will Nora pack my lunch for school, so I can take it with me on the bus like the rest of the kids?"

"I think most of the kids eat their lunch at the school," said Zachary, "but I'm sure if you want her to she'll arrange something with Mrs. March."

"I don't think Chris needs to ride on the bus." Alisa shook her head slowly as she spoke. "I can drive her to school in the morning and pick her up in the afternoon."

"No, Alisa, I want to ride on the bus," Chris protested with a wail. "I don't want to be different from the other kids."

"She's got a point, Alisa," Zachary glanced at her briefly over the rim of his wineglass.

"Yes . . ." Still Alisa hesitated, her gaze on the pleading eyes that were staring earnestly back at her, the small lips forming the word "Please."

"If that's what you want, Chris, you can ride on the school bus. But you've got to get ready on time."

Later, after Chris had raced off to check out the Bale Mill more closely, Alisa finished packing away the remnants of their meal and Zachary had stretched himself out on his side in the grass. "Stay where I can see you," she called to her sister.

"I'm glad you agreed to let her ride on the bus," he said, as Alisa curled her legs to one side and straightened her skirt. "I think it will make her adjustment to her new school and her new friends a lot easier."

"I hope so," Alisa murmured, gazing after the lively little girl. "I hope she doesn't become too attached to her new friends, or it will be hard for her to leave at the end of the school year."

"She wouldn't have to leave." Zachary's tone was deceptively casual.

"What do you mean? You and I will be getting a divorce at the end of the school year and we'll be leaving." Beneath the pale golden hair, her forehead was creased with a frown.

"OK, you'll be leaving my house, but that doesn't mean you have to leave here, does it? I think that if Christine were happy here, you would stay."

Suddenly, she knew with startling clarity that once they were divorced, she would never stay in the same area that Zachary was in. Nodding as if it was possible nonetheless, she recalled his unexpected kiss, which had almost overwhelmed her piteous attempt to resist him. The memory was as clear as if he had left a brand. And in that instant, their temporary truce dissolved. Zachary must have sensed it, too, for he rose and began packing the things away into the trunk. The serene peacefulness of the afternoon was gone.

CHAPTER SIX

The first weeks of September inched by, each day seeming to pass more slowly than the last. The flurry of activity in the mornings as Christine raced to meet her school bus was offset by the hours that stretched ahead for Alisa to fill until the bus brought Christine home in the afternoon. The grape harvest had begun. The vineyards were a hum of people and vehicles, picking and transporting the grapes to the winery on the hill above the house. And Zachary was directing the activity, rising and going to the fields before the workers arrived and staying at the winery long after they left. Alisa and Christine usually had their evening meal long before he even came back. Occasionally Zachary would join Alisa in the living room, sitting in companionable silence before excusing himself to go over his paperwork in the den.

During the first empty days, Alisa had wandered

aimlessly around the house and yard, noting the autumn colors of the grapevines changing from green to brown-gold, and the ivy on the house slowly turning flame-red. Her walks often led her in the direction of the winery, but she always stopped in the shadow of the oak trees and gazed absently at the traffic between the buildings and the vineyard. Zachary ate his lunch in those buildings, thanks to Nora. The returning half-eaten sandwiches were evidence that his attention was on his grapes.

Several times Alisa had heard the sound of hoofbeats on the gravel road. She knew of only one person who rode a horse and that was Renée, although Zachary never mentioned her. It was unlikely that he would, knowing her feelings about Renée. It angered Alisa that Zachary was still meeting her, openly defying Alisa.

The combination of inactivity, and unwillingness to meet Renée accidentally on one of her walks, had driven Alisa back to the house. She asked the housekeeper to let her help in taking care of the house, insisting that Nora had plenty to do supervising the kitchen, the laundry, the shopping and her own home without doing all the cleaning, too.

Slowly, over a period of days, Alisa took on the daily tasks herself, making beds, dusting furniture and floors, and anything else that would speed the passing of the hours.

Alisa opened the door to the master bedroom where Zachary slept and stepped inside, pulling off the plastic wrap from one of his suits just back from the dry cleaners. Her eyes trailed appreciatively around the room, admiring the ivory-colored walls and the red velvet curtains. Straightening, dusting, and making the bed in this room had become her custom. Since the first day that she had nervously entered the room and discovered its elegant Mediterranean decor, she had fallen in love with it. She had known a moment of envy that Zachary occupied the room until she remembered, with a shiver, that as his wife she could share it with him.

But the adjoining room had captured her imagination. It was too small to be considered a bedroom and too large for a dressing room. Dirty, pale cream walls spoke of its neglect, as did the two lonely pieces of furniture, a daybed and a wardrobe. Alisa had known its purpose immediately—it was a baby's room. Even now, as she opened the door and entered the room, she could see it transformed. The walls would be papered in a gentle green and white stripe to suit either a boy or a girl and the windows and woodwork would be painted with white enamel. The curtains . . . oh, airy dotted swiss for a girl, or nubby linen for a boy. In the place of the daybed, there would be a shiny white crib with dancing butterflies hanging over it. Near the window would be a rocking chair and a floor lamp. In Alisa's mind, all the details were very clear.

She stood in the center of the room, unconsciously hugging Zach's suit against her. As her head bent, the material brushed her cheek and she pulled away with a jerk. A tiny smile of embarrassment lifted the corners of her mouth at her wandering thoughts. Alisa brushed the jacket sleeve against her cheek again, wondering how many wives caressed their husbands' clothes like sentimental idiots and dreamed of the babies they would have. She turned with a cynical shrug, telling herself how glad she was that she wasn't that kind of a woman.

"I wondered how long your daydream was going to last." Zachary stood in the doorway, a hand braced against the doorjamb. "You looked so content that I hated to disturb you."

"What are you doing here? You're supposed to be at the vineyards." Her face colored slightly at his questioning look.

"I have to go into town to pick up a spare part, so I decided to shower and change first," he explained, still not moving from the door. "Now what are you doing here?" He was actually unbuttoning his shirt as he talked.

"I was just going to put your suit away. Nora picked it up from the dry cleaners this morning." Alisa hated the defensive weakness in her voice.

"My closet is in this room." His head turned slightly to indicate the room behind him.

"I know. I've been in there several times before."

"Have you?" Zachary's left eyebrow arched mockingly.

"I usually straighten things some," Alisa added, not liking the gleam in his dark eyes.

"If you don't stop crushing that jacket, it'll have to go back to the cleaners to be pressed." His glance slid from the pink spots on her cheeks to her hands that were digging into the suit.

Alisa nearly dropped it. "If you would move out of the way, I'll hang it up," she managed to say huffily.

"By all means." Zachary shifted to lean against

one side of the door, giving her just enough room to pass through.

She hesitated, wishing he would move out of the doorway altogether. Not about to let him see he riled her, Alisa left the safety of the center of the little room to walk to the door. As she was about to slip past him, his arm moved to bar the way.

"Would you please let me through?" She eyed him frostily.

He wouldn't even let her retreat. Zachary stood even closer.

"What were you thinking about a minute ago when you were standing there dreaming in the middle of the room?" he asked with a lazy regard that didn't match the fiery brightness of his eyes.

"If you must know, I was visualizing what it would look like redecorated." A trace of exasperation and frustration sharpened her words.

"Used to be a baby's room, you know."

"I assumed it was," she replied coldly. "Now, will you let me through?"

"Oh, by the way—I've noticed that you've been calling Nora by her first name. You two are finally getting along. Why the change?" Zachary ignored her request again.

"No point in insisting on formality when everyone else in this house doesn't." Alisa glared at him, angered by his relentless refusal to let her pass. "Chris started school, so I decided to help Nora around the house. It's as simple as that."

"Hmm. Interesting. I didn't know you knew how to do housework. Well, in another few weeks, the harvesting will be over and I'll have more free time."

"That should please Renée," Alisa said sarcastically.

"You're taking care of things. And you seem happier. Softer somehow. I think it must have been your perfume that's lulled me to sleep these past nights." Zachary moved closer still, shrugging off her barbed comment about Renée. "Nice. Like spring flowers." His head bent slowly towards her as she stiffened and held herself rigidly erect. Alisa could feel the feathery lightness of his touch as he stroked the side of her neck. "Where do you put it? Here, on the side of your neck?" Zachary continued his tender quest. "Or here?" His lips gently followed the trail of his words while Alisa stood motionless, determined to let him see how little his lovemaking affected her. But it was a strange and sensuous sensation that thrilled her to the core.

"Did your daydreaming include making babies?" The unexpectedness of his question startled her, although the persistent nuzzling on her neck didn't cease.

"Of course not!" Alisa breathed in a shocked whisper.

"Too bad. I guess you've noticed my great, big bed." Zachary moved away long enough to gaze deeply into her blue eyes before his lips began kissing the opposite side of her neck.

"Oh, listen to the big, bad wolf. Haven't you seen Renée recently?" Alisa asked indignantly.

"As a matter of fact, I saw her this morning." Alisa could hear the amusement in his voice. "But that doesn't answer my question. What do you suppose our baby would be like?"

Alisa was beginning to feel overpowered by his

nearness. His blue shirt was completely unbuttoned. Her hands, even if she wanted to resist, couldn't push him away without touching the nakedness of his chest. The fragrance of his cologne with its masculine earthiness grew stronger with each breath she took. But it was the delicious sensation of his mouth against the sensitive skin of her neck that was creating the most unrest inside her. She realized that she was trying to ward off a master of the art of making love.

"Please stop it, Zachary," she said sharply. "Anyway, I've never even considered a . . . a . . . baby, and least of all yours!"

"Why don't you consider it now?" Zachary tilted his head back and smiled down at her wickedly before he moved forward again, this time to claim her lips in a gentle but ardent kiss.

Determined to remain outwardly unresponsive to his touch, Alisa fought the inner fire that threatened to melt her icy reserve. When she thought she couldn't make it any longer, Zachary moved away.

"Does it give you a sense of power to know you can arouse me?" he asked.

Alisa studied him carefully. Except for the sexual heat in his gaze, there didn't seem to be any other thing to support his statement that she had aroused him. He even seemed to be laughing at her.

"Did you feel a sense of defeat when you failed to arouse me?" she returned sharply.

"Oh, I aroused you all right," Zachary smiled. "Your heart was pounding. Too bad I have to go into town, or this could have lasted longer. It would be interesting to see how long you could resist returning my kiss."

"You are the most arrogant, and vain—" Alisa began, infuriated by his assumption that she would have wanted to kiss him.

"The word is man," Zachary supplied, a confident smile on his lips.

Alisa didn't spare the time to think about what she was doing. Her hand moved faster than the thought that commanded it. Only after the sting of the contact with his cheek registered did she realize that she had slapped him. Zachary looked at her. Then, with the most irritating composure, he laughed.

"You'd better hurry up and get out of here," he chuckled. "Hang up my suit or whatever you were going to do. I came in here to shower and change my clothes. You're welcome to stay if you want to."

Alisa wished the floor were uncarpeted so that the sound of her stamping feet could echo in his ears. But unfortunately, it wasn't. She had the suit hung up and was slamming the door when, from the corner of her eye, she saw the blue shirt go sailing across the room to land on the velvet bedspread.

CHAPTER SEVEN

"I wish you'd leave those windows for one of the men to get, Mrs. Stuart," Nora called from her vantage point at the base of the ladder. "It's much too dangerous for you to be climbing around up there like that. Zachary would be so mad if he knew!"

"These windows were so dirty from all that dust flying around from the trucks that you couldn't see out of them." Alisa didn't pause as one hand clutched the ladder tightly while the other reached over to wipe a windowpane dry. "Besides, this is the last one and I'm all done."

"Well, thank goodness it's the end of October and the last field will be picked tomorrow," the housekeeper replied, firmly holding the ladder while Alisa started down.

Alisa wasn't too sure she agreed. The harvesting had kept Zachary too busy and prevented any more chance meetings. Although she had grown fond of Nora, Alisa looked forward to the end of the harvest season. After the endless hum of activity, the peace and quiet would be a welcome change.

"I just came out to make sure there was nothing else you'd be needing me for this afternoon and to tell you that your lunch was all ready whenever you get cleaned up," Nora said.

"Thanks. I can hold down the fort," Alisa assured her, reaching the bottom rung of the ladder. "You go on to town and visit your grandson and don't give a thought to anything out here."

"He's recuperating in the hospital after his tonsillectomy. He'll be home tomorrow. But you know how children are. He expects his grandma to see him."

"He's in Chris's class at school, and she said to tell him to get better in a hurry. According to her they have a really spooky party planned for Halloween," Alisa laughed, wiping her hands on her faded denims.

"If you won't be needing anything, I'll be going," Nora repeated after promising she would relay Chris's message.

"There's nothing," Alisa assured her again.

It took several more minutes of conversation before Nora was confident that she was leaving the house in capable hands and there would be no unforeseen calamities while she was gone. At last she was away, honking the horn at Alisa as she drove out the lane. Sighing heavily, Alisa gathered her rags and bucket, and trudged into the house. She hesitated inside, debating whether to shower and change before eating her lunch or just wash her hands for the time being. She decided on the latter, as the gnawing pangs of hunger increased.

As she neared the kitchen, Alisa could hear the mumbled grumblings of Mrs. March, the cook. Cupboard doors slammed loudly, combined with the clanging of utensils.

"Hello, Mrs. March," Alisa said cheerily as she swung through the door. "How are things this morning?"

"Terrible, if you must know," the woman snarled. Her brown hair, laced with gray, was drawn tightly against her skull into a bun at the back of her head. "I ain't one to complain, you know that."

Not much, Alisa thought to herself, before reminding herself what an excellent cook she was.

"But that woman,"—Mrs. March obviously meant Nora—"goes off and leaves me when she knows I'm in the middle of making a torte for dessert tonight. Why, it'll take me an hour or more before it's done!" Another cupboard door slammed shut.

"I don't understand. What's the problem?" Alisa asked, trying for a tone that would quiet the woman's barely controlled tantrum.

"Would you tell me how I'm going to do this torte and still get Mr. Stuart's lunch out to him by one?" Her voice rang shrilly through the kitchen.

"Why didn't you ask her to take it out to him before she left?" Alisa asked, a sinking feeling descending upon her stomach.

"And have her start carrying on about her poor little grandson again? Not on your life!" Mrs. March shook her head firmly. "I guess I just might as well forget all about this torte. Throw it in the garbage. Nobody in this house cares about all the time and trouble I take. They just go on about their business as if I don't matter!''

"You know how much Mr. Stuart and I appreciate your efforts," Alisa soothed in vain.

"Well, some people in this house, not mentioning any names, just don't seem to care one way or another."

"I'm sure there's a solution to this." She knew what the solution was, but Alisa dreaded taking it.

"And what would that be? Telling Mr. Stuart to come down here to eat his lunch, with him working so hard? Bet he'd skip eating altogether." A spoon clattered loudly into a bowl.

"It's simpler than that, Mrs. March," Alisa smiled. "I'll take his lunch up to him later."

"Now why didn't I think of that myself?" The dull eyes turned on her with a hint of gratitude in their depths.

"Because you were just too busy," Alisa said, a cajoling expression on her face. But her heart sank at the prospect of going to the winery with Zachary's lunch. "No, I'll just wash up and have my own lunch."

"I'll have everything fixed all up for you in the morning room, Mrs. Stuart. You're a lifesaver," Mrs. March nodded firmly.

As far as Alisa was concerned, this was a great way to ruin what had started out to be a beautiful day. But there was no other course of action open. She sighed, pushing her hands under the water from the tap and scrubbing at them briskly. There was always the possibility that Zachary would be occupied elsewhere and she could just leave the lunch for him. It was a small hope to cling to, but it was the only one she had.

Her own meal, though it looked delicious, held no appeal. Maybe the prospect of seeing Zachary had robbed her of her appetite. Alisa pushed her plate away after eating only half the food. While her resolution to take up his lunch held, Alisa returned to the kitchen and picked up the covered tray of food that Mrs. March had prepared.

The heady bouquet of fermenting wine filled the air as she walked determinedly on the tree-lined path to the winery. Alisa had no idea at all where she could find Zachary or even where his office was. Shortly after reaching the clearing, she realized that she didn't have to be concerned about it. She remained motionless for a moment in the shadow of the trees, staring at Zachary completely shirtless, his torso gleaming with a fine sheen of sweat. He resembled a bronze statue. She tried to shake away the unnerving feeling, telling herself of the many men she'd seen wearing a lot less at swimming pools and beaches. But Zachary seemed to radiate an earthy virility that was disturbingly compelling.

Finally she forced her gaze to include the man at Zachary's side. With a flash of relief, Alisa recognized Paul. So much for any forced intimacy that Zachary might have attempted. Armed now with fresh confidence to face her husband's all-encompassing vitality, Alisa walked forward with poised, sure strides.

"Well, well," said Zachary, as he turned his head in her direction at the crunching of her canvas shoes on the gravel road. "Look who's here."

"Hello, Zachary, Paul," Alisa said calmly, halting beside them. "Nora went into town to see her grandson so I volunteered to bring your lunch."

"Alisa," Paul acknowledged with a wide smile and a nod. "You look gorgeous, as usual."

"She's glowing. All that fresh air, I guess," Zachary's gaze danced over her face. "You know you look great with your hair flying every which way. Reminds me of that morning in Las Vegas when we were married."

Trust him to remember that, Alisa thought with irritation. "I wish I'd known you were here. I could have had Mrs. March get you some lunch, too, Paul."

"I had a late breakfast." His blue eyes looked at her warmly.

"Where would you like me to—" The rest of Alisa's sentence was interrupted by the sound of spinning tires racing up the hill road. All three turned to watch the bright red sports car screech to a halt beside them in a swirling cloud of dust. Alisa's lips compressed tightly as she recognized Renée behind the wheel. The convertible top was down, so instead of climbing out, Renée stood up and perched on top of the seat.

"Isn't this convenient," she exclaimed. Her dark eyes moved from Zachary and Paul to Alisa. "Guess what, guys. Papa has set the date for our party: a week from this Saturday. You all can consider it a formal invitation."

"A party?" Alisa asked.

"Papa always has a party to celebrate a successful harvest. It's informal, and lots of fun. Isn't that right, Zach?" She turned her charming smile on him, and ran a hand through her tangled hair.

"It's a little windy with the top down, isn't it?" Zachary said. An enigmatic smile played with the corners of his mouth.

"You know how I like the feel of the wind running through my hair. It reminds me of . . . well, you know what it reminds me of," Renée finished coyly.

"Where did you want me to put your lunch, Zachary?" Alisa asked sharply.

"Paul, show her where my office is," he directed before turning back to Renée. "How was your harvest?"

With rigidly squared shoulders, Alisa accepted Paul's guiding hand. Zachary had dismissed her rather smoothly, she thought with glowering anger. Shooing her off so he could go ahead and play. Her throat tightened as she heard Renée's husky laugh trailing after her.

"Doesn't she know where your office is?" If Renée hadn't meant Alisa to hear that remark, she could have lowered her voice a little. But Alisa knew she was meant to hear it, so that the point could be driven home again that she was the outsider and not Renée.

Paul led her through a large double door, down a twisting corridor amid stacks of large barrels to a small hallway. There he opened a door into a large, but sparsely furnished office consisting of one desk and chair and a large table surrounded by wooden chairs.

"Zachary's office—it sometimes doubles as a tasting room," Paul announced. "You can put the tray on his desk. He'll be in soon, I'm sure."

Alisa wasn't that sure, but she put the tray down on the desk as he had directed. She glanced idly around the room, allowing her gaze to trail out the door to where the barrels they had just passed were still visible.

"What are those barrels for?" she asked.

"They're used for wine in various stages of aging," Paul replied, stepping with her to the doorway for a better view. "All the casks you see are made out of French oak. Would you like me to show you around the winery?"

Winemaking had always seemed so mysterious to Alisa that she agreed eagerly. Besides, she wasn't exactly eager to return outside where Renée and Zachary were probably still talking.

"OK. Let's begin at the beginning with the grapes." Paul smiled, pausing at the doorway for Alisa to go first.

Again they went through the twisting corridor, only instead of ending up at the double door to the outside, they had taken a turn somewhere and were entering another building. They walked to the front of the building where grapes were being unloaded into a large machine.

"This is the stemmer-crusher, a Garolla type used by nearly all the California vineyards. It put the grape-stompers out of business," he added with a wink. "The grapes are fed into the machine either by lugs or in this case, by hopper so that our large gondolas can be emptied all at once. Paddles revolve inside the cylinder, popping off the stems of the grape and breaking their skins at the same time. On the other side of the machine, the stems are blown out. Here we're working with white grapes." He pointed to the green-gold fruit tumbling into the machine. "These will go from the crusher to a press that squeezes out the juice."

Paul led Alisa to the press, dodging workmen as they went. "And now, the miracle of fermentation," he said wryly. "Red grapes ferment first so that the desired color and other characteristics of red wines can be extracted from their skins." He brought her to a group of enormous tanks. "Here's where the fermentation takes place. The redwood tanks on this side of the building are for red wines. As you can see, or perhaps you can't," Paul laughed as Alisa attempted to stand on tiptoe and was several feet away from the top, "the top of these tanks are open. But oxygen is a deadly enemy for white wines, so their fermenting tanks are closed."

"What are those things at the base of the tanks?" Alisa asked.

"Cooling devices to control the temperature of the fermentation. We have to make sure that the process isn't too rapid. Basically, fermentation is the conversion of the sugar contained in the grape into roughly equal parts of alcohol and carbon dioxide. There are vents on the closed white wine tanks to let the carbon dioxide escape. Natural fermentation would allow the various strains of yeast that grow on the grapeskins in the vineyards to develop. But that's unpredictable, so we use yeast strains that are kept in the laboratories from one harvest, or vintage, to the next. 'Vintage wine' is really a misnomer, since vintage refers to the grapes gathered in a given year. Some years are better than others, of course. If you want to watch the fermentation process, we can go up on the catwalk overhead and look into the red wine tanks," Paul offered.

Alisa nodded quickly, intrigued. She followed Paul along to the stairs, grateful for his steadying hand as they made the steep climb. Walking near the rafters of the building, Alisa was thrilled with her new vantage point. She could look right down into the tanks to see the frothing white foam seeth-

ing on top of the juice while inhaling the heady
scent of fermenting grapes.

"It takes from one to two weeks before the major
part of the fermentation is over. For rosé wine,
they're allowed to ferment with their skins on for
only a few hours to prevent them from acquiring
too much color from the grapeskins," Paul continued. "They're drawn off into other casks, leaving
the skin sediment behind. When the fermentation
process quiets down, the new wine is moved to
regular storage tanks or casks."

After allowing her to pause and watch the process, he led her on once again, taking her down
the steps to the main floor, then to another building. Here were more enormous tanks, some made
of wood and others of shining stainless steel. "Col-
lectively these bulk containers are known as cooperage and come in various sizes and materials
ranging from wood to stainless steel to concrete.
Each winemaker has his own particular reason for
using one instead of another."

There was a sense of timelessness about this
room, Alisa discovered as they wandered slowly in
the shadows of the cooperage. All was quiet within
the walls, waiting with expectant silence. It was a
peaceful hush that held the promise of fulfillment.

"So this is where you've carried my wife off to,"
Zachary's voice echoed loudly into the silence.

Paul laughed easily—something he wouldn't
have been able to do a few short months ago, Alisa
realized.

"Hey, Zach," he answered. "Just revealing all
the mysteries of winemaking."

"Well, there's a call for you from San Francisco.

You can take it in my office." Zachary's long strides quickly brought him abreast of them.

"I got Alisa this far. You can take over from here," Paul replied. He turned to Alisa, smiling at her fondly if a little regretfully. "Zach can explain everything better than I can, anyway."

"You underestimate yourself, Paul," Alisa said softly, wishing there was a way she could tell him that she didn't want to be left alone with her husband, especially in this deserted building.

"Still keeping him on the line, huh, Alisa?" Zachary stated once Paul was out of sight. "Like a fish on a hook?"

"All we did was go through the winery. What could be more innocent than that?" she retaliated.

"I understand he's visited the house recently," he persisted.

"Yes. We sat on the patio in full view of anyone who wanted to watch." She glared at him coldly. "Can't say the same for all your visits from Renée."

"Always fighting, aren't you?" Zachary grinned. "The best defense is a good offense, right?"

"Where you're concerned, yes," Alisa replied. She turned her back to him and stared at the huge wooden tanks. "Tell me, how long do the wines stay in these containers?"

"Why are you trying to change the subject?" he laughed. "Afraid?"

"Yes."

"I didn't think you would be honest enough to admit it. Are you afraid of me ... or you?" He seemed closer to her than before, even though she had heard no sound of footsteps.

"What a ridiculous question!" Alisa walked away with a disgusted shrug of her shoulders. "I'd like to see the rest of the winery. If you're not interested in showing it to me, I'll go up to the office and wait for Paul.''

She turned to see his reaction to her ultimatum. He was watching with amused thoughtfulness. It was difficult to meet his look, but she did so defiantly.

"Are you really interested in the winery?" he asked.

"After all, it's my husband's business," she retorted with all the sarcasm she could put into the words. "You're my husband, remember?"

"Oh, right, I keep forgetting."

She wanted to smack him.

"Now, forgive me if I repeat some of the things Paul has already told you." Zachary was immediately all business, speaking in a way that captured Alisa's interest despite her antagonism. "The wines are held here in cooperage for various lengths of time depending on what the end product is to be. Young wines like Beaujolais are bottled after a few months. Other wines that are aged longer are racked or moved from one container to other, successively smaller casks. This could mean a time period of over a year to three years.''

With a firm grip on Alisa's arm, he guided her to a flight of stairs down to a cellar. "There are two reasons for changing wine containers. One is to make the wine clearer with each change and the other is to intensify the changes brought on by aging. You've already seen some of the bigger casks in the building where my office is. We store some more down here." A sweeping hand spread out before her to indicate stacks of slightly smaller barrels.

"At the far side," he led her along as he spoke, "is where we stack the cases of already bottled wine, referred to as binning. Used to be that individual bottles were stacked, but putting them in cases means fewer handlings and better protection from the light. Here again they age for a few weeks, months, or years, depending on what the wine-maker wants."

"Where do you do the bottling?" Alisa asked.

"In another small building behind the office. Let's skip it, it's too small. I hope to enlarge it next year," Zachary replied with a polite but incredibly distant smile. "OK, there are variations in the making of dessert and sparkling wines, but you have the basic idea. Now I'll take you back upstairs and point the way to the house."

"Meaning I've trespassed on your preserve for as long as you'll allow me," Alisa retorted sharply, jerking away from the hand that sought to help her up the steps.

"Meaning I haven't eaten my lunch, I'm hungry, and I have a lot of work to do!" There was a flash of anger in his eyes. "And I'm in no mood to bicker with you!"

"I get the message!" Her eyes glittered coldly.

"Good." A look of annoyance crossed his tanned face as he glanced at her briefly.

Alisa raced up the steps to the door. Stopping just long enough at the top for Zachary to point the way, she hurried down the long aisle to another door that led to the outside. Zachary didn't follow her, probably taking another exit that would lead him to his office. She took several deep breaths in the clear air, determined that no one else would see her loss of composure.

"Hello there! Tour all finished?" Paul called out from where he stood beside his car.

"Yes, it is," Alisa replied with forced lightness. "Where are you off to?"

"Nowhere in particular. I was just going to see some distributors before going into San Francisco. Is there something you wanted?" he replied as Alisa made her way calmly to his side.

"Nothing special," she breathed in deeply, glancing over her shoulder in the direction of Zachary's office. "I was just going to offer you something cold to drink since you've already had lunch."

"I can spare the time," he smiled. "Want to ride down, or shall we walk?"

"Let's ride. I've done enough walking through the winery." Alisa laughed, letting her gaze trail over his attractive face with the sandy blond hair and blue eyes. She realized she was making a petty attempt at revenge on Zachary for telling her to stay away from Paul, but she didn't care. She wanted to get under Zachary's skin and irritate him the way he irritated her. And there were a few things she wanted to find out herself. Paul would be the perfect person to supply the answers.

Once they were settled on the patio with a pitcher filled with lemonade and ice, Alisa kept the conversation on the winery and the different things she had seen. She surprised herself at the way she could manipulate Paul and the situation. She hadn't realized she could be quite so resourceful. Slowly she led the subject around to Renée and the approaching party.

"What do you know about Renée and Zachary?"

Alisa asked, adding hastily at Paul's startled expression, "before we were married, of course."

"They were together a lot," Paul replied, choosing his words carefully. "I think almost everyone expected them to marry. Especially Renée, which is probably the reason you don't see much of her."

"Why do you suppose Zachary didn't marry her?" Alisa frowned slightly. "I guess women are always curious about who their husbands knew before them. But it just seems like she would have suited him perfectly."

"True. Mr. Gautier made it clear that he wanted Zach to take over his vineyards," Paul agreed, slowly warming to the subject in spite of his reluctance to discuss it with Alisa. "It's not as if he was trying to unload an ugly daughter off on Zach either. Renée is gorgeous. A little spoiled, maybe, but gorgeous."

"Sounds like everything Zach would have wanted. I'm sure Mr. Gautier would have given him the money to modernize this vineyard." Alisa was getting nervous. Again she wondered about Zach's reason for marrying her. If he could have had all he wanted from the Gautiers, then why did he marry *her*?

"I'm sure he would." Paul shrugged. "But Zachary wants to be in total control of his own destiny. These last couple of years the Stuart Vineyard has made enough of a profit to make its own improvements. Renée is high maintenance. I guess Zach wanted to enjoy her company without getting mixed up in marrying for money."

But that was exactly what he had done, Alisa mused silently. Of course, the contract was for only one year with no option for renewal. "Paul," she leaned forward, her face earnestly expressing her desire for him to answer her next question, "how . . . how close were they?"

He turned away from her gaze. "I don't think Zach had to marry her to get, uh, that." His troubled glance moved back to study her face. "Alisa, this is past history, something we shouldn't even be discussing. Zach is married to you now. It's all over between him and Renée."

"What if . . . what if I told you it wasn't?" There was a shimmering film of pain in her blue eyes that Alisa wasn't even aware of.

"Are you serious? Zach would never do that to you. I know he comes on strong, but no matter how much running around he's done in the past, I just can't see him doing it when he's married." Paul reached over and covered Alisa's hand. "Believe me, Alisa."

"I wish I could, Paul. It's so humiliating to think that—" She stopped. She almost sounded jealous, she thought. That was ridiculous. She was just angry that Zachary would carry on like that right under her nose. "You've seen how often she comes to the winery, Paul. She never stops at the house. She only goes to the winery where Zachary is."

"Have you talked to him about this?" Paul asked.

"He refuses to discuss it with me." A hint of her former coldness crept into her voice as she stared down at her hands. "I needed to talk to someone about it. I have no one else to turn to except you."

"You know the way I feel about you, Alisa. That hasn't changed. I almost wish it were true about Zachary and Renée. If things get too rough for you, you know you can always call me if you need someone to talk to."

"This party, Paul, is it very important?" Alisa asked after smiling her thanks for his offer. "I mean, I'm not looking forward to going."

"You have to go, Alisa. The Gautiers would be insulted if you refused. They invite only a few select people, and you can't turn down an invitation."

"It was a thought." If the party was that important, Alisa knew Zachary would drag her there by the hair. There was no alternative except to go and try to show up Renée.

"I have to go, Alisa. But remember, you can call me anytime." Paul rose, still holding her hand firmly in his.

"I will, Paul. Thank you for being here." She was comforted by the open concern in his blue eyes.

CHAPTER EIGHT

Alisa adjusted the full-length cheval mirror, then stepped back to survey her reflection. After spending nearly an entire day in San Francisco, in and out of the best shops in the city, she had finally found the gown she was looking for to wear to the Gautiers' party tonight. Although she tried to appraise herself critically now, Alisa couldn't keep the glow of triumph from lighting her blue eyes.

The shimmering, midnight-blue cloth clung suggestively to her body, emphasizing the length of her legs and accenting her pale golden hair as the midnight sky highlighted the moonlight. Daring, sensuous, and elegant all at once, the gown dipped low in the back and the front. The full curve of her breasts was never exposed, yet they were shown off to bold advantage. Never before had Alisa worn anything that made such a display of her body.

But it would certainly overshadow anything Renée would wear, and that was her intention.

From the bed, Alisa picked up the matching shawl. Its fluid metallic lace discreetly concealed the bareness of her skin and the front corners could be drawn through a beautiful rhinestone ring. Her shoes were silvery, with delicate heels that set off the slenderness of her ankles.

Alisa wished that Christine were here to admire the new gown with her. But, rather than impose on Nora to stay in the house with Chris, Alisa had allowed Chris to spend the night with one of her new school friends, and her little sister had been happy to go on such a grown-up adventure.

Gathering up her rhinestone-studded handbag, Alisa cast one last look at her reflection, smoothed the sides of her pale hair where it was swept on top of her head into sophisticated curls. She had heard Zachary leave his room several minutes earlier and knew he must be downstairs waiting for her. He was just closing the door to his den when she made her way slowly down the staircase, feeling his eyes on her but refusing to meet his gaze. When he walked to the bottom step to take her arm, Alisa raised her head to look at him, silently admiring the white dinner jacket perfectly tailored to set off the wide shoulders and tapered torso.

"You look fabulous." There was an irritatingly sardonic tone in his voice that for a moment dampened Alisa's pleasure. But the obvious compliment in his dark eyes as he inclined his head towards her soon made her spirits rise again.

"You look fabulous, too," Alisa returned, a slight lift to her eyebrow as she spoke. "Are we too fabulous for this party?"

He smiled but shook his head. "Probably not."

They proceeded out the door to the car in silence. It wasn't until Zachary had pulled out of the lane on to the main road that he initiated further conversation.

"Just so you know, this is no ordinary cocktail party. The guests will be fellow vintners like myself and their families, mostly close friends of Louis Gautier," Zachary explained quietly, his eyes leaving the road occasionally to glance at Alisa to make sure she was listening to him. "They only serve champagne. It's an important tradition in the Gautier family, one that's been carried down from their first harvest season. It's a very big deal to Louis. So behave. No scenes, please."

"I wouldn't dream of it," Alisa smiled easily. "But I do hope our host's daughter agrees with you."

"I wouldn't worry about Renée," Zachary said grimly.

Before she could reply, they reached their destination. One glance at the imposing house told Alisa that this was truly a mansion. The rambling, red-tiled roof topped a spacious home; the immaculate lawn was a landscaper's dream; the whole effect was one of tasteful affluence.

Zachary parked their car in a large paved private lot already half filled with other cars of people who had already arrived. There seemed to be no further need for conversation as they walked the short distance from the car to the ornately carved doors of the main entrance. The door was opened almost the instant they reached it. A uniformed servant ushered them into a large room filled with expensive Louis XIV furniture and priceless antiques.

Their host and hostess were just inside the door welcoming their guests as they arrived.

"Zachary, how good of you to come," Louis Gautier greeted him happily, grasping Zachary's hand and shaking it enthusiastically.

"You know we wouldn't have missed your celebration," Zachary replied with genuine warmth.

"Mrs. Stuart," Louis turned his head to welcome Alisa, taking her hand to touch it lightly with his lips in a continental salute. "How lovely you look this evening. Your dress is the color of Pinot Noir grapes under clear blue skies. The very grapes from which I make my champagne."

"I'm flattered," Alisa murmured, charmed by his gallantry.

"Let us hope my champagne turns out to be as irresistible as your gown," Louis bowed in return.

"I'm sure, Louis," Zachary broke in, his hand resting lightly on Alisa's back, "that you're overrating my wife's gown and underrating your wine."

"*Mais non,*" Louis replied with courtly politeness. "Would you care to remove your wrap, Mrs. Stuart?"

Alisa removed the rhinestone ring that held the shawl in place. The older man's eyes gleamed with admiration as the blue shawl slipped down on her shoulders. There was a barely perceptible sound to her left and she turned. Renée, regally resplendent in a red velvet gown, was staring at her with open hatred. Alisa met the malevolent stare calmly enough.

"I believe it's you, Zachary, who underestimates your wife," Louis said quietly, drawing her attention to the man towering over her on her right side.

"Maybe so." Zachary stared down at her, his expression like a mask and impossible to read.

Another group of guests arrived and Zachary and Alisa wandered into the room. Strangely, Renée was nowhere to be seen. Alisa realized she had somehow won only a minor skirmish and the rest of the evening stretched ahead of her. She had expected Zachary to make some comment about her gown, but he never referred to it. Except during introductions to various couples, he hardly even glanced at her, which was difficult to understand. Only the admiring looks from the male members of the party assured Alisa that her gown was a hit, even though her own husband seemed unmoved by its daring décolleté.

The soft melody played by an accomplished string quartet in the far corner of the room came to an end. There was a brief hush in the crowd as Louis Gautier walked to the center of the room. With aristocratic self-assurance he paused for their undivided attention. Then he lifted a tulip-shaped glass in front of him. It was an obvious signal, for almost immediately a group of dark-suited waiters appeared carrying trays of similar glasses that were passed around to the guests.

"Ladies and gentlemen." His resonant voice carried to the farthest corners of the room. "Tonight marks the end of another vintage, the success of which we have come to celebrate. The cultivation of wine grapes began in California two hundred years ago by Spanish missionaries. Since that time, the vineyards and wineries have combated disease, the uncertainties of Mother Nature, and the U.S. Congress. I at least am old enough to remember Prohibition." There were quiet chuckles and nodding smiles at his statement. "But we withstood them all, we *vignerons* and the grape. Today we compete with the very best wines all over the world. Let us lift our glasses this night to the time when our sparkling California champagne captures the delicacy typical of its European namesake." There was a tinkling of glasses as all raised theirs in salute. "To our California wine," Louis said proudly.

"That concession is only made in the presence of fellow vintners," Paul whispered from behind Alisa. "In public, no one will admit that California wine isn't as good or better than those from Europe."

The effervescent liquid tingled down her throat as Alisa turned to greet Paul. Zachary watched indulgently as if he had no reason to believe that Paul was a rival. His indifference irked Alisa and she turned up the charm for Paul's benefit.

"I was looking for you, but I didn't see you come in." Her eyes seemed a deeper blue with the reflection from her shimmering gown.

"I saw you the minute I entered the room," Paul answered, his eyes devouring her appearance. "You look absolutely stunning this evening."

One of Zachary's acquaintances came up to claim his attention, though he still watched Alisa with amusement dancing in his eyes.

"What do you think of the party?" Paul asked.

"Kind of formal, isn't it?" Alisa laughed, glancing around at the richly gowned women and the elegantly groomed men.

"Winemaking is an extremely traditional and serious business." He smiled, following her glance around the room. "Notice the men. See how they let the bubbles rise in their glass, sniffing the bouquet before they allow the liquid to touch their mouth, studying the color in the light. Only the very best of the Gautier champagne is served tonight. This is a group of true connoisseurs gathering to pay homage to one of their peers.''

Alisa was barely listening to him. She was watching Renée slowly wind her way through the crowd in their direction, or more correctly, in Zachary's direction. Her arms curled possessively around his left arm as she edged herself between Zachary and Alisa, her face turning up towards his as she murmured her greeting. Alisa watched in almost furious silence as Zachary gazed down at Renée, his eyes traveling admiringly over her gown and face. They spoke so softly that Alisa couldn't hear the words. The man previously talking to Zachary moved discreetly away, which irritated Alisa even further. At last, Renée fluttered a hand up to his cheek before releasing her hold on his arm and making a swirling turn away from him. She met Alisa's gaze for a brief moment, her dark eyes flashing with an unmistakable challenge.

"Don't let her get to you," Paul prompted from her side.

Alisa turned with a start, then smiled apologetically. "I try not to," she sighed.

"Try not to what?" Zachary asked, meeting her gaze. "I noticed you didn't say hello to our host's daughter."

"I notice she didn't say hello to me," she answered sharply. "But then she was too busy gazing into my husband's eyes to see me, wasn't she?"

"Was she? I didn't notice," Zachary answered, calmly sipping from his glass.

Paul glanced uncomfortably from one to the other, while Alisa took a larger gulp from her glass. "I wouldn't drink that champagne so fast," Zachary advised quietly. "It'll go to your head."

Rebelliously Alisa drained the glass and motioned to one of the waiters for another which he quickly supplied. Her hand trembled slightly with her anger as she held the new glass in her hand.

"Zachary!" Renée called eagerly, moving quickly through the crowd to where the trio stood. "Papa said we could begin dancing now." Her voice carried clearly over the drone of conversation from the other guests. "I picked you to be my first partner."

"With your permission . . ." Zachary inclined his head towards Alisa, a wicked smile tugging on his mouth.

"And if I say no?" She spoke in a voice just loud enough for him to hear.

"Then you would be creating a scene." There was a slight underscoring of the word *you* as he answered in the same quiet voice.

Alisa had no choice but to give her permission for Zachary to partner Renée. But she refused to meet the triumphant glitter in Renée's eyes, choosing instead to turn towards Paul and smile as if nothing at all was wrong. Try as she would, though, Alisa couldn't keep her gaze from straying to the dance floor and the couple dancing so closely together. When the song ended, Zachary didn't return to her side. Instead he squired other female guests on to the dance floor, never once approaching Alisa. Twice she danced with Paul, smiling with false sweetness at Zachary when they neared him and his partner on the floor.

Alisa had finished another glass of champagne

when her host walked up to ask her to dance. Zachary was on the floor again—with Renée. Alisa quickly accepted Louis Gautier's invitation, discovering he was an accomplished dancer whose fluid movements easily matched with hers. There was even applause for them from the guests when the song ended. Louis had just insisted on repeating the dance when Zachary tapped him lightly on the shoulder.

"I haven't had the privilege of dancing with my wife yet this evening, Louis. Do you mind?"

The older man sighed expressively before bowing to Alisa and stepping away.

"I didn't think you'd noticed," Alisa declared sarcastically as Zachary's hand touched the bare skin of her back. "Or was it a case of pleasure before duty?"

"You catch more bees with honey than vinegar," Zachary replied, taking her hand in a viselike grip as he firmly guided her to match his steps.

"But then who would want to be stung by a bee?" Alisa said sharply. She was all too aware that he held her apart from him. There was none of the intimate closeness of touching bodies when he danced with her. Even when avoiding another couple on the floor, he managed to do so without drawing Alisa closer to him.

"With some people, the bee doesn't sting."

"Like Renée?" Alisa asked.

"Renée could be one." Zachary smiled mysteriously at her, his gaze roving almost indifferently over her face.

"You didn't say whether you liked my gown," Alisa went on, nodding towards Louis, who was dancing with his wife.

"Didn't I? It's very nice. A little daring for you, though," Zachary jeered, taking amusement at the quick flash of anger in her eyes.

"How would you know?" she retorted, just as the song ended. She would have walked away except that his hand still maintained its hold on hers. He solemnly escorted her to the edge of the dance floor where Paul was standing.

"You've been determined to keep me at arm's length, remember, Alisa," Zachary smiled.

He nodded towards Paul, then moved off to claim Estelle Gautier for the next dance. Alisa walked away from the floor with Paul following anxiously behind her. A waiter offered her a glass of champagne which she accepted.

"Alisa . . ." he began hesitantly.

"I will not be treated like this!" she exclaimed, her angry eyes glaring back at the dance floor to see Renée breaking in on Zachary and her mother. "I'm not going to let him ignore me whenever he chooses and remember when he feels it's his duty!"

"Alisa—" Paul began soothingly.

"Look at how he dances with her!" She attempted to lower her voice, although she didn't hide the venom. "They're almost making love right there on the floor!"

"Not exactly," Paul protested, at his wits' end as to how to cope with her.

"I'm not staying here another minute." She was ready to cry. "Paul, will you take me home?"

"You can't leave. It would look terrible if you left without Zachary."

"Would it? How inconvenient for him," Alisa said, swallowing the last of the liquid from her glass, and handing it to a nearby waiter.

"Alisa, be reasonable."

"I am being reasonable. Now either you take me home or I'll walk."

"I'll take you," Paul sighed reluctantly.

He went to get the car while Alisa waited for a member of the staff to bring her shawl. She paced restlessly in the hall, half afraid that Zachary would appear and stop her and half hoping that he would try. But only Mrs. Gautier appeared, concerned that Alisa was leaving so early.

"I have an awful headache," Alisa lied, "I don't want to leave such a wonderful party but it just won't go away."

Mrs. Gautier nodded understandingly, telling Alisa that she would explain to her husband. Alisa was relieved to see someone arrive with her shawl and said her good-byes quickly before she hurried out the door to Paul's car.

"Let me know if you change your mind, Alisa," Paul said as he put the car in drive. "I'm sure it isn't as bad as it seems. After all, Zachary has to be polite to Renée."

"I didn't see you dancing with her," Alisa replied, fighting the light-headedness from all that champagne. Paul smiled a little sheepishly. "I don't want to talk about it."

She turned to stare out the window at the star-filled sky. She was so confused, filled with anger, self-pity, indignation and resignation. The lump in her throat made speaking almost impossible. When the wheels of the car rolled to a halt on the driveway of her home, Alisa stared at it absently. It seemed so long ago that Zachary had brought her and Christine here. The future had looked very different then. She'd thought she could cope with anything, but she couldn't begin to cope with Zachary. He had blocked her at every turn.

Paul got out of the car and walked around to open her door. "Do you want me to walk you to the door?" he asked.

"No," she answered shortly, fighting her overwhelming emotions.

Taking the hand he offered, she stepped on to the sidewalk. He held her hand to keep her beside him, gazing helplessly into her face. She wanted to reassure him that everything was going to be all right, but she didn't believe it herself.

"Alisa." Paul breathed her name in a caress, pulling her into his arms where he held her tightly against him. "I wish there was something I could do or say." She made a protesting little move in his arms that brought his hand to her chin. Gently he tilted it level with his, leaning forward to touch her lips in a soothing, controlled kiss. Then, almost regretfully, he released her, standing aside while she walked slowly towards the house.

She turned once to wave to him and watched from the doorway as he drove away before she closed the door and entered the large foyer. The shawl hung heavily on her shoulders, so she pulled it off, and tossed it on the bureau. The click of her heels echoed loudly in the empty house as Alisa walked across the hall into the living room, her arms hugged about her tightly to ward off the chill that seemed to be creeping through her.

"That was a very short good-night."

Alisa's head lifted to see Zachary seated in one of the armchairs in the darkened room.

"How did you get here?" she gasped.

"As soon as I learned my wife wasn't feeling well,

I took the shortcut through the vineyards,'' he answered calmly, rising to walk towards her.

"I suppose you're angry," Alisa sighed, suddenly not caring whether he was or not.

"At you for leaving the party without telling me? Or for kissing Paul just a minute ago?"

"For both, I guess," Alisa answered.

"The first gave me a good excuse to leave the party myself." His eyes mocked her glance of surprise. "And the second reminded me how inexperienced you are at making love."

"The kiss meant nothing," she shrugged.

"Every kiss means something. I think it's time I showed you what I'm talking about. There are all kinds of kisses, each with a different purpose."

Alisa was confused. She hadn't expected this kind of reaction from Zachary. Even as his hands moved to rest on her arms, the very lightness of his hold made moving away from him a ridiculously childish gesture. Instead she turned her face up to him, curious to discover what he was going to do.

"First of all, there's the duty kiss, much like the one you gave me on our wedding day." His lips brushed hers lightly, a surprising coolness in the contact. "Then there's a kiss between two friends." Again the contact was light, but this time there was some warmth to it. He didn't seem to be expecting any resistance from Alisa and she wasn't giving any. "Of course, we have the gentle good-night kiss, too." As his lips descended again on hers, there was a slight pressure that Alisa found pleasing. The slowness with which his lips left hers left a feeling of regret behind.

"The next kiss is, I imagine, the type of kiss that Paul gave you." His hands left her shoulders and moved to her back where he could pull her into his arms, kissing her easily, but without any real passion. It was a lot like the way Paul had kissed her except that she didn't feel the same way, so it couldn't have been the champagne. Something was happening and Alisa wasn't sure she liked it. As he released her, she tried to pull away. "Not yet," he reproached her softly. "There's one more. You can resist one more."

"This . . . this is silly," Alisa stammered.

"One more." His coaxing tone weakened defenses that had already been eroded by the champagne. "The kiss that a man gives to a woman he loves." There was only the slightest trace of resistance now as he drew Alisa slowly into his arms. She watched the sensuous curve of his mouth as it lowered towards hers. A flash of exquisite sweetness seared through her at the incredibly persuasive ardor in the kiss, her own lips parting almost at once. At this tiny spark of response, Zachary's arms tightened their hold about her, his hands moving down to the small of her back, arching her against him.

She tried to remember that she shouldn't respond, that she shouldn't show him that for the first time in her life she was enjoying being kissed, that she felt just plain wonderful in his embrace. But it was no use. Her fingers curled around the lapels of his jacket as he increased the passion in his kiss and she answered it with her own. Almost reluctantly, his lips left hers even though she involuntarily moved forward to try to recapture them again.

She stared up to his face, barely visible in the waning light. There was no mistaking the fiery passion burning in Zachary's eyes as he looked down upon her. An inner trembling was coursing through her and her heart was pounding faster than its normal rate. Through his suit she could feel the quickened pace of his heart. A tremulous thrill grew inside her that he had reacted to her as well.

"Is that all?" Her voice came out all husky and thick and he smiled at the sound of it.

He shook his head, just once. "When a man wants to make love to a woman, he sometimes kisses her like this."

Love—*love*. Her mind reeled. Why did he keep using that word? This time there was no initial gentleness when his mouth descended on hers. Immediately Alisa was overwhelmed by the demanding power of his kiss. But she was more frightened by the strange feeling that was taking over her own body, the growing heat that was spreading through her until she seemed deprived of the strength to do anything but surrender to whatever he wanted.

There could only be one reason for this, her mind cried out. *You're in love with him.*

Yes, yes, I am, her heart replied, as she gave herself up ecstatically to his kiss.

It didn't matter how much she had scoffed at love before. She had never known what it felt like, that it could bring such a wondrous joy and happiness with it. Her arms slid around his neck as she stood on tiptoes, crushed against his body and loving every part of him that touched her. Abruptly he broke away from her lips, his chest rising and falling heavily.

"Zach, Zach," Alisa murmured, burying her head in his coat, shy and afraid to meet his eyes after baring her feelings so openly in her response to his embrace.

"You learn very quickly. This isn't the champagne, is it?" Alisa made a small negative move of her head. His hand became entangled in her hair as he forced her to look up to him. She gazed at him in open adoration. "I knew when I saw you in that dress that I wanted to hold you like this." He inhaled deeply at the look in her eyes. "Don't look at me like that, Alisa. I don't want to get my hopes up."

"I didn't know . . . I didn't know it could be like this," she whispered. Her arms tightened around his neck.

Zachary moaned softly before he covered her mouth with his, forsaking it to rain kisses over her eyes, nose, ears, and neck before coming again to claim her lips. At the same time his hands were moving over the bare skin of her back as if trying to find a way to mold her even closer to his body, the aching need of both of them trying to transcend the limits of physical ability. As his hand moved between them, slipping into the neckline of her gown to cup her rounded breast, Alisa emitted a gasp of fear and pleasure. Almost immediately his hand moved away as his mouth slowly left hers.

"No!" she protested weakly.

Zachary's voice was rough with desire. "Alisa, you don't know what you're doing. We either stop now or—" He left the obvious hanging in the air.

"I know," she said, surprising herself with her own calmness, even as she reached up to touch his lips with her own.

In one movement, he covered her lips and swept her off her feet into his arms. He had carried her to the stairs and his foot was on the first step when the phone rang shrilly. Zachary gazed down at her, caressing the arm that encircled his neck.

"Shall we let it ring?" he asked.

Alisa hesitated. "It might be Chris. Something could have happened."

He sighed with a reluctance that sent Alisa's heart pounding wilder than before. In the light of love, she understood so many things about their relationship in the past and her unaccountable dislike of Renée.

"I wish I'd torn the damn thing off the wall," Zachary muttered, setting Alisa reluctantly on her feet.

"I'll get it," she smiled, so happy that he felt as sorry as she did.

His head bent to touch her lips sweetly before she hurried to the hall phone and picked up the receiver, her eyes returning to stare admiringly at this tall, handsome man who was her husband, and whom she now loved so deeply.

"Hello?" she said into the receiver.

"I'd like to speak to Zachary, please," Renée's voice demanded.

Alisa's heart stopped cold. She began swallowing convulsively as she tried to answer. A wave of cold shame washed over her as she realized that never once had Zachary said he loved her. How often had she told herself that men don't have to be in love to make love?

"Alisa, what's wrong?" At the stricken look on Alisa's face, he walked swiftly to her side. "Who is it?"

"Renée." The word was practically torn from her throat. "I suppose you forgot . . ." The hurt was so excruciatingly painful that she could hardly talk. Zachary seemed to sway in front of her in the misty tears that were blocking her vision. ". . . another rendezvous."

In the next second she was shoving the receiver into his stunned hand and racing up the stairs to her room. She heard his strident order to come back, but she ignored it. When she heard him direct his words to the phone, her flight to escape increased its pace. Not until she reached her room did Alisa pause, leaning against the closed door, her head moving from side to side in the agony of her shame.

She wanted him; she loved him; and she wanted him still, even knowing he was unfaithful, even knowing that he might never be faithful. That was her shame, her humiliation. But she knew, no matter how much she wanted him, she could never do it without love.

Her hands fumbled at the doorknob. There was no lock! In a matter of minutes, Zachary would be coming up the stairs. She glanced around the darkened room until her gaze stopped on the straight-backed chair in the corner. Swiftly Alisa raced across the room, bringing it back and propping it under the handle of the door. From the hallway came the sounds of his sure strides. Slowly she backed away from the door, unknowingly holding her breath as he came closer. Her back touched the wall beside the window where she stopped. Her gaze was fastened on the doorknob.

"Alisa?" The golden knob turned, releasing its catch while the door moved a fraction of an inch before it was held by the chair. "Alisa!" Zachary's voice was angry and demanding as his fist pounded on the door. "Open this door!"

She bit her lip to keep from crying out. She wasn't going to answer him.

"Alisa, I want to talk to you." He made an attempt to control the anger in his voice. "Renée called to make sure everything was all right. I never had any intention or plan to meet her tonight."

Sure, Alisa thought bitterly, *she just wanted to make sure everything was all right. Then why didn't she ask me?* she cried out silently.

"Alisa, open the door!"

So Zachary was angry. She wanted him to be angry—wanted him to feel the disappointment that she felt. What would he do? she wondered. Would he break down the door? With the chair that would be practically impossible. There were several more minutes of silence until she finally heard his muffled swearing and his footsteps moving away from the door. Slowly, with every muscle in her body aching with pain, Alisa turned to stare out the window. She longed for the release that tears would bring, but there was none. She curled her arms about her waist, rocking slowly from side to side trying to comfort the hurt that was too deep to be comforted.

There was a click and the room was illuminated with light. Spinning around, Alisa saw Zachary standing in the room near the doorway to the bathroom that connected her room to Christine's. She had forgotten. Foolish of her. Her pain-filled eyes stared into the black fury in his.

"Would have been simpler if you'd just opened the door," Zachary said sarcastically.

Her eyes closed briefly as she turned her back to him to stare out the window.

"Damn it, why won't you talk to me? I can explain if you'd give me the chance!" His long, lithe strides carried him swiftly to her.

"Get out of here, Zachary." Her words came out with all the frigid coldness of her former self.

"And forget what happened downstairs?" His question mocked her more effectively than his voice.

"Mark it up to champagne and moonlight," Alisa said bitterly. "After all, what's a few wasted moments?"

"That was real. That happened. I won't accept—" His hands reached out and captured her shoulders. With surprising violence she wrenched herself away from him.

"Don't touch me! Don't ever touch me!" All her control was lost.

Zachary stared down at her, the angry fire in his eyes meeting the blue sparks of hers. For a moment she thought he was going to hit her but instead he stalked to the door. He stood in front of the chair that had previously barred his entry before picking it up and turning towards Alisa.

"You won't need this tonight." His jeering voice was a combination of anger and sarcasm. Then he flung the chair across the room as if it were a toothpick before slamming out the door.

The resounding crash of the wooden chair against the wall sounded like an explosion in the room. Alisa's hands covered her ears at the splintering sound. A shudder quaked through her body as she surveyed the damaged chair and wall. Then, almost staggering to the bed, she collapsed on the coverlet, all her energy drained and her spirit dead. In a trancelike state she heard Zachary leave the house. She didn't even spare a thought to where he might be going. He was going to Renée. A wave of jealousy convulsed her body knowing that he would be there with her.

It was nearly dawn when sleep finally claimed her, carrying her off into a nightmare world where Zachary kept moving out of her reach.

CHAPTER NINE

Alisa gazed out of her window. The noonday sun shone brightly on the autumn colors of red and gold. The rays danced in the window, picking up the shimmer of the ruby on her left hand until it appeared as red as her broken heart. The light of the new day didn't bring any fresh perspective on her situation. After awaking at nearly ten and making sure that Zachary wasn't in the house, Alisa had gone downstairs, sipped indifferently at her coffee, and tried to think of a logical solution. But her heart wasn't ruled by logic. There only seemed to be one choice.

Sighing heavily, she turned from her bedroom window and walked to the cupboard. From the far corner, she brought out her suitcases. There was no longer any way that she could stay in the same house with Zachary. An annulment would be simple enough, she could start the proceedings as soon as she left the house. With leaden movements, Alisa opened the suitcases on her bed and began transferring the clothes from her drawers into the empty bags.

Outside the closed window she heard a car crunch to a stop and the sound of slamming car doors followed by the opening and closing of the front door of the house. In her lethargic state, her mind registered little else except that it wasn't Zachary's footsteps she heard on the stairs. It really wasn't until Christine came bursting into the room that Alisa remembered that it wasn't a schoolday.

"Hi! I had a great time. Was the party fun?" The excited voice stopped and the exuberant steps slowed as Christine saw Alisa meticulously folding clothes into the suitcases. "Where are you going?"

"We're going on a little trip," Alisa answered calmly. "What did you and Mary Ann do last night?"

"Nothing really," Chris answered absently. Her happiness faded away. "Where are we going to go?"

"Oh, we'll probably go see your cousin Michael." Alisa tried to smile confidently as if it was really going to be an enjoyable time.

The brown eyes inspected Alisa closely, too intense for Alisa to meet the gaze squarely. The small hand trailed idly over the railing at the foot of the bed, as Chris wandered to the opposite side. Then she saw the chair sitting in the corner, its broken leg crumpled beneath it. Seconds later she saw the wall where the plaster had been gouged out.

"What happened to the chair? And the wall?"

Alisa hesitated nervously, her hand crushing the

slip in her hand. "It got broken," she replied casually.

"Who broke it? Did you?"

"No, I didn't."

"Then who did? Did Zachary?" Chris persisted.

"Yes." Alisa slammed the dresser drawer shut harder than she intended.

"This trip we're going to take—when it's over, are we going to come back here?"

Alisa tried desperately not to see the troubled expression on her sister's face. "Really, Chris," she laughed, "you ask so many questions!"

"We're not coming back, are we?" The small face crumpled with her cry. "We're not ever going to come back!"

"Chris dear, it's so hard to explain." The lump was back in Alisa's throat, but the little girl didn't wait for explanations as she ran sobbing out of the room.

For a moment Alisa started to follow her before deciding that it would be best for Chris to be alone, to cry out the hurt as she had not been able to do. She turned back to her packing, trying to block out the accusing look in her sister's face. Angry screams from downstairs halted her. She dropped the clothes in her hand on to the floor and dashed out of the room to the head of the stairs. At the base of the staircase, Christine was screaming and kicking at Zachary, her arms flailing at him ineffectually.

"I hate you! I hate you!" Her cry was a sobbing scream. "You broke Lisa's chair! I hate you!"

"Christine, stop that at once!" Alisa called sharply, hurrying down the stairs.

"What did you tell her?" Zachary glared accusingly at Alisa now that Christine's fury had begun to subside.

"You broke her chair," Chris sobbed, "and now we have to leave. And we're never going to come back!" Her face, twisted with pain, was turned on Alisa. "I know it. We're never coming back!"

"You are not leaving, Chris," said Zachary, his eyes holding Alisa's gaze firmly. When Chris started to protest, he interrupted, "I don't care what your sister says, you're not leaving. Now go outside, so I can talk to her in private."

Christine glanced hesitantly towards Alisa, who nodded for her to obey. She hadn't intended to confront Zachary with her decision to leave. She had hoped to leave him a note—a coward's way, she realized, but the easiest way. Now that was denied her. Alisa tried to regard him in a detached way. Although it was difficult, she succeeded.

"Let's go into the den." The tight rein on his temper was evident in the way he tried to speak calmly, even though anger danced in his eyes.

"There's nothing to discuss," Alisa said coldly.

"You have a choice, Alisa. We can stand here in the hallway and discuss your 'nothing' or we can go into the den and do it in private. Make up your mind." His ultimatum was clear, and she had to agree. He took her arm as if adding insurance that she would accompany him. Once inside the room with the doors closed behind them, he released her arm and stepped away. The silence lengthened unbearably.

"Why are you leaving?" Zachary finally spoke.

"That's a stupid question," Alisa answered.

"No, it isn't. I want to know why."

"Because I'm not going to spend another minute in this house," she paused for effect, "with you!"

"I won't let you leave."

"If it's the money you're worried about, you don't have to. The money was yours the day you married me. That was your condition, remember?" Alisa said bitterly.

"I thought you'd bring that up." Zachary walked to the desk, opened a drawer, removed a bank statement from it and tossed it to her. "There's your money, all of it plus interest. I never touched a penny. I never needed to touch a penny. I'm not rich, but I'm sure as hell not poor."

Alisa stared at the closing balance on the statement in dumbfounded silence. "I don't understand." She replaced it on his desk as though it was too hot to touch. "It doesn't change a thing. I'm leaving."

"Last night, I told Renée I didn't ever want to see her again. I haven't wanted to for a long time, if I ever really did." Zachary took a step towards her.

"Don't burn your bridges behind you," Alisa retorted, turning to leave the room. This conversation was more than she could bear.

But Zachary grabbed her by the shoulders and twisted her around to face him. Alisa couldn't help cringing at the rage etched on his face. He gave her a short, hard shake.

"Have you forgotten the reason you married me in the first place?" he snarled. "It was so you could have Chris. You told me your mother's will stated that you had to reside with your husband for one year. You still have a little over eight months to go."

"You wouldn't," Alisa gasped. "I know you care a little bit for her. What goes on between you and me has no bearing on Chris! You wouldn't tell Marguerite."

"Wouldn't I?" He released her, walked to the desk and picked up the telephone receiver. There was a pause as Zachary dialed. "I need a number for a Roy Denton in Oakland, California. On Hawthorne Street . . ."

Alisa stared at him in disbelief. His mouth curved wickedly as she tore the receiver from his hand and slammed it back on its rest.

"How can you be so cruel? How can you do this?" she sobbed.

"I won't let you go, Alisa." She could no longer doubt that he meant it. The uncompromising expression on his face made it unbelievably clear.

"Why? Why?" Her voice was a mere whisper.

Zachary reached out, gripping her shoulders so tightly that she moaned unwillingly at the pain. He crushed her against him, his hand forcing his head against his chest.

"Because I'm a fool," he growled. His hand roughly stroked her head. "Because I need you. Because last night I saw all the cold reserve leave you and you became a woman—my woman, Alisa. I'll make you mine again."

"Please," she begged, pushing weakly against him in an effort to free herself. "Don't humiliate me anymore. Isn't it enough that you made me love you? Leave me my pride."

"You do love me." He took her face between his hands. Passion and desire filled his eyes as he greedily inspected every curve and angle of her face. "I don't want to take away your pride, angel," he murmured. At the startled and surprised expression in her eyes, he laughed softly. "My beautiful wife, you think I merely wanted to have you last night. I did, make no mistake about that. But that's because I love you more than my own life."

He leaned forward to kiss her lips, but Alisa stepped away, not willing to believe what he was saying.

"Please, Zachary, don't play with me. Don't use me." She stepped away again as he moved towards her. The glint in his eyes became harder to resist. She put up a hand to ward him off. "Why did you marry me?"

"I had no intention of marrying you," Zachary smiled. "That night in the casino I went along with you to see how far you would go, to see just how much you would do to get your sister." At her indrawn breath, Zachary looked at her tenderly. "I knew how you'd treated Paul. But the following morning when I went to tell you what I thought of you, I saw you all soft and tousled by sleep, looking so vulnerable and alone, and I knew I *was* going to marry you. I told myself that I would make you fall in love with me so you would know some of the pain that Paul went through, never knowing that I would go through it myself. I must have fallen in love with you that morning."

This time she didn't resist when he took her in his arms, murmuring over and over again how much she loved him but her words were constantly being silenced by his kisses. A small sound from the doorway brought Zachary's head up, though he didn't loosen his loving hold on Alisa.

"Are we leaving?" Chris asked hesitantly from the door.

"No," Alisa answered softly, gazing adoringly into Zachary's face.

"Maybe for a few days, as a sort of belated honeymoon," Zachary corrected her before turning to the auburn-haired child at the door. "Come here, peanut." He gathered Christine into his arms and lifted her up so that all three were encircled in the same embrace. "We're a family now."

THE
MATCHMAKERS

CHAPTER ONE

"Your supervisors at the hospital recommend you very highly, Ms. Darrow." The interviewer glanced up from the papers in her hand and smiled politely at the young woman seated in front of her desk. "What prompted you to quit?"

"Actually, it was a combination of reasons." Kathleen Darrow folded her hands primly in her lap, silently wishing she didn't feel so defensive. "I had four years of nurse's training and three more years working as a nurse. So for the last seven years my life has revolved around the hospital. There's more to the world than that, and I'd like to see what there is."

"In the form you filled out for the agency, you mentioned the night work as a reason. I suppose that might interfere with your social life."

Kathleen guessed that her interviewer wasn't much older than she was. The name plaque on her desk identified her as Lorna Scott. She was a good-looking woman, dressed in a beige linen jacket and top that complemented the tawny blond of her hair. Her aura of sophistication and poise made Kathleen feel unsure of herself. It was a ridiculous sensation when she knew how well her own outfit showed off her slender figure. Its rich olive green set off her hazel eyes and even accented the fiery auburn highlights in her brown hair.

"Oh, that," Kathleen replied with a self-deprecating smile, "well, you have to have a social life before your work can interfere with it."

The blond interviewer's laughter flowed easily and musically. "You're destroying my illusions about nurses! I always picture them fighting off a geriatric Romeo with one hand and fending off the advances of a young intern with the other."

"There are some patients who hope a massage will lead to something else," Kathleen admitted, "but very few in my experience. And as for interns, ask me about bedpans and I could probably tell you more," she added with dry humor.

Saying that she had no social life wasn't exactly the truth. There was always Barry. The problem was, Kathleen regarded him as more of a distant cousin than a boyfriend. He was Mr. Reliable, always there to pick up the pieces when a romance ended. Lately there hadn't been any pieces to pick up, but Barry was good company and an always available escort.

"What type of position would interest you? Obviously you want to stay away from a hospital environment." Lorna Scott smiled with understanding.

"I honestly don't know what kind of work I would like," Kathleen admitted, shaking her head in faint bewilderment. "My experience is strictly in nursing, but I'd like to get away from the medical profession for a while. I don't really know what other type of position I'm qualified for."

"Let me see what openings are available," Lorna Scott suggested, pulling up job files on her computer. "I'm sure we'll find something."

I hope so, Kathleen thought silently as the woman studied the screen. Her friends, nearly all fellow nurses, had thought she was crazy to hand in her resignation without having another job lined up, but Kathleen had chosen not to listen to their well-meaning advice. There was enough money in her savings account to keep her going for a few months. If she didn't make a complete break from the hospital while she was determined to do so, she knew she would never do it.

As for her future employment, she was open to any suggestion: sales associate in a department store. Waiting tables in a restaurant—whatever. She knew she could always return to nursing.

It wasn't as though she didn't enjoy her work or find it rewarding. Her life had simply fallen into a rut and she wanted to do something different. With luck this employment agency would offer her a new horizon. Anything was better than her view of the old one.

"Have you had any experience as a caregiver?" The other woman's question broke in on Kathleen's train of thought. "For kids, I mean."

"I've worked in the pediatrics ward." A smile tugged at her mouth, bringing a pair of dimples into play. "And I'm the oldest of seven children, so I suppose that gives me some experience."

An amused smile touched Lorna Scott's face as

she selected a computer file. "We have a client who's looking for someone to take care of his two children. Let's see." She consulted the screen again. "They're both girls. One is twelve and the other is ten."

"It sounds as if it's more supervision than actually taking care of them," Kathleen commented, her interest mounting as she thought it over.

"Our client is away from home often and the job would require that you live in. It also means some housekeeping and cooking." Lorna Scott tipped her head to the side in resignation. "I can't say that would help your social life."

"No, that's true." Yet there were some obvious compensations. While she wouldn't have a lot of free time, there would be enough for her to spend as she wished. Two girls who were almost teenagers wouldn't require her constant attention or need to be entertained twenty-four/seven.

Her mother had always declared that Kathleen was a homemaker at heart. She did enjoy working around her small apartment, cooking and cleaning and redecorating every time she watched *Trading Spaces*. She had always looked forward to the day when she would have a home of her own. Of course, her dream had always included a husband. And there wasn't any applicant for that position on the horizon, unless she counted Barry, which she didn't.

"Still," Kathleen added after several seconds of consideration, "the job does sound interesting."

"Your experience and background sure do meet the requirements. And the salary is generous. You'll have one day off a week and one weekend a month. The girls will stay with a relative during those times.

Once the summer vacation is over and they're back in school, you'd have more free daytime hours to yourself."

The more Kathleen thought about it, the more appealing the job sounded. Summer days with two girls would invariably mean a lot of time spent at the beach, swimming and lazing in the sun. It wouldn't be much different from playing around with her younger sisters—except she'd be paid for it. It was worth looking into.

As Kathleen started to say she wanted to do just that, her interviewer spoke. "The only problem you might run into is that Mr. Long did request that the woman be older, more mature. A mother image, I guess, as opposed to a sister. Unfortunately we haven't been able to find a qualified woman who wants to leave her own home and live in, so perhaps he'll concede on that point. If you're interested, I can phone for an appointment."

"I *am* interested," Kathleen stated definitely.

"Excuse me a minute while I see what I can arrange." Lorna Scott rose from her desk, closing the computer file before she left the small room.

Kathleen waited silently, concealing her impatience. As a nurse, she had learned to control her emotions, whether anger, joy or sorrow. The first was not always easy, since the glint of red hair indicated a temper as quick to flare as a match.

It had surfaced often as a child, but with six other children, her parents hadn't had the time or the patience for any tantrums. Generally Kathleen counted to ten, waited until she was alone, then vented her wrath on some inanimate object. For the most part it had been a successful method for releasing her frustrations, but it was kind of hard on the sofa pillows.

"Good news," said Lorna, stepping back into the office. "I've arranged an interview for you this Saturday at one-thirty."

Kathleen leaned forward eagerly, wanting to remove any obstacle in her path. "What did he say when you mentioned my age?"

"Mr. Long is out of the country. I talked to Mrs. Long, his aunt, and I didn't get a chance to say more than that you were younger than he had requested. But there've been so few applicants for the position that Mrs. Long is willing to see anyone. She's staying with the girls until someone can be hired. Her only comment was that she was too old to keep up with two active girls." She smiled reassuringly. "I think that bodes well for you."

"It might." Mentally Kathleen had crossed her fingers, discovering that she really wanted the job, providing that everything was as it seemed on the surface.

A slip of paper was handed to her. "Okay, here are the directions to Mr. Long's home. It's out in the country near the coast of Delaware Bay. Not too difficult to find, I hope."

Glancing at the written directions, Kathleen nodded agreement. "I'm familiar with the coast roads. I think I know exactly where this is."

"In the meantime, I'll check through the rest of our openings to see if I can't find something else you might be interested in, just in case this one doesn't work out. I'll phone you at your apartment if I find anything," the other woman promised. "I assume you have voicemail."

"I'm a nurse. I have to have voicemail." Kathleen slipped the directions into her bag.

That evening she was seated at a large oval table with three of the nurses from her old hospital and the ever-present Barry. The remnants of a pizza were in the middle.

"Oh, Kath—!" The last syllable of her name was lost in hooting laughter from Maggie Elliot. "You'd be nothing but a glorified nanny and housekeeper. Don't you want something more exciting than that?"

"It isn't excitement that I want so much as a complete change of scene. I want to get away from regimentation and set hours and schedules," Kathleen tried to explain.

"Yes," Maggie sighed mockingly. "She probably wants to carry on intelligent conversation with the normal people. Imagine never having to explain again, 'The operation is over, Mrs. Gallbladder. You're in the recovery room now and you're going to be just fine.' Sometimes I think they should have a recording of that to play over and over again."

Darla, the more serious of the trio, spoke up. "Do you really think you'd like a job like that, Kathleen?"

"Why not?" she shrugged in answer.

"If those two girls are anything like my sister," Betty inserted, "I can give you a reason. They're probably know-it-all little brats who've been spoiled rotten."

"It's possible," Kathleen conceded. The same thought had occurred to her, but she was prepared to keep an open mind.

"Did you ask what happened to the last nanny?" teased Maggie. "Maybe those kids are like the little creeps in the Addams Family movie."

"I don't think so," Kathleen said with a good-natured smile. "The only thing I know is that Mr. Long's aunt is taking care of them now. She evidently feels she's too old to make it a permanent arrangement."

"I bet I'm right then." There was a knowing nod from Betty. "If their aunt can't control them, they really must be holy terrors."

"What about their mother?" Darla asked. "Is she dead or is she divorced from this Mr. Long?"

"I really don't know. I didn't ask," Kathleen answered.

"What about Mr. Long?" Maggie tipped her head to one side, a curiously bright light in her blue eyes. "What does he do for a living, Kathleen?"

"I don't know." She was beginning to repeat herself. "The woman at the employment agency said that he traveled a lot and that he was out of the country now, but she didn't mention the type of business he was in."

"Weren't you curious?" Maggie grinned with amazement.

"Not really, I—"

"Maybe he's tall, dark and handsome," Betty interrupted. "Imagine living in the same house with someone like that!" She rolled her eyes suggestively.

"Or maybe he's short, fat and bald," Kathleen laughed.

"Honestly, you girls are hopeless. I haven't even been interviewed yet. I don't even know for sure if I'll take the job if it's offered to me."

"You're crazy if you do." Maggie took a quick sip of her Coke. "It's one thing to be tied down to a home and children when you're married and another to do it voluntarily in someone else's home and with someone else's children. Big responsibility and it's all yours!"

"It wouldn't be any more responsibility than the health and welfare of a patient in the hospital." Kathleen airily waved aside that argument.

"It might not be so bad if you were going to be living in town," Betty murmured sympathetically, "but out in the country, there just won't be anything for you to do."

"I love the country," Kathleen protested. "You're all forgetting that I was born and raised outside the city limits of Dover. It won't be anything new for me."

"You haven't said a word, Barry," Maggie commented. "What do you think about it?"

Barry ran his fingers through his sandy brown hair, a stalling gesture to gain the time to consider his answer. In all the years Kathleen had known him, he rarely said exactly what was on his mind.

"Kathleen is old enough to know what she wants. If she thinks this job is what she wants, I hope she gets it," he answered slowly.

"Yes, but you'll hardly ever see her. It'll be worse than when she worked the night shift," Betty pointed out. "Really, Barry, is that what you want?"

"I don't know why I won't be able to see her as often as I do now," he said, clearing his throat nervously, "unless there's some restriction about her having visitors."

"That's one of the things I'll have to find out, *if* I'm offered the job and *if* I decide to take it,"

Kathleen inserted, emphasizing the fact that they were all discussing something that might not happen.

"Well, you're going to have to find a job sooner or later," Darla remarked. "Your savings account isn't going to last forever and everyone's 401K is tanking."

"Do you know what I'd like to try?" Maggie studied the ice in her glass with quiet contemplation. "I was thinking of applying for a job as a nurse on a cruise ship. Why don't you do that, Kathleen?"

"No way. I get seasick," she laughed.

"If you can't find a job, you know you can always come back to the hospital," Darla reminded her.

"All that training, Kathleen," Betty sighed. "It's a crying shame to let it go to waste."

"Nothing is a waste. And who knows?" Kathleen lifted her hands palm upward. "I might not like it on the 'outside' and go right back to being a nurse."

"Or you might get married," Maggie twinkled, casting a sideways glance at Barry.

Darla offered the first intelligent suggestion that Kathleen had heard yet: go back to the university and get a teaching certificate. The subject was officially changed from Maggie's hints of a possible marriage between Kathleen and Barry.

Kathleen hoped that was the last of that until she and Barry were sitting at the small breakfast table in her apartment having coffee. The other three had gone to a hit movie at the ten-plex.

Barry ran his fingers through his hair and slid a tentative glance from his coffee cup to her. "Kathleen, would you—like to get married?"

A frozen feeling held her motionless for an

instant. His careful wording brought a silent sigh of relief. At least he had suggested marriage and not actually proposed.

"No, I don't think so, not right now anyway. Besides"—she smiled crookedly—"why should we spoil a beautiful friendship?"

It was a half-truth. She wanted to get married, but not to Barry. The problem was, Mr. Right hadn't come along. In her heart, Kathleen believed that Barry knew this, although she had never explained it in so many words.

It was a shame in a way that she wasn't in love with him. Barry was a nice, sensitive and fairly attractive man. He would make an affectionate husband and a loving father. But for someone else, not her. Nothing happened when she was with him, not even a warm glow. When she married, it would be for love and no other reason.

When Barry left a half an hour later, satisfied with a light kiss at her apartment door, Kathleen couldn't believe that he was in love with her either. Being together had become a habit, that was all— a habit they were both reluctant to break since it kept the loneliness at bay.

No doubt Maggie's comment about marriage had thrown Barry off balance. He thought Kathleen quitting her job at the hospital was impractical and illogical. He hadn't really understood her restless need to seek change and to grow. Neither did she completely. The hesitant offer of marriage had probably been made because Barry thought that might be what she wanted.

Kathleen sighed. Escaping her long, arduous shifts left her with a lot of time to think. In some respects that was good, but she would be glad when she was working again. There had never been any time for idleness in her life, not in childhood when being the oldest of seven meant she had to help her mother to keep house and care for the younger children, and not as a nurse.

She hoped her Saturday interview would go well—she *wanted* this job.

The Long house was easy to find, as she had known it would be. A mile from Delaware Bay, it was an old white clapboard house, two stories high with black shutters at the windows. There was a quiet elegance about it, with its well-kept lawns and large shade trees.

The atmosphere around it was friendly, even hospitable. Kathleen had the strange sensation of coming home as she halted her small VW Bug in the driveway. Remembering Betty's warning that the two girls were probably spoiled brats, she smiled. It was impossible to believe it when she gazed at the home they lived in.

Curiosity moved her to the front door. She wanted to see the inside and find out if it lived up to the promise of the welcoming outside. It was barely past one o'clock when she rang the bell. Her hazel eyes sparkled with a brighter green, her pretty features animated by the excitement of anticipation.

The door was opened by a slender girl, a few inches shorter than Kathleen. Her tawny blond hair was cut short and spiky but it flattered her face and its tip-tilted nose. Smoke-gray eyes ran over Kathleen in cool appraisal.

This had to be one of the girls, obviously the

older, Kathleen decided. There was nothing rude in her gaze, only a considering kind of curiosity. For the first time Kathleen wondered how the two girls would react to a stranger looking after them.

"Hello, I'm Kathleen Darrow," she introduced herself, a warm smile curving her mouth. "I have an appointment for an interview at one-thirty."

"We've been expecting you," the girl nodded, an enigmatic light suddenly entering her gray eyes. "Come in, please." The door was swung open wider to admit Kathleen. "I'm Annette Long. Come this way."

Kathleen stepped into the small entry hall and glimpsed the handsome walnut wainscoting on the walls before she was ushered through a doorway on her left.

It was a study, casual and comfortable with plush carpeting of olive green. A fireplace of gray brick faced a small sofa upholstered in tartan plaid of olive green and black against an ivory background.

The slender girl walked to the walnut desk that almost filled the narrow side of the room. Kathleen's attention shifted with her, noting the pair of chairs covered in ivory leather. One was occupied by a younger girl with medium-length dark hair and a cute dimple in her chin. Her eyes were blue and she gazed apprehensively at Kathleen.

"This is my sister Marsha," Annette Long announced, settling into the black swivel rocker behind the desk and resting her forearms on its top. "Marsha, this is Kathleen Darrow. She's here about the job."

Something in the inflection of her voice seemed to put more meaning in the casual announcement. Or was it the tension Kathleen detected in the younger girl? Marsha did not have her older sister's confidence.

Their coloring, the contrast between blond and brown hair, and gray and blue eyes, seemed to deny they were sisters. Yet their delicate features were very similar. Kathleen wondered briefly which girl took after which parent.

"Hello, Marsha," she said. "You must be the youngest."

"I'm eleven. Annette is twelve." Marsha nibbled slightly at a corner of her lip and tried to smile.

"Actually Marsha is ten and a half," Annette corrected her. With a wave of her hand she indicated the empty chair in front of the desk. "Please have a seat."

Kathleen took the chair and set her bag on the floor beside her. "Thank you. You have a very lovely home." She glanced around the room again, silently wondering where the girls' aunt, Mrs. Long, was.

"We like it," Annette shrugged. "How old are you, if you don't mind me asking?"

"Twenty-five." As Kathleen answered, she noticed Marsha's gaze skitter questioningly to her sister, who merely smiled and nodded as if the reply was satisfactory.

"And you were a nurse before you applied for this position, is that right?" Annette continued.

"Yes, that's right. I've been a registered nurse for the last three years," Kathleen replied.

"What made you give up nursing?" The blond girl leaned back in the swivel rocker, clasping her hands in front of her, totally composed.

Kathleen hesitated, covering up her confused frown with a smile. "Excuse me—it's not that I object to answering your questions, but I'm supposed to be interviewed by your aunt, Mrs. Long. I'm sure she'll ask the same questions you have. Perhaps we should wait until she joins us.''

"Actually, Helen is our great-aunt," Annette pointed out, not the least put off by Kathleen's suggestion. "She married our grandfather's brother. He died ages ago." She pushed herself out of the swivel chair and walked around to the front of the desk, leaning against it to study Kathleen with a solemn face. "Helen won't be joining us immediately. You see, we—that is, Marsha and myself—are screening applicants for her.''

"I see." Kathleen wasn't exactly certain if she did see. It was a novel experience to realize she was about to be interviewed by a twelve-year-old girl.

"It's very logical and practical, actually. After all," Annette continued, "whoever's hired to look after us is going to be living here day after day. Naturally we want to be certain that whoever gets the job is going to be compatible with us. It will make things much easier all the way around, don't you agree?''

Kathleen wanted to laugh, amazed and amused by the turn of events, but she couldn't do that when both girls were so serious. Besides, there was a lot of truth in the idea.

"Yes, I do agree," she admitted, feeling the dimples deepen in her cheeks as she tried to conceal her amusement.

"I'm glad." Annette smiled, with a youthfully charming grin. "That gets us off to a good start right away. Tell me, what are your hobbies?''

"I enjoy swimming, playing tennis, reading,

cycling, listening to music, and sewing. Not necessarily in that order of preference."

"What kind of music do you like?" Marsha spoke up. "Rock? Hip-hop? Rap?"

"Basically I like all kinds of music, except rap. Too monotonous," Kathleen said. The girls nodded solemnly, as if some extremely important point had just been settled.

"Did you leave nursing because of a man?" Round gray eyes watched Kathleen's startled expression with unblinking innocence.

The frankness of the question stopped Kathleen from replying for a split second. "No, it wasn't a man or love affair," she answered, remembering how romantic her own younger sisters had been at that age. "I just decided that I wanted to see something more of the world than the walls of a hospital."

"You're young and really pretty." Again Annette ran an appraising eye over her. "You must have boyfriends."

"Well—" Kathleen hesitated. Did Barry count as a boyfriend? "Yes, there is a man I've been dating recently."

"Are you going to marry him?" The abrupt question was immediately followed by an explanation. "You see, Ms. Darrow, if you're in love with the man and are planning to marry him any time soon, then it's pointless to consider you for the position. A few months from now we might have to go through this same rigmarole again."

"We're good friends, that's all. I'm not contemplating marriage with anyone at the present time." Kathleen again checked the smile that tugged at the corners of her mouth.

"Don't you want to get married?" Marsha looked momentarily worried as her dark eyebrows drew together in a slight frown.

"Yes, some day, when I meet the right man."

"Naturally, that's what all us girls want," Annette declared in a pseudo-adult voice, sending a quelling look at her sister. "Do you have any brothers or sisters?"

"Six of them," Kathleen admitted, curiously glancing from one to the other. "Four sisters and two brothers. I'm the oldest."

"Does your family live near here?"

"About sixty miles away. I usually try to see them once a month."

"Would it bother you, living out here in the country? I mean, with just us two when Dad's away?" Annette questioned.

"Aunt Helen is terrified someone will break into the house," Marsha explained hastily. "Every night she runs around locking all the doors and windows, peering out at every car that passes by."

"I live alone in an apartment in the city. I don't think I would feel insecure here. My home, where my parents live, is on the outskirts of a small town, so I'm used to not having any close neighbors," Kathleen replied. "Is your father away a lot?"

Annette nodded nonchalantly, as if it was a fact she had become accustomed to a long time ago. "He works for an oil company as a troubleshooter, and they send him wherever they're having problems. Sometimes he's gone for a week and sometimes months. He's somewhere in the Middle East now."

"He's traveled all over the world," Marsha pointed out with pride.

"Do you girls ever go with him?" Kathleen wondered what the answer would be.

"We used to—during summer vacations," Annette answered.

"And holidays. We never spend a holiday apart," Marsha rushed to assure her. "If Daddy is away for Christmas or Easter or Thanksgiving or our birthdays, we always fly to wherever he is to celebrate with him. It isn't fair for him to always spend them alone. I mean, Annette and I have each other."

Blinking her hazel eyes in astonishment, Kathleen decided not to feel sorry for the two girls who were so often left alone by their father. They were more concerned for him. Marsha's unselfishness surprised her, though she sensed that the younger sister was much more timid than Annette.

"What about summer?" Kathleen asked. "You don't spend it with him anymore?"

"Oh, yes," Annette nodded decisively. "He arranges his vacation to be with us."

"One year the company had a really bad problem and they tried to persuade Daddy to cut his vacation short, but he wouldn't do it. He said if it was really bad, it would wait until he came back to work and if it wasn't, they would solve it themselves without him." Marsha sat forward on her chair.

"Actually he did help," the older sister said patiently. "He made a lot of telephone calls and consulted for days with the man the company sent out. He just didn't go himself. Now"—she breathed in deeply—"the agency did explain that you would do the cooking and some light cleaning. We have a woman who comes once a week to do the whole house. Marsha and I take care of our own rooms and help with the other stuff."

"That was explained to me," Kathleen said, silently marveling at how quickly the girl switched the topic away from her father.

"Actually—may I call you Kathleen?" At Kathleen's nod, Annette continued, "Actually, Kathleen, I think the three of us will get along very well. We'll give Aunt Helen a copy of the application the agency supplied, as well as our endorsement of you. I can't think of any more questions we need to ask."

The interview was obviously concluded, as far as the girls were concerned. Kathleen had thought she would see Mrs. Long before she left, but that evidently was not the case. It seemed unusual that such an important decision would be made without her ever having spoken to an adult in the family, and she wasn't leaving until she did.

"Annette!" The voice calling from the hallway raised an octave on the last syllable.

The girl winced visibly while Marsha murmured in a low groan, "Aunt Helen!"

CHAPTER TWO

Annette recovered swiftly, smiling at Kathleen as if butter wouldn't melt in her mouth. "That's our aunt. She'll see you now." She turned to her sister and motioned her up. "Marsha, let Aunt Helen know we're in here."

With obvious reluctance, the other girl slid to her feet, her blue eyes glancing uncertainly at Kathleen. Noiselessly she hurried over the carpet to the hall door. The door stayed ajar as she stepped through, allowing the older woman's voice to carry clearly into the study.

"There you are. Is your sister with you, Marsha?"

Marsha's answer couldn't be heard, her voice sounding as only a low murmur. But the aunt's response made it clear that she had been informed of Kathleen's arrival.

"And you girls have been entertaining her? That was very thoughtful."

As the door opened, Kathleen rose to her feet to greet the older woman who followed Marsha into the study. She was in her early seventies, rather plump, and wearing orthopedic shoes. The blue flowered dress she had on intensified the blue rinse she used in her gray hair. She moved slowly as if walking was difficult for her.

A glance at the swollen joints of her fingers indicated to Kathleen that the woman suffered from arthritis. It probably plagued the joints of her legs, too, and the extra weight only aggravated the condition. She understood more fully why the woman didn't feel capable of keeping up with two active girls. There were probably mornings when it was a chore to get out of bed.

"Aunt Helen"—Annette came forward—"this is Kathleen Darrow. The employment agency sent her over. This is our great-aunt, Mrs. Helen Long."

"Good afternoon." Kathleen offered her hand in greeting. It was held briefly and released.

Mrs. Long's friendly but keen blue eyes swept over her, not missing one detail. Her gaze rested briefly on Kathleen's brown hair, her expressive hazel eyes and their dark lashes, the strong cheekbones and straight nose, her appealing smile and the generous curves beneath the professional-looking suit.

"I hope I haven't kept you waiting too long, Miss Darrow," the older woman said politely.

Kathleen glanced at her watch, about to say she had only been there a few minutes. In fact, her interview with the girls had taken almost half an hour.

"Not at all," she replied, not wanting to get the girls in any kind of trouble.

"Very good," Helen Long answered sincerely. "I should hate to have you make the trip all the way out here and wait for me as well. Especially . . ."— she paused and Kathleen noticed Annette's mouth tightening into a grim line—"Well, the agency did warn me that they were sending out someone who was younger than Jordan—Mr. Long—had requested. I assumed they meant someone in her thirties. But you, Miss Darrow, you can't be more than—" One eyebrow lifted expressively.

Kathleen filled in the blank. "I'm twenty-five, Mrs. Long."

The woman sighed, indicating that her answer had settled the matter. "I'm so sorry. We really must have someone older for the job. I feel that it's my fault for not asking more questions when the girl from the agency phoned."

"That's all right. I understand," Kathleen assured her, but her mind was racing.

A few minutes ago Annette had all but promised the job would be hers, that age was not a problem at all. Now, neither girl was saying a word, just standing silently beside their great-aunt. She was crazy to have believed them even for an instant. It was just that, after meeting the girls and seeing the home, Kathleen wanted the job even more.

"May I offer you some tea or coffee?" Mrs. Long murmured apologetically.

"No, thank you. I really must be going," Kathleen refused gently. Glancing at the two girls, she smiled. "I enjoyed meeting both of you. Maybe we'll run into each other again some time."

Marsha gave her sister a covert look behind her aunt's back, her expression resigned and defeated.

Annette's pointed chin raised a fraction of an inch. Her smoke-colored eyes were full of determination.

"Nice to meet you, Ms. Darrow," she responded. "I'll walk you to the door."

There was a brief exchange of goodbyes and another apology from Mrs. Long for wasting Kathleen's time, then she was walking into the entry hall toward the front door.

"I wouldn't worry about the job, Kathleen," said Annette, reverting casually to her first name. "Marsha and I can talk Aunt Helen into anything." She made the statement with an almost comical self-assurance. "You know how it is when a person gets old. Everyone under thirty is like a kid to them."

"I think Mrs. Long made up her mind," Kathleen cautioned. "And it is her decision, you know." It was better that the girls didn't count on changing their great-aunt's mind.

"You do want to come here and live, don't you? With us?" The gray eyes stared unwaveringly at her.

Pausing at the front door, Kathleen considered her words carefully before answering. "I think it would have been fun and I really like you two. But I'm sure Mrs. Long will find someone older, and you girls will be happy with whoever she chooses."

"Trust us," Annette declared earnestly. "If we can't get around Aunt Helen—well, the final decision rests with Dad. He'll listen to us. Promise not to take another job until then? Please?"

Biting into her lower lip, Kathleen hesitated. "I have to find work. I can't wait very long."

"Two weeks. Give us two weeks."

There was something about Annette's attitude. She wasn't whining for what she wanted; she was just positively confident that Kathleen couldn't ignore the request. But what was she doing, listening to a twelve-year-old?

"All right, two weeks." The concession was made before Kathleen realized what she was saying. She resigned herself to keeping the promise, come what may.

Two weeks wasn't so very long. Despite Annette's optimism, Kathleen didn't believe she would be offered the position. Mrs. Long had been definite and she was carrying out her nephew's instructions.

"You'll hear from us," Annette promised with a satisfied smile on her face. Mrs. Long stepped out of the study and the blond girl slipped a politely bland mask over her expression. "Bye for now."

As Kathleen walked to her VW, she didn't attempt to suppress the smile that surfaced. She liked the two girls, but she also realized she'd have to be on her toes all the time to stay ahead of them. More so when it came to Annette than Marsha. Annette was the leader and Marsha was the follower. They were a formidable pair, but she had a feeling that their father and their great-aunt were fully aware of it.

Closing the door, Annette turned toward her sister and great-aunt, an expression of careless unconcern on her face. She walked lightly past them, almost skipping to the stairs that led to the second floor.

"I'm going up to my room to listen to my new CDs," she declared. "Are you coming, Marsha?" At her sister's nod of agreement, Annette paused at the door. "You'll be watching your soap opera, won't you, Aunt Helen?"

"Yes, I suppose so. Why?" The woman gave her a curious look.

"Oh"—the girl shrugged her shoulders casually—"I just wanted to know. If you're watching television, I didn't want to turn the boombox up too loud. Come on, Marsha."

Annette took the steps two at a time, not stopping until she reached her room and Marsha closed the door. She flopped onto the bed, signaling her younger sister to play the CD already in the boombox. As the close harmonies of 'N Sync filled the room, Marsha joined her on the bed, sitting cross-legged near the foot.

She sighed heavily. "What are we going to do now, 'Nette?"

Annette was sprawled on the bed on her stomach, her fingers drumming the floor in time with the music.

She rose slightly, propping herself up on her elbows. "We'll have to revise our plan, that's all," Annette said firmly. "We might as well start now. You sneak downstairs and get her application so I can start tracing it onto the blank form."

"Did you really like her?" Marsha frowned anxiously.

"Yes." Annette rolled onto her side, supremely confident and self-assured. "I always know as soon as I meet someone whether I'm going to like them or not. You gotta admit she was friendly and really nice. What choice do we have, anyway? You know Aunt Helen is going to recommend the dragon lady." Marsha grimaced. "If we want to have our way, we're going to have to break a few rules."

"But she's so young," Marsha persisted. "How are you going to change her age on the paper without getting caught?"

"Simple. I'll just invert the numbers of the year she was born so it looks like a mistake. Now go downstairs and get the application from the study desk. And don't let Aunt Helen catch you."

Marsha shook her head. She had many more misgivings about the plan than her older sister had. "Are you sure we won't get in trouble?"

"Sooner or later Dad is going to find out about it," Annette acknowledged with blissful unconcern. "But once it's done, that's that. You'll see!"

Kathleen didn't relate the full details of her interview to Barry or her friends. All she told them was that she didn't think she would be offered the job. She didn't mention her promise not to accept another position. It seemed just plain ridiculous when she thought about it, but she couldn't disappoint those kids. A promise was a promise.

Still, when she was offered a well-paid job the following Tuesday as a consultant to a firm that designed medical uniforms, Kathleen asked for time to think it over. It was granted, since the job involved moving out of state, something she would be reluctant to do in any case. She chided herself for being impulsive enough to go along with Annette's whim in the first place. If she lost an interesting and challenging opportunity because of it, there would be no one to blame but herself.

The employment agency set up appointments for several more interviews. Fortunately, none of them were even close to what she was looking for and only one company tentatively offered her a job.

She had only a few more days to wait. . . .

"Do you have the envelope?" Marsha whispered as Annette tiptoed through the hall door into the kitchen.

With a triumphant grin, Annette held up the thick manila envelope and carefully closed the door behind her. "Has the water started to boil yet?"

"No." Her brown curls danced as Marsha shook her head.

"Be careful, dummy!" Annette exclaimed in a hissing whisper. "Hold the lid back on the teakettle or it'll whistle when it starts boiling. If it wakes up Aunt Helen, she'll come in here to find out what we're doing."

"It's too hot to hold it back," Marsha said defensively.

"Well, tie it back with a string or something. There's some in the catchall drawer, I think." Once the teakettle's lid was haphazardly tied open, steam began to rise. "The envelope flap is unstuck at the corners. Won't take long to steam it the rest of the way open."

Annette's tongue darted out one corner of her mouth as she concentrated on exposing the partially sealed envelope flap to the rising steam. Her fingers kept moving along the edge of the thick envelope to avoid the burning heat. Marsha picked up the two sheets of paper lying on the counter.

"You really did a neat job, Annette," she murmured. "I can hardly tell which is the original and which is the one you did."

"All I had to do was trace over her handwriting and make the changes we wanted. Just don't get them mixed up and stick the wrong one in the envelope," Annette warned with a frown. Her prying fingers lifted the flap, its sealing glue loosened by the steam. "Got it!"

Turning off the gas beneath the kettle, she quickly withdrew the contents of the envelope. Marsha handed her the completed application form, but Annette checked it to make sure it was the right one. She slid it in the middle of the other forms.

"Now for Aunt Helen's letter," she breathed out slowly. "Good thing she uses that old typewriter and not the computer. All I have to do is fake the signature, no biggie." Annette read it over. "She recommended the dragon lady to Dad. Ugh! Helen doesn't know it, but"—her gray eyes sparkled wickedly—"she's about to recommend Ms. Kathleen Darrow as well."

"You aren't going to leave the dragon lady's name in there, are you?" Marsha moaned. "She'd send us to bed at eight o'clock every night."

"I have to leave her in. She sounds so highly qualified and experienced that Dad would be suspicious if Helen didn't say something about her," Annette explained impatiently.

She set her great-aunt's letter to one side and removed several folded sheets of paper from the pocket of her jeans. "I wrote Dad a letter, too. In the beginning, it's just stuff about us, but here's the way I signed off. 'Just to let you know what me and Marsha think about the women who applied for the job. All of them were all right, but the nicest one was Ms. Darrow. We can hardly wait until you come home.' Et cetera. That should do the trick. Do you have some of Helen's stationery?''

"It's right here." Marsha pointed to the floral bordered paper on the breakfast table. "How soon will Daddy get this?''

"Helen's taking us into town tomorrow morning and dropping the envelope off at the company office. Their private jet is leaving tomorrow afternoon, so Dad will have this soon. Then he can look it over and hire Kathleen," she replied, crossing her fingers.

"But what if Aunt Helen says something about her being so young?''

"You know how Helen is," Annette sighed. "She doesn't argue with Daddy. She has old-fashioned ideas about men making the decisions.''

"I hope you're right," was the doubting response.

"Oh, Marsha, you're such an alarmist!" Annette declared with a disparaging roll of her eyes. "Bring the envelope and come with me to the study. I'm glad Helen types badly. I won't have to worry so much about mistakes.''

"This is so sneaky," Marsha whispered as Annette peered around the kitchen door, listening for some sound of their great-aunt's stirring.

"Well, of course it's sneaky," Annette hissed, shaking her head hopelessly. Her younger sister had absolutely no sense of adventure.

The chair teetered slightly, and Kathleen grasped the back of it to regain her balance. Using the closet shelf for support, she again tried to reach the box at the far end of the shelf. Her fingertips brushed it, but she couldn't stretch far enough to reach it.

"How on earth did I get it in there?" she muttered aloud to herself.

Straightening, with her hands on her hips, she surveyed the situation again from her stand on top of the chrome chair from the breakfast set. The sleeves of her bulky gray sweatshirt were pushed back to her elbows. A blue scarf kept her auburn hair away from her face. Below the snug-fitting blue jeans, her feet were bare.

"If I could remember what was in that stupid box, I wouldn't have to go through this," she sighed.

Her gaze fell on a wire hanger. Reaching for it, she decided to try to hook the box and pull it closer until she could reach it. But before she could find out if her plan would work, the apartment doorbell rang. With a frustrated sigh, she hopped down from the chair, tossing the hanger among the cluttered pile of discards on her bed.

Saturday afternoon had seemed like a perfect time to clean out the closets, a task she had been meaning to get to for the last two years. But there had been one interruption after another. Maggie had phoned, then her mother. Someone hoping to get her to sign a petition for a cause she'd never heard of had appeared at her doorstep and Kathleen thought she would never get rid of him.

Her hand paused on the doorknob. "Who is it?" If it was that petition guy again, she had no intention of opening the door.

"It's me, Barry."

In double quick time, she unlocked the door and

flung it open. "You're a lifesaver!" She grabbed his hand and without a word of explanation led him into the small bedroom of her flat.

"Looks like a hurricane blew through here," he commented.

"One called Hurricane Kathleen," she laughed, pausing at the closet. "I can't reach that box on the top shelf. Will you get it down for me?"

"Sure." Obligingly, he reached up, tall enough to snag it without the aid of a chair. "What are you doing?"

"Going through closets and drawers and getting rid of everything I don't wear or use anymore." She knelt beside the box as he set it on the floor. "I can't believe the way things accumulate in no time."

"Things don't accumulate," Barry corrected her with a good-natured smile. "People accumulate things."

"That's true." Kathleen opened the box flaps to view the contents. "My high school scrapbook!" she exclaimed, then, "my photo album and my Barbie collection. I thought all of this was in the attic at home." She put everything back, resisting the impulse to go through it, and closed the flap. "Okay, put it back on the shelf, only not so far that I can't reach it this time."

The jarring ring of the living room telephone distracted her. Grumbling at yet another interruption, she hurried to answer it.

She picked up the receiver on the fourth ring. "Kathleen Darrow speaking." She used her crisp, professional voice that had worked so well on patients who wouldn't take their medicine. Whoever it was, she wanted them to know she was in no mood to chat.

There was a pause, and a crackle of long-distance static.

"Ms. Darrow, Jordan Long calling." The voice was brusque and low-pitched, and very masculine.

"Yes?" The name was familiar, but for an instant she couldn't place it. It was the kind of voice no woman would ever forget if she heard it before.

He must have caught the blankness in her tone. "Is this Kathleen Darrow who applied for the position in my home looking after my daughters?"

"Yes, Mr. Long." The name fell into place. "I'm sorry—I didn't mean to sound like—" Like I was about to bite you, was what she almost said.

"No problem." The voice smoothly interrupted her. "My aunt, Mrs. Long, forwarded me your application and list of references. You seem to be a highly responsible and intelligent woman. My daughters also seem to like you."

"We did have a long talk," Kathleen acknowledged, still trying to take in the fact that he had actually called her. Annette had said that they would let her know one way or the other, but she wasn't actually in charge of the Long household, no matter how much she acted like she was.

"Would you be able to start on Monday? My aunt will stay for a few days until you settle in."

There was a chair nearby and Kathleen gratefully sank onto it. "Do you mean you're offering me the job?" Her training as a nurse had schooled her well. Very little of her surprise crept into her voice.

"Yes," was the clipped answer. Then he asked, "Are you still interested in the position?"

"Yes, but—" Her teeth sank quickly into her lip. She was on the point of asking him about the age requirement, since he hadn't mentioned it. Maybe it was no longer an issue.

She wanted the job, and he had obviously looked into her background and been satisfied that she was capable.

"Is something wrong, Ms. Darrow?" The compelling quietness of his voice seemed to cross the miles to pin her down.

Kathleen shrugged off her uncertainty. "Not at all, Mr. Long," she answered smoothly. "I was thinking over everything I need to do by then. I can start on Monday." It would mean a lot of racing around, but she could do it.

"I assume the agency explained about your salary, days off, and all that."

"Yes."

"Mrs. Long will go over the household budget with you and any other domestic details you'll need to know. I'll let her know she can expect you some time on Monday." His abruptness was slightly unnerving.

"Am I allowed to have friends over occasionally to spend an evening or an afternoon with me?" Kathleen asked.

"I don't see why not," Jordan Long agreed blandly. "Is there anything else?"

"I don't believe so. I'm sure Mrs. Long can answer any other questions that might come up," Kathleen replied.

"Fine. It'll be another two weeks or so before I'm back in the States. I look forward to meeting you then, Ms. Darrow." It was a polite statement, and his tone was reserved.

"Thank you. See you then," she replied, with a bit more sincerity than politeness in her comment, since she was curious to know what the man who belonged to that voice looked like.

The thought made her smile as the line went dead. The last time she had been curious about a man's voice, she had been sorely disappointed. The sexy male voice that had called the nurse's station every day for a week, to ask after a patient on Kathleen's floor had belonged to a man who looked like a stork, all arms and legs and a beaky nose.

"Who's Mr. Long?" Barry's question surprised Kathleen as she replaced the receiver in its cradle.

She turned slightly to see him standing in the bedroom doorway. She had completely forgotten he was there. His attention was focused on the bemused smile on her lips.

"Do you remember the job interview I had last week, taking care of two girls?" she asked. Barry nodded. "Well, I've just been offered it."

"I thought you said you weren't even being considered," he frowned.

"I thought I wasn't," she said, shrugging her shoulders to communicate her own surprise. "I guess it proves you should never underestimate the power of a child. The oldest girl, Annette, said I would get the job as I was leaving," she explained, "even though the aunt flatly told me I was too young. It seems the father trusts his daughters more. After all, I'd be taking care of them. I start Monday."

"You accepted?" Barry didn't look very pleased at the news.

"Yes, I did," she said. She suddenly realized all the things she had to do before Monday and walked briskly toward the bedroom. "Wait until you meet the girls, Barry," she began chatting, dragging an empty box to the middle of the room. "The oldest is blond and fair with big gray eyes. Her sister is dark with blue eyes. A complete contrast—an angel and a devil, but I think the roles are reversed. You'll like them. I already do."

"Annette and Marsha! Your father's on the phone!" Helen Long called up the staircase. "He wants to talk to you!"

"This is it!" Annette hissed excitedly as she and her sister tumbled out of her room and charged down the steps. "Now we'll find out if our plan worked. Let me talk first."

In the living room, Annette quickly took the receiver from her great-aunt's hand while Marsha shifted nervously beside her. Taking a deep breath, she met her sister's anxious look. Two of the fingers holding the phone's spiral cord were crossed.

"Hi, Dad! How are you?" she said brightly. "You usually only call on Sundays. What's up? Are you coming home sooner than you thought?" She winked at Marsha as she bit a corner of her lip.

"I'm afraid not," Jordan Long replied. His voice wasn't brusque, but warmly indulgent instead. "I phoned to let Aunt Helen know I've decided on someone to take her place."

"Oh? Who?" Annette tried to make her voice sound mildly interested, but her heart was jumping all over the place.

"The one you girls recommended, Kathleen Darrow."

A grin split Annette's face as she gave Marsha a

joyous thumbs-up. "Oh, yes, she was nice," she said, suppressing the urge to giggle and keeping her back turned to her great-aunt. "Aunt Helen can phone her this afternoon to let her know."

"That won't be necessary." There was a crackle of interference on the line and Annette only managed to understand the last part of his statement. "—talk to her myself."

"You don't have to talk to her, Dad," she rushed on. Panic sprang into Marsha's blue eyes as she listened to only one side of the conversation. "We can call her just as easily from here."

"I said I've already talked to her," he repeated with amused patience. "She'll be there on Monday."

"You've already talked to her?" Annette repeated slowly, swallowing tightly as she wound the receiver cord nervously in her fingers. "What did she say?"

"Nothing very much. She accepted the job and said she would be there on Monday."

"What did you think of her?" She held her breath, her gaze locked to her younger sister's.

"She seems well qualified." There was an underlying current of curiosity in his tone and Annette understood that she was asking too many questions about his reaction to Kathleen.

"Yeah, I guess so," she agreed indifferently, and launched into a falsely enthusiastic account of the things they had been doing the past few days. By the time she handed the telephone to Marsha, whatever suspicions her father might have had were forgotten.

"That was a close one," Annette sighed when she and Marsha were once again in her upstairs bedroom. "I never dreamed Daddy might call her himself. But it's hard to judge a person's age just by their voice, and he doesn't suspect a thing."

"He isn't going to be happy when he finds out," Marsha reminded her.

"Oh, stop being such a worrywart!" Annette exclaimed impatiently. "Everything's going to be fine."

CHAPTER THREE

There really hadn't been much settling in for Kathleen to do. Almost from the minute her clothes were unpacked and hung in the closet, she had felt at home. She had been given an upstairs bedroom near the girls' rooms. Helen had used the room off the kitchen, originally the cook's quarters, because it was so difficult for her to go up and down stairs.

Surprisingly, the girls were domestically inclined, especially when it came to cooking. They loved to experiment in the kitchen, trying new dishes. Between them and Helen Long, Kathleen now knew where everything was. She had spent a frustrating hour looking for the dishwasher, but the old-fashioned kitchen had none. Apparently Mr. Long believed that doing the dishes built character.

When it came time for Helen to move back into her small house in town, the four of them made almost a party of the task. Kathleen had been given the keys to the Lexus in the garage, but she felt more at ease driving her own car.

With everyone and everything squashed into the VW, Annette's appointing herself the Chief Sardine in the Can had them all laughing. And the happy mood didn't change all through the unpacking and putting away.

Without their great-aunt around, the girls were even livelier. More activities and outings were possible now that they were not restricted by the older woman's physical limitations. Not that Kathleen spent most of her time chauffeuring the girls. School was out and they sometimes stayed with friends.

At the end of her first week, Kathleen decided things were working out better than she could have hoped. The girls squabbled every now and then, sometimes jointly testing her will, but mostly they regarded Kathleen as a big sister with authority.

The last of the Sunday dinner dishes were cleared away, and Kathleen wandered into the living room. Marsha was standing at one of the windows, gazing silently through the panes. Annette was slouched in one of the large cushioned chairs, a leg dangling over one of the arms while she flipped through the pages of *Teen People*.

"It's a beautiful day," Kathleen commented, looking from one to the other as she sensed the vague restlessness in the air. "Why aren't you outside?"

Annette closed the magazine and tossed it onto the coffee table, then slouched deeper in the chair, swinging her leg in the air. "Dad always calls on Sunday."

On cue, the telephone rang and Annette jumped up from her chair to answer. After her initial hello, her gaze shifted to Kathleen and she held out the phone to her.

"It's for you," she announced, with an air of impatient resignation. "A man."

Kathleen took the receiver and Annette slumped into her chair again, with Marsha taking up a position behind it. "Hello," Kathleen answered, guessing that the only man who could be calling would be Barry.

"Hi." She was right, it was Barry. "Just thought I'd phone to see how you were doing."

"Fine," she replied. The last time she'd talked to him, Helen had still been living with them. None of Kathleen's friends had visited yet. She had decided to wait until she knew the girls a little better.

"Do you have anything planned for this afternoon? I could drive out and take you and the girls to the beach," Barry suggested.

"Maybe another time." Kathleen glanced at Annette, who was absently chewing her lower lip. "Do you mind if I phone you later, Barry? The girls are waiting for an overseas call from their father."

"No, no, I don't mind," he agreed, but there was an underlying reluctance in his voice.

"Talk to you soon," she promised. " 'Bye!"

His goodbye sounded into the room as Kathleen replaced the receiver in its cradle. She walked to the green and yellow print sofa, its airy spring colors repeated in the rest of the room's decor.

"Was that your boyfriend?" Marsha asked.

Kathleen checked the impulse to explain her

platonic relationship with Barry and merely nodded. "Yes. His name is Barry Manning."

"Do you like him very much?" Annette gave her a thoughtful look, the expression in her gray eyes unreadable.

"Yes, he's very nice," Kathleen answered truthfully.

"What does he do?" Marsha tipped her head on one side, a wing of curling dark hair falling across her cheek.

"He sells insurance."

"Is he cute?"

Before Kathleen could answer Annette's question, the phone rang again—which was just as well, because she didn't have a clue as to how to describe Barry. She had never actually thought about his looks all that much.

Annette pounced on the telephone and said "Hello?" followed immediately by, "Hi, Dad, how are you?" Marsha moved quickly to her side, not displaying as much excitement as her older sister.

"This Friday! You're coming home this Friday!" Annette exclaimed. There was a long pause during which Annette seemed to hold herself motionless. When she spoke, it was with false enthusiasm. "Oh, no, it sounds like a great idea. I was—just thinking about Marsha, that's all." She twisted her fingers in the coil of the receiver cord and turned her back toward Kathleen. "Well, you know how she is about flying. I mean, maybe it would be better if we postponed it until you're home and we can drive over there for a couple of days . . . Who? Ms. Darrow?"

Annette's back visibly stiffened and Marsha's eyes widened apprehensively. "Oh, I don't think so,

Dad, I mean . . . yes, all right," came the grudging agreement.

The squared shoulders turned, a bland expression on Annette's face as she looked at Kathleen. "Dad wants to talk to you."

Kathleen walked to the telephone. Her palms were sweating, although there was no reason for her to be nervous. She wiped them dry in a smoothing motion over her jeans. There was something in the offing that she sensed Annette didn't like, a trip of some sort.

"Yes, Mr. Long?" She spoke with professional crispness into the phone.

"Hello, Ms. Darrow. Are you settling in all right?" The low pitch of his voice was the same, but it lacked the brusqueness of their previous conversation. The note of friendly interest made it all the more pleasing, and Kathleen felt herself warming to its sound.

"Yes, thanks. I feel like I'm at home," she admitted. "I overheard Annette say something about you returning this coming Friday."

"I'm flying into Washington, D.C., on Friday," Jordan Long explained. "I've been promising the girls a tour of the capital for several years, and I decided this would be a good time to keep that promise."

"I see. You're going to have the girls fly in to meet you." Her hazel eyes shifted to the two girls listening intently to her conversation.

"Yes," Jordan said. "Have you ever been to Washington, by the way?"

"A while ago," Kathleen replied. "My parents took me and my brothers and sisters when I was sixteen."

"Then you'll enjoy seeing it again as much as the girls." Before Kathleen could comment, he continued, "Marsha hates flying—she usually gets airsick. I'd like you to go with them."

"I'd be happy to." At long last she would meet the man who belonged to this deliciously sensual voice. Then she concentrated her thoughts on the details of the trip. "How long will we stay there?"

"Over the weekend. We'll leave on Monday afternoon. I've taken care of the hotel and plane reservations and you can pick up your e-tickets at the airline counter."

He gave her the name of the airline, the flight number and its departure time. Kathleen jotted the information down on the message pad beside the phone before Jordan Long asked to speak to his youngest daughter, Marsha.

It was a short conversation. And when Marsha hung up, Annette took her by the arm and hurriedly led her away.

"Come on, Marsha," she ordered. "Let's go and pick out the clothes we're going to take."

Kathleen watched them rush toward the stairs. A faint smile touched her mouth. Annette's initial reluctance seemed to have disappeared.

Her own thoughts were running along similar lines. What clothes did you pack for a weekend with a single dad and his two adorable daughters? Practical ones, she told herself firmly.

Annette swept into her bedroom, angry frustration glittering in her silver-gray eyes. She grabbed the bright throw pillow from the top of her bed and crushed it against her stomach as she spun around to sit on the bed.

"Why did he have to do it?" she demanded. Marsha was silent. "Why? Why? Why?" The slam of the pillow against the soft bed punctuated each question. "All of our strategy has just been thrown out the window!"

With the explosion released, Annette rose to her feet and began pacing the room, the pillow still in hand. She nibbled at her lower lip, deep in thought.

"What are we going to do?" Marsha asked urgently.

"I'm thinking!"

Friday morning found Kathleen scurrying around the house dusting and cleaning, trying to make each room neat as a pin. She had just put fresh sheets on the large bed in the master bedroom and was smoothing the beige coverlet over the top.

The chocolate brown carpeting was thick and soft beneath her bare feet. She liked this room, she decided as she glanced around it again. The walls were an ivory beige with walnut woodwork. Drapes, the same shade as the bedspread, hung at the windows with insets of ivory sheers. The walnut furniture was bulky and solid, befitting the masculine aura of the room. A cushioned armchair sat in one corner of the room with a reading lamp beside it. It was a cozy touch that kept the room from being too male or austere.

A louvered walk-in closet took up nearly one whole wall of the room. Kathleen had investigated it on the sly during her first week at the house.

There were some clothes in it, shirts, pants and suits, a few pairs of shoes. She'd guessed that Jordan Long had taken most of his wardrobe with him.

The clothes had told her a few things about him, though. He was neither short nor fat and had excellent taste. Except for more casual wear, his suits were all expensively tailored—a fact that didn't surprise Kathleen. She had already noticed that the clothes the girls wore were top quality and made to last.

Kathleen still wondered about the absence of photographs in the bedroom. There were several in the study, all of them of Annette and Marsha. She had not seen any of Jordan Long or of his wife who, Kathleen had learned, died when Marsha was three. Neither of the girls had seemed inclined to talk about her and Kathleen had stifled her natural curiosity.

Both girls talked often about their father, usually stories that involved the three of them together. But Kathleen still knew very little about him, except that he was fond of his children and dedicated to his job. But in spite of his business travel and the time he spent away from his children, they didn't seem to resent it. So Kathleen decided they had resolved the conflict on their own somehow.

A sigh caught in her throat. She didn't really have time to daydream and wonder about her employer. There was still lunch to prepare, and she wanted to shower before changing into the ivory linen suit she'd picked for the short flight. She had supervised the packing of their suitcases yesterday, minus the last-minute items. Both girls had known just which outfits they would need to take. Clearly, they were more experienced travelers than Kathleen.

Thinking about the girls made her realize how mature they were for their age. In many ways, they were remarkable kids. She doubted that the credit belonged to her predecessor, whoever that was, or to their great-aunt. No, all the roads seemed to lead back to Jordan Long, and late this afternoon she would finally be meeting him face to face.

Pushing Marsha ahead of her, Annette slipped into the aisle of the plane ahead of several other disembarking passengers. Kathleen had to struggle with their carry-on bags and lagged two passengers back, as Annette had planned.

"Remember what I told you," she whispered fiercely in Marsha's ear, her face looking even paler against her dark hair. "The plan we use depends on how Dad reacts. If he looks angry when he sees Kathleen—you know, that icy-cold look when he's really mad—then we'll start yakking about the things we've been doing, and how well we're getting along with Kathleen and stuff. But, Marsha, don't screw up!"

"Okay," Marsha nodded lethargically, a result of the motion-sickness pill she had taken before the flight's departure.

Annette's hand closed over Marsha's shoulder. "We'll wait for Kathleen here." She guided her sister between two seats to let the departing passengers by, then joined in the line in front of Kathleen.

"Stay close, girls," Kathleen warned as they emerged from the plane. "I don't want to lose one of you in the crowd."

After she said it, she wished she hadn't even voiced the nightmarish idea. Here she was, anxious to impress her employer. Imagine informing him that one of his darling daughters had wandered away. Kathleen shuddered. What a way to make a great first impression.

In the last three hours, Kathleen hadn't had a minute to worry about meeting Jordan Long. Between locking up the house and making sure nothing had been left behind, then driving to the airport, figuring out how to pick up e-tickets, boarding the plane, and soothing Marsha's anxious nerves during the flight, she had been completely frazzled. Now she could feel the tingle of anticipation begin.

According to the timetable Jordan Long had given her, his flight should have arrived an hour earlier. Somewhere in the hustle and bustle of the international airport, he would be waiting for them. Kathleen wished she could take a minute to freshen up, but she could tell by the tense expressions on the girls' faces that they were anxious to see their father. She couldn't blame them for being so eager after their long separation.

Leaving the plane walkway, they entered the small waiting area of the flight gate. Annette breathed in sharply and hesitated a step before breaking into a wide smile.

"There he is!" She dashed from Kathleen's side with an exuberant Marsha following seconds later.

It was a moment before Kathleen figured out which of the many strangers was the object of their attention. Then her gaze separated the man in a summer suit and white shirt from the rest of the crowd.

She had a brief impression of height, somewhere around six feet, before he bent toward the two girls rushing toward him. Thick, slightly wavy black hair was brushed carelessly across his forehead. His face, boldly and ruggedly carved, was tanned and healthy-looking. There was a cleft in his chin that seemed to deepen as he smiled, which he was doing now.

Strong arms encircled the two girls hugging him. The open happiness and affection between the three was a beautiful thing to see. Kathleen felt a lump forming in her throat at the sight. But years of training enabled her to conceal her emotions as she walked slowly toward them, giving them the time to enjoy a private reunion.

Before she reached them, Jordan Long's gaze focused on her with very masculine approval. Kathleen's confidence grew. The afternoons she had spent at the beach with the girls had brought a golden tint to her skin, which the ivory suit set off to perfection. The sheer fabric of her blouse was in vibrant greens and golds, intensifying the glitter of green in her eyes and the shimmer of fire in her hair.

Several steps closer, Kathleen saw the color of his eyes—charcoal gray, outlined with thick ebony lashes. The impression of black smoke was all the more apparent because of the searing warmth in his admiring gaze. Her heart skipped a beat as he directed a smile right at her. She responded to it with a dimpling one of her own.

Then his attention returned to the girls and Kathleen heard him say, "And where is the wonderful Ms. Darrow? You didn't shove her out of the plane, did you?"

"Oh, Dad!" Annette laughed, but she shot an anxious look over her shoulder at Kathleen. "Here she comes now," she answered.

The smile on Kathleen's face faded slightly. Since she had realized who he was, she had automatically assumed that Jordan Long had guessed her identity when he had smiled at her. The discovery that his attention had been solely that of a virile man admiring an attractive woman caught her off guard.

His gaze flickered past Kathleen, then returned with lightning swiftness as the fact registered that she was the only woman in the vicinity. The black smoke of his eyes became a color more like cold steel. For a split second Kathleen faltered, then recovered her poise to walk the last few feet to the group.

"Are you Kathleen Darrow?" There was pure ice in his voice as he made the question sound like an accusation.

Forced by his superior height to tip her head back to look into his face, Kathleen felt intimidated, but she had faced too many head nurses, doctors and irate relatives to let it show.

"That's correct," she answered pleasantly. Her mind raced, trying to find the cause for this sudden switch from approval to icy displeasure. "It's a pleasure to finally meet you, Mr. Long."

She offered a hand in greeting and received a fast, no-nonsense shake in return from his tanned fingers. There was an unmistakably sardonic twist to his mouth.

"I'm sure it is," he responded dryly.

Kathleen had the uncomfortable sensation that there were several more scathing comments he intended to make, but, fortunately, Annette chose that moment to give him another quick hug.

"It's so good to have you back, Dad," Annette sighed. "We thought we'd have to search all over the terminal to find you. How did you manage to meet us at the gate? I thought only passengers were allowed in this area."

"I got clearance from airport security to be here to meet you." The warmth was back in his voice and expression as he smiled down at his daughter. "Your old dad has a few connections."

Marsha had inherited her father's dark coloring and the dimple in his chin, while Annette appeared to have only Jordan Long's gray eyes. Yet Kathleen had the impression as she studied the rapport between the father and his oldest daughter that there was much more of Jordan Long in Annette than in Marsha.

"How was your flight?" Annette asked, then rushed on before he had a chance to answer. "Ours was really bumpy, but Marsha didn't get sick once. Kathleen—she's a nurse, you know—she gave her some airsick pills when we got to the airport and sat with her all the way. Actually I think it's all in Marsha's mind, don't you?"

"I doubt if Marsha thinks so," Kathleen said with a gentle smile at the little girl's wan face. Instantly she wished she had kept silent as Jordan's piercing gaze focused on her once more.

"What hotel are we staying at?" Again Annette distracted his attention. "Are we going to do anything tonight? Ooh!" she exclaimed, her gray eyes widening as she glanced at Kathleen. "We still have to pick up our luggage! If they lost our bags, I'll just die! We went shopping the other day and Kathleen helped me pick out this really amazing outfit. I look totally great in it and I can hardly wait until you see me wearing it. You don't think they would have forgotten to unload our luggage from the plane, do you, Dad?"

"We'll have to go to the baggage claim area to find out, I guess," he replied indulgently.

As they all turned down the corridor, Kathleen followed a step behind and to one side. The two girls flanked him, with Annette walking with her usual buoyancy on his left and the more reserved Marsha on his right.

"I got a new outfit, too," Marsha spoke up. The weakness in her voice betrayed the tranquilizing effect of the motion-sickness pill. "It's blue. Kathleen said it matched my eyes."

There were two truths in her statement. Marsha did have a new outfit and it was blue, but Kathleen couldn't remember making any comment about it matching her eyes.

"You never did say what we were going to do tonight, Dad," Annette reminded him.

"Nothing," Jordan Long replied. "By the time we get your luggage, drive from the airport to the hotel, check into our rooms and have dinner, it will be late enough for you girls to be in bed."

"Translation: you're suffering from jet lag and are too tired to take us anywhere," Annette teased.

"Right on the first guess," he chuckled.

Annette kept up a steady stream of chatter all the way to the baggage claim area while Kathleen unobtrusively studied her employer. Now that she had met him, she could well understand why the company found him so invaluable in the role of a troubleshooter.

He had the same total self-confidence that she had noted in Annette. He was intelligent and vital in a very male way, and clearly someone who could assess a situation and come to a quick decision. The aura of strength about him would command the respect of men and attract the admiration of women. Kathleen had been exposed briefly to his masculine charm in those few minutes before he had realized who she was. She knew its potency.

The abrupt change in his manner allowed her another glimpse of his character. Obviously he could deal quite ruthlessly with any adversary. She was still puzzling over the reason for the change, but she had the uneasy feeling that before the night was over she would find out why.

There was a large crowd milling about the baggage claim area when they arrived. As a nurse, Kathleen had learned to anticipate the needs of others, both doctors and patients. She had the claim tickets ready when Jordan Long asked for them. His hard expression was icy and aloof; his mouth set in a grim line.

All their luggage was accounted for. A porter wheeled it to an exit door and waited with Kathleen and the girls for Jordan to drive up in the luxury car he had rented for the weekend. Annette immediately hopped into the front seat with her father while the porter stowed their luggage in the trunk with Jordan's. Kathleen and Marsha were relegated to the backseat.

Kathleen thought her position behind the driver would isolate her, but she hadn't counted on the rear view mirror. It provided her with a clear view of the strongly etched features of Jordan Long and an equally unobstructed view for him of her. As he shifted the car into gear, their glances locked in the mirror. His seemed to challenge Kathleen to look away, but she couldn't keep her gaze from straying to the ruggedly handsome face in the mirror during the drive to their hotel. She paid little attention to the conversation flowing between Annette and her father. From the look of absent concentration on his face, she guessed that Jordan Long wasn't giving it his undivided attention either.

A sixth sense warned her that she was the object of his harsh contemplation. The sensation reinforced the few times her gaze inadvertently caught the growing fire in his.

Okay, so he was angry about something. If he wanted to tell her about it, he would, sooner or later.

Checking in at the hotel didn't take long. Jordan had reserved a VIP suite. Kathleen's small room was connected to the girls' by a shared bathroom. Theirs was separated from his by a small sitting room. The decor was faultless, but Kathleen didn't have much of an opportunity to enjoy it as she unpacked her clothes and helped the girls dress. She had only a few minutes to freshen up before it was time to go down to the hotel restaurant for dinner.

CHAPTER FOUR

The food served was delicious, but Kathleen would've enjoyed it more if she had been less aware of the undercurrents of anger coming from Jordan Long. The rare comments he directed at her were polite but tinged with thinly disguised hostility nonetheless.

Fortunately both of the girls had seemed oblivious to his attitude toward her. Marsha had picked nervously at her food, leaving most of it on her plate, but Kathleen hadn't blamed it on the tension in the air. She doubted that the young girl had fully recovered from the flight. As for Annette, nothing seemed to faze her.

It was a relief when Jordan finished his coffee and suggested it was time they went up to their rooms. As it turned out, Kathleen's relief was short-lived.

When they entered the small sitting room, Jordan instructed, "You girls go into your room and get ready for bed. Ms. Darrow and I are going to have a little talk." His gaze flicked to her with the sharpness of a whip.

"It's too early, Dad," Annette said.

"It'll be nearly ten by the time you change and crawl into bed, so don't talk back," he said in a tone that would not tolerate any arguments.

Grumbling beneath her breath, Annette sulked toward the door to the bedroom she shared with Marsha. Her younger sister seemed almost eager to leave. Kathleen wished she could join them when she cast a sideways glance through her lashes at the uncompromising hardness etched in Jordan Long's face.

At the click of the latch indicating that the door was tightly closed between the two rooms, he turned toward her, his gaze coldly sweeping over her. Kathleen kept her expression composed, although a bewildered light entered her eyes.

"Have a seat, Ms. Darrow." The command was clipped.

Kathleen obeyed. "What was it you wanted to discuss with me?" she inquired calmly.

He had remained standing, increasing the sensation that he was towering above her like an angry avenger. Having to look even higher up at him put her at a greater disadvantage, as she guessed he knew it would.

He didn't immediately respond to her question. Long, smooth strides took him to a small table sitting against the wall. A briefcase was on top of it. He removed a folder and separated a paper from the others. Walking back, he handed it to her.

"Would you please explain the meaning of this?" Jordan challenged coldly.

A muscle twitched in the strong jaw. Kathleen sensed that the anger that had been building since they met was now held in check by a very slim thread. Her gaze slowly withdrew from its study of his face to examine the paper he had thrust in her hand.

She recognized the writing on the form instantly—it was hers. She was even more bewildered when she looked at him again. "I don't understand." She frowned in confusion. "This is my application."

Fire smoldered in his charcoal eyes at her admission. "How old are you, anyway?" he accused.

Her frown deepened. "Twenty-five." Were they back to the age problem?

"What does your application say that your age is?" Jordan Long demanded tightly.

Kathleen glanced at the section of the form where her birthdate was. She looked at it once, blinked and looked at it again. It wasn't possible!

"I . . . I'm afraid there's been a mistake." An abrupt, self-conscious laugh accompanied her words.

"A big mistake, I would say." The words of agreement were drawn out slowly and precisely.

"The last two numbers for the year I was born are inverted," she murmured, looking back at the application when she was unable to bear his piercing gaze.

"Were you aware of my requirements when you applied for the position?" The softness of his accusing voice filled her with dread.

Her tongue nervously touched a corner of her mouth.

"You're referring to the fact that you had wanted someone older, aren't you?" Considering how upset she was, her voice sounded remarkably composed, even to her.

"Then you did know," Jordan Long returned with pinning hardness.

"Yes, I was aware of it—" She was about to say that she'd understood her qualifications had overridden the age factor, but he didn't give her the chance.

"Which is why you deliberately lied about your age."

"That's not true!" Kathleen protested sharply.

"Is that your handwriting?" he retorted.

Her temper flared and she quickly counted to ten. "Yes, it is my handwriting," she admitted evenly, "but the date written here is simply an honest mistake. The numbers are right, but in the wrong order."

"Hmm. I almost believe that explanation." His mouth twisted into a mocking smile. "You knew I would find out eventually. What did you hope to gain by a lie like that? Enough time to settle into my home and get acquainted with my daughters, to show me how capable and reliable you are so that even when I knew the truth, I wouldn't be inclined to fire you."

"I didn't do it deliberately!" Kathleen repeated forcefully. "I wasn't trying to deceive you just to get the job." Her hand waved in a hopeless gesture toward the bedroom. "Mrs. Long and your daughters were aware of my age. If I had been trying to trick you, then why would I tell them the truth?"

His expression didn't change as he ignored her question. "Must have been easy to charm an old lady and two young girls. Since I was out of the country, there would only be their comments and your falsified application for me to review. It was a very smart plan, Ms. Darrow."

The temperature in the room seemed to be rising steadily. Kathleen unbuttoned her ivory jacket and rose to her feet. She was beginning to get a crick in her neck from looking up at him all the time.

"I did not plan this," she insisted.

"Why were you so eager to take this particular job?" His gaze narrowed thoughtfully, black lashes veiling the dark smoke of his eyes.

"Because I thought I would like it and I do," Kathleen said, thoroughly irritated. "There was no ulterior motive."

"Wasn't there?" Jordan Long said jeeringly. "You're a trained nurse, an excellent one if your references were true. There's no lack of work for a good nurse."

"I wanted a change." She began breathing slowly to control her growing temper. "Nursing and hospitals were becoming my whole life, and that wasn't what I wanted. Besides, nurses are not that well paid."

"I see, then it was money. It must have sounded like a cushy job, looking after two nearly grown girls, getting free room and board and a generous salary from an employer who wasn't there a lot of the time."

"I didn't look at it that way at all," she replied tightly.

"Oh, come on," he said, his head tilting to an arrogant angle. "If it wasn't the money, then why would you take a job with so little free time? Did you want to be isolated in the quiet countryside with only two young girls for company? Were you jilted by some guy from the big, bad city, and decided to run away to nurse your broken heart?"

"I wasn't jilted, and my heart isn't broken." Her voice trembled in anger. "If I'm doing any running then it's to a new way of life. I like the country and I like your daughters. And I don't really care whether you believe that or not!"

"And that's the only reason you lied about your age? Do you expect me to believe you?"

"I didn't lie about my age!" His steely gaze moved to the application still in her hand. Kathleen thrust it onto the small table where the briefcase lay, as if the paper had scorched her fingers. "Not on purpose I didn't," she qualified, since the evidence so obviously pointed to the opposite. "And I don't see why age is such a factor. I'm just as capable of taking care of your daughters and your home as someone twice my age. I take my responsibilities seriously. I don't consider this job as a sort of vacation."

"You can't be that naive, Ms. Darrow." He towered beside her, the material of his jacket brushing the thin fabric of her blouse sleeve. His gaze held hers for a moment, then traveled slowly down the front of her blouse, dwelling on the agitated rise and fall of her breasts beneath the thin fabric. "Can't you think of one reason why it might not be appropriate for a woman as young and attractive as you are to stay in my house?" Jordan Long spoke softly and suggestively.

No woman could possibly remain indifferent to the almost physical touch of his eyes. Kathleen was not an exception as hot flames licked her cheeks. She took a quick step away. A wicked glint of laughter danced in his eyes, and she hated herself for betraying her awareness of him.

"Were you hoping I would be a balding middle-aged man that you could twist around your finger?" he mocked. "Someone who would be dazzled by your auburn hair and that flash of green in your eyes? What was your plan B? Were you going to appeal to his baser instincts?"

"You're disgusting!" Her temper aroused at last, Kathleen didn't try to regain control of it. "The only way I intended to 'please' my employer was to do my job well and conscientiously. I was hired—by you, Mr. Long—to look after your daughters and your home. Nothing else! You're my employer, and that's the only relationship we have or ever will have!"

"Oh?" His maddening composure wasn't disturbed by her outburst. "That smile you gave me at the airport sure looked like an invitation to get to know you better."

"It was not!" she denied vehemently and turned away. That wasn't exactly true, since her reaction to his admiring look had been strictly feminine and not that of an employee meeting her boss for the first time.

"Maybe I read something more into it," Jordan Long replied in a voice that didn't believe her denial.

"You certainly did!"

"It doesn't really matter, because you won't be around long enough to find out which of us is right. I shouldn't have delegated the responsibility of interviewing applicants to someone else. It's a mistake I won't repeat. But I kept the other applications—''

With her ear pressed against the connecting door, Annette listened intently to the conversation in the sitting room. She grimaced at her father's words and glanced at Marsha.

"He's going to fire her," she said in a moaning whisper. "We've got to do something."

"What?" Marsha's lower lip trembled. "He'll just get madder if he finds out what we've done."

Annette flashed her a speaking glance. "I don't think he can get much madder than he is right now, do you?"

"Poor Kathleen," Marsha murmured sympathetically. "I was really beginning to like her a lot."

"So was I," came Annette's whispered agreement. "There's just got to be something we can do to gain time."

"I'll just die if he hires the dragon lady."

A scheming light flashed in the gray smoke of Annette's eyes. "You won't die. You'll be sick!"

"What?" Marsha blinked her blue eyes.

"Come on. We don't have much time," Annette whispered urgently.

On tiptoe, she hurried to the bathroom with her curious and confused younger sister right behind her. Turning on the hot water tap in the sink, Annette slipped a washcloth under the faucet.

"What are you doing?" Marsha persisted, frowning at her sister's action. "What did you mean when you said I'd be sick?"

"Just what I told you," she answered quietly. "You're going to pretend you're sick. It's the only thing I can think of to make them stop arguing, so at least I'll have time to think of something else," Annette explained. She wrung most of the water out of the washcloth. The mirror above the sink was steaming. "Hold this cloth on your face. It'll make your skin feel hot, like you had a fever."

"It's hot!" Marsha protested, making a face as the cloth touched her skin.

"Do you want Kathleen to leave?" Annette's hands were on her hips.

"No," the younger girl sighed, and gingerly wrapped the washcloth around her cheeks and her forehead.

Annette waited for a few seconds to see the results. With a satisfied nod, she soaked the washcloth again in hot water and handed it back.

"Now, hop into bed. All you have to do is be real weak. Every once in a while you can moan like you don't feel very good. But don't overdo it," Annette cautioned in a fiercely low voice. "When I call them into the bedroom, you ask Kathleen to stay with you."

"Yes." Marsha bobbed her head as Annette led her to one of the twin beds in the room. "Why does it have to be me? Why can't you be sick?"

"Because"—Annette's patience was wearing thin—"I never get sick and you do." She rumpled the bedcovers as Marsha slid between the sheets, then mussed up her own bed and ruffled her short blond hair. "Are you ready?"

"I guess so," Marsha mumbled.

"Throw the washcloth under the bed." Annette started towards the connecting door. "Here goes emergency plan plus two!"

* * *

"You're planning to fire me before you've even found out whether I'm capable or not," Kathleen said angrily. "There's only one reason you would do that. You're the one who doesn't trust himself to have me in the house. You're one of those jerks who have to try to make every woman they meet to prove to themselves that they're really men."

"Interesting theory. But it doesn't apply to me." His lips curled contemptuously. "I don't like it when people take advantage of me or my family. And I don't like liars."

"I've told you over and over that the mistake on the application was just that—a mistake. I—"

"Kathleen!" Annette's voice called frantically from the connecting room, followed immediately by a knock on the door before it burst open. "Kathleen, Marsha's sick. Come here!"

Kathleen was already reacting to the alarm in Annette's voice and was halfway to the door before Annette said much more. She was vaguely aware of Jordan Long following her as she hurried into the adjoining room.

Marsha was lying in the far twin bed with her eyes closed. She opened them as Kathleen bent over her. The blue eyes were wide and slightly frightened, and Kathleen smiled reassuringly.

"What's the matter, Marsha?" she asked softly, placing a hand against the girl's flushed cheeks.

"I don't feel good," came the murmured reply.

The hesitant blue eyes swung past Kathleen, then the lashes fluttered weakly down. The hands gripping the covers trembled slightly. Kathleen glanced sideways, her gaze catching the broad chest of Jordan Long and rising quickly to his face. Simultaneously, his gray eyes flicked from the face of his daughter to her.

The anger of a moment ago was forgotten. Kathleen easily slipped into her previous professional role, responding to the concern in his face.

"She seems to have a slight fever." She answered the unspoken question in his gaze and looked at Marsha again. "Is your stomach upset, Marsha?"

The lashes opened to reveal rounded eyes and Marsha managed a small nod.

Annette moved around to the opposite side of the bed. "Is this because of the plane ride, Kathleen?" she asked. "I mean, she gets so nervous and all."

"I don't think it's anything serious," Kathleen agreed, giving Marsha a gentle smile. "Have you thrown up?"

"No," she answered weakly, then moaned softly as Annette sat on the bed beside her. "But I kinda feel like I might."

"Well, just lie there and be quiet for a while. Breathe slowly." Kathleen took hold of her wrist and checked her pulse. With a glance at Jordan, she said softly, "It's normal."

"Will—will you stay with me, Kathleen?" The blue eyes gazed at her imploringly.

"Of course I will," she agreed. She glanced around the room, her gaze settling on a chair in the corner. "I'll sit right here beside you until you go to sleep. How's that?"

"Fine." A tiny smile curved Marsha's mouth.

While Kathleen moved away from the bed to fetch the chair, Jordan Long stepped closer to his daughter. He leaned over and lightly kissed her forehead.

"Everything will be all right, honey," he murmured and smiled, deepening the cleft in his strong chin.

He turned as Kathleen came back carrying the chair. Taking it from her, he set it next to his daughter's bed. When she started to walk past him, he moved slightly to block her way for an instant.

"We'll finish our discussion in the morning," he said quietly.

Her chin raised a fraction of an inch. "Of course, Mr. Long," Kathleen agreed curtly.

There was really very little left to discuss. He had made it clear that he was going to fire her. As he walked from the room, she sat down in the chair, taking the hand that Marsha held out to her and holding it lightly in her own.

With the excitement over, Annette returned to her own bed and crawled beneath the covers. "I'm glad you were here, Kathleen," she said simply. "Marsha gets a little frightened when she doesn't feel good."

"So does everyone," Kathleen smiled. "Good night, Annette."

"Good night."

"And you try to sleep," Kathleen told Marsha in a voice that was genuinely loving.

"I will," Marsha agreed obediently. "Thank you for staying with me."

"You don't need to thank me." She shook her head slightly. "Good night."

"Good night." And Marsha closed her eyes.

It was nearly an hour before Kathleen was satisfied that Marsha was sleeping soundly. She was still clutching Kathleen's fingers. Gently she pried her hand free and tucked the covers around the sleeping girl before quietly returning to her own room. She left the door slightly ajar so she could hear Marsha if she called for her in the night.

Very quietly, Annette pushed back the covers and reached for her watch on the night table between the two beds. The luminous dial revealed that the time was two-thirty in the morning. She slipped from her bed and walked silently to her sister's.

"Marsha!" She shook the girl's shoulder until she got a response.

"Wh—"

"Ssh!" Annette held a silencing finger to her mouth. Tiptoeing to the door Kathleen had left open, she closed it very carefully, then tiptoed back to the bed. "You're going to have to be sick again," she whispered.

"Why?" Marsha frowned sleepily.

"Because you heard Dad last night. He said they'd finish their talk in the morning, and we're going to have to convince Kathleen that you're still sick. We have to keep them apart for a while longer."

"What do I have to do this time?" Marsha yawned and rubbed her eyes as she pushed herself into a sitting position.

"Come on. We're going into the bathroom," Annette instructed.

Reluctantly Marsha climbed out of bed and followed her older sister. "It doesn't seem fair to trick Kathleen this way," she mumbled.

"If we don't, then she'll leave and we'll never see her again," Annette pointed out. "Now you sit down there by the toilet and look sick."

Scurrying like a silent mouse, Annette hurried to open the connecting door to Kathleen's room, leaving it ajar the way it had been.

Kathleen stirred beneath the covers, her subconscious prodding her to waken. At the urgent call of her name, she was instantly awake, flinging back the covers and slipping out of bed. Static electricity molded her nightgown to her figure.

"Kathleen!" Annette was in the doorway. "Marsha's in the bathroom."

With Annette leading the way, Kathleen hurried into the bathroom. Marsha was sitting on the floor and leaning against the bathroom wall. She looked exhausted and weak as she glanced up.

"I'm sorry, Kathleen," she murmured.

"You don't have to be sorry," Kathleen soothed. "You couldn't help it."

She knelt beside her, noting the slight pallor in the cheeks that were cool to the touch of her hand. Marsha's respiration seemed even, although there was a faint skip to her pulse.

"Would you like to go back to bed now?" Kathleen asked.

There was a wide-eyed nod of agreement. Annette stepped forward as a door opened and footsteps approached. Kathleen turned slightly.

"Maybe we should help her," Annette suggested. "She seems awfully weak."

"Yes—"

Jordan Long stood in the doorway, his gray eyes

sweeping over them in quick assessment. He was wearing only a pair of dark pants. His dark hair was tousled from sleep, spiked up in a way that was incredibly attractive. Kathleen couldn't help looking at the amazing sight of his bare, muscular chest. Then it was her pulse that suddenly began behaving erratically.

"Marsha was sick again," she explained unnecessarily, averting her gaze and struggling for composure. "We were just about to help her back to bed."

"I'll do it." He stepped into the small room, seeming to fill it with the force of his presence. His hard shoulder brushed her arm as he moved toward his youngest daughter, searing her skin with its warmth.

When he had gathered Marsha in his arms, Kathleen moved swiftly into the girls' room and pulled back the covers on Marsha's bed. With Marsha in bed, Kathleen sat on the edge, tucking the covers around the girl.

"Show me where it hurts, Marsha," she asked.

The little girl pointed to the right side of her abdomen, then the left. "It just doesn't feel good," was the answer.

Glancing up at Jordan standing beside the bed, Kathleen queried, "Has she had any appendix trouble?"

"It's already been removed—when she was eight," he answered briskly, eliminating that possible explanation. The steel gaze raked harshly over Kathleen. "Kathleen, I think my daughter will survive long enough for you to go and put a robe on."

Her head jerked back with a start, a hand instinctively moving to the open neckline of her night-gown.

She blushed and a resentful sparkle of green flashed in her hazel eyes. She wasn't about to hurry as if she'd done something wrong again and turned instead to Marsha.

"I'll be right back," she promised, and returned, swaddled in a long robe, a few minutes later. Jordan Long departed immediately.

The next morning Marsha still felt sickish, or so she said. There weren't enough physical indications for Kathleen to recommend a visit to a doctor. She didn't think it was still a nervous reaction to the plane ride and said as much.

"Maybe," Annette said hesitantly, glancing at her father who was standing in the far corner of the girls' room, "she's worrying because she has to get back on the plane the day after tomorrow."

"Is that what's bothering you?" Kathleen looked at the little girl inquiringly.

Marsha glanced sideways at Annette before nodding silently that it was. Inwardly Kathleen sighed. It was so difficult to tell a child not to worry about something that seemed terrifying.

"Dad, I've been thinking," Annette said. "Maybe we should go back to Delaware. I mean, seeing Washington was a great idea, but—well, let's face it, Marsha has really put a damper on the trip. We can come another time by car, can't we?"

"I think that, under the circumstances"—his gaze narrowed briefly on Kathleen—"you're right. None of us is up for sight-seeing. I'll change our return flight to today."

"I'll pack your clothes, Marsha." Annette was already walking toward the closet.

"It will all be over in a little while, Marsha," Jordan said, moving toward the door.

Prophetic words, Kathleen thought, since once they had returned, it *would* all be over for her. She imagined that Jordan Long would make her pack up and leave before the day was over.

In just two short weeks, she had become fond of Marsha and Annette. His accusations were false, but there was very little she could do to prove she wasn't lying. Even if she could, considering how obnoxious he'd been, she didn't want to try.

CHAPTER FIVE

The two girls were already at the door when Jordan Long laid a hand on Kathleen's arm, restraining her without much effort.

"Don't bother to unpack your things," he murmured as she glanced up to meet wintry gray eyes.

"I didn't intend to," she replied coolly, understanding exactly what he meant by that remark and determined not to give him the chance to insult her. "I cleaned the house thoroughly before we left and there's plenty of food in the kitchen. I'm sure you and the girls can fix your own meal tonight."

His mouth thinned into a grim line. "If you'll step into my study, I'll write you out a check for the time you've worked."

Lines from a nursery rhyme sprang into her mind. *Will you step into my parlor? said the spider to the fly*. Kathleen felt decidedly like the fly, only more wary.

Ignored by the adults conversing in low tones in the entry hall, Annette and Marsha paused on the first steps of the stairs. Annette was nibbling again on her lower lip, her expression one of deep concentration.

"What are we going to do?" Marsha whispered. Grimacing a little, she added, "Do I have to be sick again?"

"We'd never get away with it a third time." Annette gave her sister an impatient frown. "No, we're going to do something different this time. Just follow my lead and agree with whatever I say, okay?"

Kathleen remained standing while Jordan Long walked around the walnut desk to sit in the swivel rocker. Her mind flashed back to the day when Annette had sat there and begun the interview. Now the girl's father was terminating the job with his signature on a check.

She would have liked to tear up the check and throw it in his face, but starting a scene would be pointless. It would accomplish nothing but to arouse his anger. No, she would accept the check with all the dignity she possessed. Despite what he thought of her, she had earned it.

There was a knock at the study door before it swung open. Annette strolled nonchalantly into the room with Marsha shadowing her. Without a word, Annette sat at one end of the small sofa and Marsha at the other.

"I thought you girls had gone upstairs to

unpack,'' Jordan Long said pointedly, his hand poised above the checkbook.

"We decided to do it later,'' Annette shrugged, plucking aimlessly at the cord edging of the sofa's arm.

"Would you mind leaving the room? Ms. Darrow and I are having a private discussion.'' His gaze flicked briefly to Kathleen, then back to Annette.

"Actually''—Annette seemed to be summoning up her courage as she met his commanding look— "it seems to me that what you're discussing is family business. Since Marsha and I are part of the family, we should take part in it, too. What is it that you're talking about?''

There was a tightening of his jaw as Jordan swerved his attention to the checkbook on the desk. He didn't reply immediately, pausing as though he was choosing his words with care. Kathleen remained silent.

"I've decided that Ms. Darrow isn't a suitable person to be looking after you girls,'' he said finally.

"Why?'' Annette asked calmly.

"We like her,'' Marsha added.

"She's too young,'' was his terse reply.

"But you knew how old she was when you hired her,'' Annette pointed out, her eyes widening in confusion.

"No, I wasn't aware of her age.'' Jordan Long shot Kathleen a look, plainly designed to remind her of the application. She smoldered inside but revealed none of her irritation. "I was under the impression she was older.''

"You could have asked us.'' Annette glanced at her sister. "Marsha and I knew how old she was. So did Aunt Helen. Besides, we liked her better than the others who applied for the job—and now that we've gotten to know her, we like her even more.''

"I'm sorry." His tone was clipped. "But she's too young.''

"What's age got to do with it?" Annette frowned. "With Kathleen it's like having an older sister to take care of us. You know how Aunt Helen was, and Mrs. Carmichael before that was a regular tyrant. And Mrs. Howard was so absentminded she'd forget where we were. Why can't Kathleen stay?''

His patience was vanishing at an alarming rate. "Annette, you're old enough to realize a few facts about life. It's not appropriate for a young woman to live in this house.''

Annette looked at him blankly for a moment before a light dawned in her eyes. "Oh, I get it!" she exclaimed. "You think that other people might think you and Kathleen are having an affair. Really, that's ridiculous, Daddy!" she laughed.

"Is it?" A black eyebrow arched indignantly at his daughter's open amusement.

"Of course it is," Annette insisted with a wide grin still on her face. "You're much too old for Kathleen ever to be interested in you that way. Da-ad, you're thirty-seven years old!" she exclaimed, as if he was approaching antiquity instead of being a man in his prime. "You're practically old enough to be her father!''

Kathleen pressed her lips tightly together to conceal the smile teasing the corners of her mouth. Covertly, she glanced at Jordan through her lashes. He didn't look very pleased with his daughter's assessment.

Annette wasn't finished. "And Kathleen isn't anything like the women you usually date. You prefer the blond, sophisticated type. And Kathleen is, well"—she seemed at a loss to find the words to describe her—"Kathleen is nice," she concluded lamely. Pricking Kathleen's ego, she went on with, "She's pretty in her own way, but she just isn't right for you, Dad."

His gray eyes glittered with sardonic amusement at Kathleen's expense hearing her cut down to size as he had been a moment ago. Kathleen guessed that what Annette said was true. She could easily visualize Jordan Long with a cool, elegant blonde on his arm.

"Besides, Dad," Annette continued, "nobody who sees you would ever for one instant think you were a dirty old man always chasing young girls. Not only that, Kathleen already has a boyfriend."

"Is that true?" A disbelieving look mocked Kathleen.

No doubt he still believed she was running away from a broken affair. For once in her life, Kathleen was actually glad to claim Barry as her boyfriend and puncture Jordan Long's theory.

"Yes, it is," she answered crisply.

With a wave of his hand, he dismissed it as unimportant. "You're not going to get your way, Annette. We need someone older and more experienced, and that's that."

"But what about me and Marsha?" Annette protested. "Don't we have some say? After all, we're the ones most directly involved."

"Yes, and we want her to stay," Marsha chimed in.

"I understand the way you girls feel, but . . ." He began, patiently but firmly, to refuse their request.

"But you don't understand, Dad," Annette interrupted. "We know you're only doing what you think is best for us, but look at it from our point of view. You're hardly ever home. I know you can't help it and that it's your job," she conceded. "Marsha and I understand that. Since you have to be away so much, we just want to stay with someone we like. And that someone is Kathleen. You can't argue that she isn't qualified for the job, because you know she is."

"We would still miss you as much as ever, Dad," Marsha added earnestly. "But we wouldn't be so lonely if Kathleen lived here with us."

She could see by the grim expression on his ruggedly handsome features that the girls had backed him into a corner. As much as she liked the job, she didn't want to keep it simply because he had been pressured into reversing his decision.

"Listen," she spoke up hesitantly, glancing at the girls in turn. "I appreciate your support and the fact that you like me well enough to want me to stay, but I really think it might be best if I didn't. Because of a misunderstanding, your father and I—well, we don't get along."

"But he'll like you as much as we do, once he gets to know you," Annette insisted.

"Please, don't go," Marsha begged openly. "No one else has ever cared about us as much as you do. If Daddy says you can stay, please promise that you will."

Tears welled in the pleading blue eyes, one spilling out at the corner and trickling down Marsha's cheek. A person would have to be made of stone to resist that appeal, and Kathleen was not.

"Oh, Marsha!" she sighed, smiling against her will and helplessly looking at Jordan Long.

The tearful gaze switched to him as well. "Please, Daddy, say that Kathleen can stay."

Breathing in deeply, he stared at the checkbook on the desktop, then flipped it shut. "One more month," he conceded grudgingly, glaring at his daughter. "Then if I decide that it isn't working out, I don't want to hear any more about it from you girls. Agreed?"

"Thank you, Daddy!" Marsha burst out, her face wreathed in a smile as she nodded agreement.

"You won't be sorry," Annette added.

"I hope not," he muttered, his wintry look sliding to Kathleen. "Is that all right with you?"

"I don't seem to have much choice," she answered, since, when it came right down to it they had both given in to the emotional blackmail of the girls. "Yes, I guess so," she replied, although she doubted the arrangement would last a week, let alone a month.

"Come on, Marsha. Let's go and unpack for Kathleen," Annette suggested in a triumphant voice, and the two girls raced happily from the study.

But Kathleen was not yet dismissed. "I hope you understand that I'm not condoning the trick you used to get the job in the first place."

Kathleen was tired of telling him that she had done no such thing. He wouldn't believe her anyway.

"It never occurred to me that you were," she replied.

"I have a week's leave coming and then another

week of work before my vacation begins," Jordan Long continued.

"That should work out well," Kathleen interrupted. "You'll have plenty of time to find an older and more qualified replacement for me—and without having to rely on pieces of paper," she said, letting him know that she was aware the new agreement was only to make the girls happy.

A humorless smile curved his mouth.

"I'm glad we understand each other."

"So am I." When she turned to leave, he didn't stop her.

"What a performance!" Annette exclaimed, throwing her arms in the air and spinning around Kathleen's bedroom. "Oh, Marsha, you were amazing! Those tears were perfect. I never knew you were such a good actress! 'I would miss you, Daddy, but I wouldn't be so lonely if Kathleen was with us,' " she said, mimicking her sister's plea and giggling.

Marsha self-consciously wiped away the wet trail on her cheek. "I wasn't acting. I meant every word I said," she replied stiffly.

Annette tipped her head to one side, the gleeful amusement gone from her expression as she regarded her sister with wide-eyed wonder.

"You really do like Kathleen that much, don't you?" she said.

"Yes," Marsha mumbled, watching her hand trailing over the suitcase on the bed.

"Well"—Annette shrugged—"that's all the more reason why we have to be sure that she stays."

"Daddy is so angry about that application. He

hates it when people lie," came the sighing words of defeat.

"He'll get over it," Annette answered confidently. "We'll see to that and so will Kathleen."

"I hope you're right," Marsha murmured doubtfully.

"I know I am."

The temporary truce that followed put Kathleen on her mettle. Although she was going to be fired no matter what, Jordan Long wasn't going to be able to fault her work.

As she and the girls cleared the Monday evening dishes, she noticed with satisfaction that he had eaten everything on his plate. It was a compliment to her cooking, whether he wanted to admit it or not.

The telephone rang in the living room. Since his return, there had been a lot more calls. Kathleen ignored the ring, aware that he was in the living room and the call was undoubtedly for him anyway. It was something of a surprise when she picked up the tray of dishes and saw him standing in the dining room.

"Phone call for you. I believe it's your boyfriend," he added dryly.

"I'll take the tray." Annette appeared at her side. "Marsha and I will take care of the dishes. You go and talk to Barry."

"Thank you." Kathleen handed the tray to her, wondering why she suddenly felt so self-conscious. She was, after all, entitled to get a phone call now and then.

As she walked into the living room, she was aware

that Jordan followed at a leisurely pace. He paused at one of the windows to gaze at the purpling dusk. Warily, Kathleen glanced at his strong profile, tucking her auburn hair behind her ear as she picked up the phone. His expression was one of absent concentration, seemingly oblivious to her presence. She wished she could say the same.

"Hello." She turned her back to Jordan, hoping that she could ignore him if she didn't see him.

"Hello, Kathleen." Barry's voice returned her greeting with considerably more enthusiasm. "Was that your Mr. Long who answered the phone?"

Your Mr. Long. Oh, no, he's not, she thought silently. "Yes," she admitted. It was impossible to correct him, not when Jordan could overhear her.

"Was he anything like you expected?" he asked curiously.

She hadn't ever had the time to imagine what Jordan Long would look like, but she doubted if she would ever have visualized the tall, vitally attractive man in the living room with her now.

"No, I guess not."

A low chuckle sounded over the receiver. "I take it by your tone that he's in the room with you."

"That's right." Kathleen laughed softly at her carefully worded answers, designed not to let Jordan Long guess that he was under discussion.

"So how was your trip to Washington, D.C.?"

"It ended almost before it began," she explained. "Marsha got sick and we came home on Saturday morning."

"Nothing serious, I hope." There was instant concern in his voice.

"Just nerves, I think. She's afraid of flying, and I guess that upset her. She was fine after we came home." Kathleen was unaware of using the word home. Subconsciously it was the way she thought of the Long house.

"I was going to suggest that I come out to see you tonight, but I suppose it's not a good idea, with your boss being there and all," he sighed.

"Well, no, it's not," she agreed, "not tonight, anyway."

"Ms. Darrow," Jordan Long's voice interrupted briskly, causing Kathleen to pivot sharply toward him.

"Excuse me a minute, Barry," she said into the telephone, then covered the receiver with her hand. "Did you want something, Mr. Long?"

"I'll be taking the girls with me to Dover on Thursday. You're free to do whatever you want for that day," he informed her, obviously assuming that she would want to spend the time with Barry. Kathleen held his steady gray look for several seconds as she removed her hand from the receiver. "Barry? Mr. Long says I can have Thursday off this week. Let's go out to lunch, okay?"

There was a glitter of contempt in Jordan's gaze as he looked her up and down before he turned away. She guessed that he disapproved of women who asked for what they wanted. He undoubtedly liked to do all the chasing, even when he knew the object of his attention wanted to be caught. And she couldn't imagine any woman, with the possible exclusion of herself, who wouldn't want to be caught by him.

"Sure, I'm free on Thursday," Barry replied.

"I'll meet you at twelve-thirty at your office," Kathleen suggested.

"Make it eleven-thirty instead," he replied.

"Then you can tell me all about your new boss," he added.

"Yes, yes, of course," she said quickly, unsure at this point of how much she wanted to tell. "I'll see you on Thursday."

There was no other comment from Jordan Long when Kathleen hung up the receiver. In fact, he didn't even glance her way as she left the living room for the kitchen, but continued staring out the window, preoccupied with thoughts she couldn't begin to guess at.

On Thursday morning, a gloomy, cloud-covered sky promised nothing but rain. It was hardly the type of day that made a person want to go out, Kathleen sighed to herself. She sipped at her coffee, but not even the fragrant aroma seemed to perk up her spirits.

Annette drained her orange juice glass and sat back in her chair at the breakfast table. Marsha was still eating her bowl of cereal and Jordan was hidden behind the morning newspaper opposite Kathleen.

"Why don't you drive into Dover with us, Kathleen?" Annette suggested. "Aunt Helen said she invited you to come with us the other day when you talked to her. She did, didn't she?"

"Yes—"

The newspaper rustled as Jordan folded it down to gaze curiously at Kathleen. "You talked to Mrs. Long recently?" he asked with an arrogant arch of his eyebrow.

"On Tuesday," she admitted.

"Kathleen calls her or has one of us call her every other day," Annette explained. "Just to make sure Aunt Helen is all right and to keep her from being lonely or thinking that we might not care about her anymore."

"How thoughtful."

But his smoldering charcoal eyes emitted an entirely different message. Kathleen guessed that he thought she was doing it simply to impress him. She wasn't in the mood to convince him otherwise.

"Tell Mrs. Long when you see her that I've made other plans for today. Maybe I can stop by another time." She addressed her reply to Annette.

"You're welcome to come with us. I can drop you off in town if you like." The paper was once more erected between them. It was a subtle and unnecessary reminder that he didn't particularly care whether she accepted or not.

"No, thanks," she refused. "I have some errands to run and I wouldn't want you to go out of your way. Besides, I have my own car."

"It wouldn't be any trouble," Annette protested. "Tell her, Daddy, that you don't mind."

"This is Ms. Darrow's day off, Annette," Jordan reminded his daughter from behind his paper barricade. "She would probably like to spend it away from you girls."

"Can I ask you something, Daddy?" Annette scowled at him. "How come you keep calling Kathleen 'Ms. Darrow'? It sounds kinda cold. And not very friendly."

"I beg your pardon." The paper was folded up and placed on the table. Mocking gray eyes were focused on the auburn-haired young woman across the table from him. "I didn't intend to sound unfriendly."

"It doesn't matter," Kathleen answered tightly, picking up her cup and drinking the remaining coffee. Annette was overly optimistic in thinking that her father would ever accept her, and Kathleen knew it.

"Is it true that you want to get away from Marsha and me?" The blond girl looked curiously at her.

"Not exactly," Kathleen said.

"The fact is, Annette," Jordan pointed out, "Kathleen has a date with her boyfriend today. She wouldn't want you two girls as chaperones."

He used her given name so casually that for an instant Kathleen didn't realize he had said it. It sounded very different spoken by that low-pitched, masculine voice.

Annette took the news blandly, accepting the explanation. "I hope we get to meet Barry some time. He sounds nice."

"Have you finished yet, Marsha?" Jordan glanced at his youngest daughter. "I'd like to leave before lunchtime," he teased lightly.

Marsha scooped out the last spoonful of cereal and announced that she was finished. As the three rose from the table, Jordan paused to look at the still seated Kathleen.

"You can leave the breakfast dishes, Kathleen." This time there was a sardonic emphasis on her name. "The girls will do them when we come back tonight." Without waiting for her reply, he turned away.

A few minutes later, the girls were calling their goodbyes as they slipped out through the side door into the closed garage.

There was plenty of time for her to do the dishes before she had to leave to meet Barry. Kathleen was inclined to do them, except that she knew Jordan Long would think she had washed them to make points with him. So instead she stacked them neatly on the counter beside the sink.

As she walked into the living room, laughter bubbled in her throat. She wondered what his reaction would be if she started calling him Jordan. She doubted that he would interpret it as a gesture of friendship. If anything, he would probably assume she was attempting some kind of female scheme to persuade him to change his mind about her.

Kathleen was suddenly reminded of the way Jordan had looked at her at the airport, and a warmth seeped through her at the picture in her mind. She wondered idly what their relationship might have been if there hadn't been that embarrassing mix-up about her age. It was a troubling thought.

The telephone rang as she walked past it, and she jumped at its strident ring. Scolding herself for being silly, she came out of her momentary daydream to answer it. It was Barry.

"Sorry, but I have to break our lunch date. It's a business commitment. I'm meeting a client," he explained quickly, as if Kathleen needed to be reassured he wasn't breaking a date with her to keep one with another girl.

"That's all right," she insisted, smiling at his almost painful earnestness. "I understand." Her gaze slid to the window and the rain misting the glass. "The weather is really awful today, and I didn't think I'd find a parking place close to your office," she laughed, since it was a near impossibility.

"I—I have a committee meeting tonight or I'd suggest that we have dinner instead of lunch together. Any chance you'd be free Friday or Saturday night?"

"No." But Kathleen assured him again that it was no problem. Secretly she felt glad. She spent too much time bolstering his confidence, anyway. At the moment she needed someone to boost her own.

They talked for several more minutes until Barry got a phone call on another line and had to hang up. Kathleen took a deep breath and glanced out the window. She had an entire day off with nothing to do.

There were no errands to run. She had made up that excuse for Annette's benefit and to avoid being pressured into accepting Jordan's offer of a ride that she knew he didn't want to make. There were a few things she wanted, personal items, but they could be picked up when she did the household shopping.

As she walked toward the staircase, Kathleen contemplated visiting her parents, but it was her mother's day for her church committee, so that was out. Maggie, Darla and Betty were working the day shift at the hospital, so she couldn't visit them. And the drizzling gray weather meant staying indoors. She certainly couldn't visit Helen Long, not with the girls and Jordan Long there.

In her room, Kathleen changed out of her bright yellow track suit, worn to make up for the lack of sunshine. Donning her old standby favorite of faded denims and bulky gray sweatshirt, she picked up the book on the bedside table and retraced her steps downstairs.

There was no point in going out, since there was nowhere to go. It was her free day to spend as she chose, she reminded herself. If she spent it alone in the house, reading a book, it was nobody's business but her own.

Curling up on the sofa in the living room, Kathleen opened the book, but the gloomy weather outside seemed to press into the room, making it melancholy and depressing. She built a small fire in the fireplace, hoping the cozy sound of crackling flames would chase away the dreariness.

For a while the fire helped as she fell under the spell of the book she had read many times before. She began identifying with the heroine, Jane Eyre, until she realized it was Jordan Long she was picturing as the brooding Rochester, and she closed the book with a snap.

Rising, she began to pace the room restlessly. Forced idleness was not something she enjoyed. Mentally thumbing her nose at Jordan, she walked into the kitchen and washed up the breakfast dishes. He could think what he liked about her reasons.

She thought of something better to do as she was putting the dishes away. The kitchen cupboards needed cleaning and there was new shelf paper in the pantry. Kathleen had bought it last week with the intention of having Viola Kent, the cleaning woman, do them on Tuesday.

The whole day was before her—it was barely ten o'clock. She could easily clean all the cupboards and put down fresh paper before the Longs returned, and Jordan would never be the wiser. If he didn't know it, he couldn't possibly accuse her of doing it to impress him.

Considering his cynical attitude toward her, he would never understand the satisfaction she got from the simple act of cleaning house. To Kathleen, the end results more than justified the work. But she didn't mind a certain amount of clutter. And she'd never gone over the edge and become a compulsive doorknob polisher and picture straightener.

With the decision made, she set to work, flipping on the radio to fill the room with music and chase away the gloomy mood. Slipping out of her shoes, she put them out of the way under the breakfast table. It was a quirk of hers. She liked to be barefoot whenever she did any cleaning.

CHAPTER SIX

Starting with the cupboards holding canned and packaged foods, she unloaded the shelves, removed the old paper and began wiping them out with a damp sponge. The work went quickly and she found herself humming as she cleaned.

The last cupboards were located above the refrigerator. Even standing on a chair in front of it, Kathleen still couldn't reach the top shelf or the back of the lower shelf, so she opted for a somewhat precarious perch, using the chair and the adjoining countertop to reach the shelves.

A matching set of glasses, goblets and punchbowl were stored on the two shelves. All of them were dusty and Kathleen washed them before putting them back.

With a knee on the counter and a bare foot waving in the air for balance, she stretched across the refrigerator top to set a goblet on the shelf. The radio was blaring in her ear.

"What are you doing?" a voice barked loudly from the direction of the side door into the garage.

Startled, Kathleen spun around. Her elbow hit the edge of an open cupboard door, sending needles of pain down her arm, momentarily paralyzing her fingers. The goblet tumbled from her hand, striking first the countertop, then breaking on the chair seat and shattering glass onto the tile floor.

"Don't move!" Jordan called out.

But the warning came too late. Instinct had already made Kathleen react quickly and try to catch the expensive crystal goblet before it broke. The sole of her bare foot came down on a piece of glass on the chair top. A stifled gasp followed the piercing contact.

Not daring to move from the safety of her perch atop the counter, she sat down on the formica top, twisting her leg to view the injury to the bottom of her foot. There was a telltale smear of red and a stabbing pain.

"I thought I told you not to move!" Glass crunched under his shoes as Jordan strode angrily to her side.

Kathleen glanced at his face, etched with impatience and concern. "You did."

"What happened?" Annette appeared in the doorway to the garage, her gray eyes rounded with curiosity. Marsha was right behind her.

"Kathleen broke a goblet," Jordan answered abruptly. "Get a broom from the closet and sweep it up before someone else gets cut." He turned his attention back to Kathleen, more specifically to her injured foot. "Let's see how bad it is," he ordered grimly.

"Guess what. I'm still a nurse," she reminded him curtly as he pushed her probing fingers out of the way. "And I'm more than qualified to deal with a simple cut."

Steel gray eyes briefly met the stubborn flash of her gaze. "Point taken. But I have some first aid experience, and unless you're a contortionist, I can see better than you whether there's glass in the wound."

Kathleen let him look at her foot. "What are you doing back so early anyway?" she muttered, then winced when he plucked out a splinter of glass.

"Four o'clock isn't exactly early." With the glass removed, the blood flowed more freely from the cut.

Deftly he wrapped his white handkerchief around her foot. Kathleen was still trying to register the fact that it was much later than she had thought when he slid an arm under her knees and another around her waist and back.

"What are you doing?" she protested in astonishment as he lifted her from the counter and cradled her against his chest.

Instinctively her arms went around his neck, as if afraid that at any moment he would drop her. But he seemed to find her weight no burden. The two girls were watching with wide-eyed looks.

This close, his smoldering gaze flustered her completely. "I was going to carry you into the other room, unless you wanted to walk barefoot over more glass," Jordan replied mockingly.

Pressing her lips together, Kathleen refused to comment on his remark and averted her gaze to the rolled collar of his white turtleneck. Her side vision saw his mouth twitching in an ill-concealed smile.

"Be careful. And be sure to get all that glass cleaned up. Use a damp paper towel to pick up the little bits, not a broom." he reminded the girls before he carried Kathleen through the door into the dining room. "Would you mind explaining to me what you were doing?"

"I wasn't stealing the crystal, if that's what you were thinking," she retorted. He didn't stop in the dining room but continued to the living room. "I was cleaning the cupboards. I was just putting the goblets back when you shouted at me."

"Cleaning cupboards on your day off? Aren't you conscientious." There was an underlying tone of ridicule in his voice.

"There was nothing else to do," Kathleen snapped in her own defense.

In the entry hall, she realized Jordan was carrying her to the master bedroom. It was on the tip of her tongue to remind him that the downstairs bathroom was much closer than the private one off his room. Then she decided to say nothing. After all, she had been in his bedroom any number of times, although never when he was there.

"Nothing else to do?" Jordan repeated her phrase. He looked curiously down at her. "What happened to the lunch date with your boyfriend?"

"Canceled. He had to meet a client."

Her senses were beginning to take notice of the steady beat of his heart and the intoxicating fragrance of aftershave lotion on his face. She could feel the rippling muscles in the arms that carried her. She didn't like being suddenly reminded of his striking masculinity just as he was about to prop her on his bed.

"Wait here," he ordered when she was seated on the beige coverlet, and walked into the adjoining bathroom.

Rather than think about the uncomfortably intimate aura of the manly room, Kathleen crooked her leg to rest her injured foot on her other knee, removing his handkerchief bandage to investigate the wound. Jordan was back in seconds with disinfectant and bandages.

"Then aren't you meeting—what was his name, Barry—this evening?" he questioned as he knelt on the floor beside her.

"No, Barry has a committee meeting tonight," she replied, straightening slightly to watch the competent, strong hands clean the cut.

He smiled crookedly. "So you decided to vent your frustrations by cleaning the cupboards. My mother used to say that cleaning was the best way to get rid of anger."

"Really?" Kathleen tilted her head curiously to one side. "I just can't stand being idle. When I lose my temper, I count to ten and then throw something."

"Remind me to stay out of your line of fire," he chuckled, and Kathleen found herself warming to the pleasant sound.

"I generally choose an inanimate object for a target," she laughed. Her laughter was cut short by the sting of the disinfectant. She immediately leaned forward to get a better look at the injury to her foot. "It isn't very serious, is it?"

"No. It isn't as deep as it looks, but it's going to be sore to walk on. Did you actually think you had a chance of catching that glass?" Jordan mocked gently, turning his head slightly toward her.

The hostility between them vanished. His sexy mouth was inches away from her own. Kathleen was suddenly aware of how dangerously close it was, and her heart began drumming against her ribs at the darkening glow in his eyes. The force of his male attraction seemed to be holding her captive.

As if he just realized that he had come too close, Jordan retreated into aloofness again. Quickly he smoothed the adhesive part of the bandage over her foot and straightened up, ending that moment of bantering friendliness.

"From now on, I suggest that you wear your shoes," he said curtly.

He couldn't have made the dismissal any plainer if he had ordered her out of the room. Kathleen put her weight on her other foot, favoring it slightly as she hobbled from his bedroom.

The shooting pain from her wound mingled with the pangs from his withdrawal. They were back to that uneasy truce. The brief glimpse she had had of what it could be like between them made her dislike the state of emotional cold war all the more.

At lunch on Saturday, Jordan announced that he wouldn't be home that evening. He was dining out, and Kathleen and the girls could plan whatever they wanted for supper.

"Let's have pizza," Marsha suggested immediately.

"If you want," Kathleen agreed, smiling. She knew pizza would be the main course every night if Marsha had her way.

"Who are you going out with, Dad?" Annette

asked, pushing the cold crab salad around on her plate with a fork.

"Kay Peters," he replied.

At the mention of the woman's name, Annette made a disgusted face as she glanced at Marsha. Kathleen saw it, but if Jordan noticed it he made no comment. And the subject was dropped.

That afternoon Jordan took the girls to the beach. Kathleen didn't go. Her cut was healing nicely and she didn't want to risk an infection. Instead she stayed at home and did the few pieces of ironing from the wash.

Barry called, asking if he could come out to see her that evening. Kathleen had put him off so many times that it was difficult to refuse him again. Besides, Jordan would be out for the evening.

She told Barry to come around eight o'clock. Jordan would be gone by then. She also warned him that they wouldn't be able to go anywhere because of the girls. But he said he'd be happy just to see her, and accepted the invitation.

Somehow Kathleen never got around to mentioning to Jordan that Barry was coming over. First of all, the girls claimed most of her attention with their elaborate plans for pizza supreme. Then Jordan was in his room, showering and changing into evening clothes.

Before she knew it, he was gone and she hadn't told him. She tried to reconcile her guilty conscience with the fact that he had already given permission for her to have visitors once and that she didn't need to obtain it again.

Barry arrived promptly at eight. The girls were openly curious about him, pestering him with questions until Kathleen began to feel sorry for him and came to his rescue.

"Annette, why don't you and Marsha fix some popcorn and cold drinks for the four of us?" Kathleen suggested.

"Let's all go and fix it," Annette countered.

Kathleen slid a sideways glance at Barry, who smiled wryly and said, "Why not?"

With Annette organizing the project, they all trooped out to the kitchen. Marsha got the old-fashioned popper out of the cupboard and put in oil and popcorn. Barry was delegated to fill the glasses with ice cubes while Kathleen made sweet tea and Annette melted butter in the microwave.

When the last kernel had popped and the salt and butter had been sprinkled over the top, they all sat around the breakfast table in the kitchen, munching from individual bowls. The homey atmosphere put Barry at ease.

"I haven't done this in years," he smiled at Kathleen. "Not since I left home, anyway."

"It's fun, isn't it?" Annette chimed in. "Dad loves to fix popcorn, especially in the winter when it's cold and dreary outside, and we have a fire roaring in the fireplace. Then we'll sit around in the evening fixing popcorn or roasting marshmallows."

It was difficult for Kathleen to visualize Jordan Long actually having fun, but she only had to remember his affectionate manner toward the girls to realize there was another side to him than the one she usually saw.

"He's always doing things like that with us when he's at home," Marsha inserted.

"Sounds like you have a close relationship with

your father," Barry commented, and Kathleen caught the trace of envy in his tone. Barry had always felt he had been a disappointment to his parents.

"We do," Marsha assured him. "He used to say we were the Three Musketeers."

Kathleen wiped her buttery fingers on a paper napkin, suddenly curious what the girls thought of Jordan going out without them. "Does it bother you when he goes out for an evening?"

There was a quick, measuring flash in Annette's astute gray eyes. "You mean with some woman? No, it doesn't bother us. After all, he is a man," she declared in a worldly way. It was a point Kathleen wouldn't dispute. "Actually, he dates a lot, but this is the first time he's gone out since you came to live with us, Kathleen."

"Have you girls ever met any of the women your father dates?" Barry's question had been on Kathleen's mind, although she was reluctant to voice it.

"Oh, yes," Annette nodded. "We go along sometimes when he takes some woman to the beach or sailing."

"It must be nice for you girls to be included," Barry said.

"It's awful," came the mumbled response from Marsha, who was staring grimly at her popcorn. "They always pat us on the head and tell us what pretty girls we are and what a wonderful father we have. They're all phonys."

The vehement statement surprised Kathleen. She had never expected that type of jealous reaction from the two girls. They had always seemed so unselfish where their father was concerned.

"Actually," Annette explained archly, "Father's taste in women is abominable. Of course I've tried to explain to Marsha that he doesn't date them for companionship, but she's a little too young to understand, if you know what I mean."

She darted a knowing look at Kathleen, who found herself uncomfortably imagining Jordan romancing some impossibly gorgeous blonde. Barry's hand covered his mouth to hide a smile.

"But I think the real reason he goes out with that type of woman is because he doesn't want to get married again," Annette continued, absently stirring the popcorn in the bowl with her fingers. "He says he doesn't want to be tied down again and that we're the only females he needs in his life. He doesn't seem to realize that in a few years we'll be grown up and he'll be all alone. We think he should get married again—but not to anyone he's seeing now." She shuddered eloquently. "It would be nice if he married someone like you, Kathleen." At Kathleen's start of embarrassed surprise, Annette added, "She would have to be closer to his own age, of course."

"Yes, of course," Kathleen agreed somewhat self-consciously. The last thing she wanted to do was point out that twelve years was not exactly a gigantic gap.

Her position in the household was tenuous enough as it was. She didn't need the added burden of the girls touting her to Jordan as their candidate for a perfect stepmother.

"I have a great idea!" Annette exclaimed, and Kathleen's heart just about stopped. "Let's all watch the late movie together." Kathleen sighed inwardly with relief. "It's supposed to be really good. It isn't a weeknight. We can stay up, can't we, Kathleen? It's called *Horror of Horrors*."

"Sounds wholesome. I don't see why not," Kathleen smiled.

"Come on, Marsha, let's clean up this mess." Annette was already scrambling from the table, taking the emptied tea glasses with her while Marsha stacked the bowls.

Later, as they were all making their way back to the living room, Barry murmured to Kathleen, "They're quite a pair."

"Yes, and they're a lot of fun, too." Although sometimes, she thought, Annette's adultlike perception was unnerving.

"Don't turn out all the lights," Marsha protested as Annette switched on the television in the living room, then walked around turning off all the lights.

"It's better if the room is dark," Annette stated. "It sets the atmosphere for the movie."

"But it's scary when it's dark." Marsha curled into a ball in an overstuffed armchair, a green pillow clutched in her hands.

"I like being scared," Annette declared airily, taking a pillow from the couch and lying down on the floor in front of the television. "Besides, it's only a movie, and Kathleen and Barry are going to watch it with you."

As Kathleen sat on the couch beside Barry, she smiled wryly at how different they were. Yet Annette the adventurous and Marsha the meek were remarkably close.

The movie was good, highlighted by stunning special effects. As the suspense and terror began building to the climactic conclusion, Barry bent his head toward Kathleen, his arm resting companionably around her shoulder.

"Take a look at Marsha," he whispered next to her ear. Kathleen's glance saw that Marsha had her face buried in the pillow, unable to watch what was happening. The background music of the film was rising to a crescendo. "She stayed awake all this time and now she's going to miss seeing the end!"

The overhead light suddenly switched on, flooding the room with light. Marsha screamed and Annette sat up. Kathleen moved guiltily away from Barry's encircling arm even before she saw the tall, dark-haired man in the dining room archway.

Gray eyes as stormy as the Atlantic in winter were focused on her. She felt her cheeks pale under their cold censure. Her mouth was dry.

"Dad!" Annette exclaimed with a sigh. "You shouldn't startle us like that. You just about scared Marsha to death."

"Shouldn't you girls be in bed? It's nearly one o'clock." His gaze moved pointedly to Barry. There was nothing subtle in that silent message. It was time he left.

"Kathleen said we could stay up and watch the late movie," Annette explained, plumping her pillow and resuming her former position on the floor in front of the television. "It's nearly over."

Kathleen darted a hesitant, sideways glance at Barry. The arm that had been around her shoulders was now self-consciously at his side. She knew Barry somehow had the impression that Jordan Long would be much older and less handsome than the man glaring coldly at him now.

"I'm glad you're home, Dad," Marsha murmured, letting the protective pillow fall to her lap.

"The End" flashed across the television screen and Jordan strode to the set. "It's over now." He snapped it off. "You girls get to bed."

"Oh, Dad!" Annette grumbled, and rose to her feet.

Barry ran his fingers through the side of his hair. "It's late. I'd better be going, too."

"I'll walk you to the door," Kathleen murmured nervously, joining him as he rose from the couch.

Jordan remained in the living room while the four of them entered the hall, the girls heading for the staircase and Kathleen and Barry moving toward the front door. Barry had seen the forbidding look in Jordan's eyes and accepted her rather hurried good night.

"I'll call you next week," he promised, and kissed her lightly on the cheek, then left.

Taking a deep breath, Kathleen closed and locked the front door, then turned around. Jordan was standing in the hall, darkly handsome in his evening suit.

"I take it that was your boyfriend." There was a contemptuous ring to his voice.

"Yes, that was Barry." Kathleen tried to reply evenly. "Obviously he came to see me." Her response bordered on defiance, a natural reaction to his intimidating manner.

"You knew he was coming?" It was really more of a condemning statement than a question.

"Yes," she admitted, lifting her chin a fraction of an inch.

"But you didn't mention it to me?"

"I didn't see the point." Kathleen shrugged self-consciously. "You'd already told me I could have visitors. I didn't think it was necessary to obtain your permission again, or to let you know in advance when they were calling."

His mouth tightened to a thin line. "When I gave you permission it didn't occur to me that your visitor would be male, or that you would be sitting with him on the couch necking in front of my daughters."

Kathleen breathed in sharply. "We were not necking!"

"You weren't?" he jeered. "Looked like you were practically sitting on top of him when I walked in."

"I was not!" Her temper was fast reaching its boiling point. Muttering aloud, she started to walk past him, hoping to end the conversation before she lost control of her anger. "Of all the—"

His fingers dug into the soft flesh of her forearm. "Do you deny that he was nuzzling your neck?"

"I do!" she flashed. "Believe it or not, he was merely whispering something to me!"

"Really? What?" Jordan mocked. "Did he want you to hurry the girls into bed so he could make love to you?"

Her free arm swung in a lightning-fast arc toward his face, her open palm striking his cheek with a resounding slap. "You have a dirty mind!" she spat.

A savage anger glittered in his eyes, Kathleen had a moment to doubt the wisdom of her attack before an iron hand closed over hers.

With her hands straining against the solid wall of his chest, she tried to push herself away, but his superior strength overpowered her efforts and crushed her against his length. The harsh imprint of his muscular body against the softer curves of hers weakened her resistance.

Kathleen's involuntary surrender brought a sensual change to the bruising pressure of his mouth. Its firm yet persuasive touch started a wildfire that raged through as Jordan's lips parted hers. She shuddered with uncontrollable desire at his intimate exploration. The arousing caress of his hand over her back and hips made her arch even closer to him, molding her flesh to his.

The stairwell door in the entry hall was partially open. Like two little mice, Annette and Marsha sneaked down the stairs, slinking along the edge of the steps so the boards wouldn't creak and betray their presence.

Annette crouched on the lowest step, while Marsha leaned forward above her to peer through the crack between the door and its frame. They both spotted the embracing couple at the same time. Marsha straightened away from the door in embarrassed surprise, while Annette watched for a second longer.

Quickly but silently, Annette turned away and motioned for her sister to go back upstairs. Not until they reached the top did she let the excitement burst from her.

"It's working!" Annette whispered gleefully. "I told you it would."

"But he was so angry when he came home." A puzzled frown creased Marsha's forehead as she tried to understand.

"It doesn't matter what he was like when he came home." Annette shook her head impatiently. "That was a kiss of passion if I ever saw one."

Marsha tilted her dark head. "Have you ever seen one?"

Annette ignored the inconvenient question, holding a finger to her lips. "Ssh, I thought I heard something," she whispered. "We'd better go to our rooms, just in case Kathleen is on her way up."

When Jordan lifted his head, Kathleen remained motionless, her fingers desperately clutching the lapels of his jacket. Her eyes were closed, her lips moist and trembling from his kiss. Her senses were still reeling from the passionate assault that had shaken her so.

"Now, Ms. Darrow"—his sarcastic voice spilled over her like an icy bucket of water—"convince me that you wouldn't want a man to make love to you if you were alone with him."

For a frozen second, she could only blink at him in disbelief. Then the shame of her wanton response to his embrace washed over her with sobering force. Wrenching free of his hold, she raced for the stairs, humiliated beyond words that she had let him see how susceptible she could be to masculine charm. If his opinion of her had been low before, it was even lower now.

CHAPTER SEVEN

Sunday was a nightmare. Although Jordan didn't once mention the embarrassing episode the night before, it was all Kathleen could think about. She couldn't look at him without her gaze being drawn to his sensual mouth and remembering how expertly he had kissed her.

Later in the afternoon, Jordan left to drive to the Greater Wilmington airport. He was flying to Louisiana to straighten out some regulatory problems on one of the offshore rigs. It was his last assignment before his vacation officially began.

Kathleen had volunteered to drive him to the airport, but he'd declined her offer, preferring to leave his car at the airport and drive himself home when he returned. Since Kathleen had her VW Bug, it was a practical arrangement.

The week dragged by slowly. On one hand, she dreaded the approaching weekend and Jordan's return, wanting to prolong the harmonious days with the girls.

On the other, she wanted to get the trial month over with, an agreement she now wished she hadn't made.

She'd arranged with Mrs. Long to have Wednesday off, and left the girls at their great-aunt's to spend the better part of the day with Maggie, who relayed all the latest gossip at the hospital to Kathleen.

There had been no phone calls from Jordan. When he left, he'd said only that he would be home the following weekend, not naming a specific day.

On Sunday, Kathleen and the girls drove into town to go to church with Mrs. Long. Then Kathleen invited her to have Sunday dinner with them and spend the afternoon. She wondered if she wasn't subconsciously trying to protect herself against Jordan's arrival. When the dinner dishes had been washed and put away, the girls brought out their Monopoly board and set it up on the kitchen table. Kathleen couldn't concentrate on the game, listening constantly instead for the sound of Jordan's car pulling into the garage.

Within a half an hour, she was bankrupt and out of the game. She stayed at the table for a while, but was too restless to sit idly and watch. She doubted that the three players even noticed when she left the table.

She decided to change out of her Sunday dress. It was one of the more feminine garments in her wardrobe, a light, summery material in an apricot color.

In the entry hall, Kathleen remembered that the bulb in the hanging lamp overhead had burnt out.

She'd intended to replace it this morning, since the fixture provided the only light in the hall, but had forgotten to do it.

Before she could forget a second time and be forced to replace it in the dark, she retraced her steps to the kitchen, hearing gleeful laughter from Marsha when Annette landed on her Park Place. Amidst the confusion, Kathleen took a new bulb from the cupboard and walked back to the entry hall, pausing in the dining room to carry one of the chairs with her so she could reach the lamp.

Setting the bulb on a side table, she positioned the chair under the hanging lamp. Afraid that the heels of her shoes would catch in the needlepoint cushion of the chair, she slipped them off and climbed onto the chair seat.

Stretching on tiptoes, she could just reach the burnt-out bulb.

As she started unscrewing the bulb, the front door opened, and her hazel eyes darted to Jordan in surprise. A few more turns and the bulb would be free. She didn't dare let go of it or it might crash to the floor, yet she couldn't tear her gaze from him or move from her position.

Dressed in a dark business suit and tie, he stepped into the hall, closing the front door behind him. His compelling features were etched with tiredness as he set his briefcase and luggage on the floor. Kathleen's heart was doing flip-flops at the way the gray eyes were mercilessly examining her from head to toe, dwelling for several seconds on the shapely length of her legs below the skirt of her dress.

His mouth quirked. "I see you chose to ignore my advice."

"Advice?" Kathleen echoed blankly. There was a tremor in her voice at the disturbing gray light in his eyes.

"No shoes." He looked pointedly at her stockinged feet.

Another turn and the bulb was free. Auburn hair fell forward across her cheeks as she stepped down from the chair and walked to the side table for the new bulb.

"You'll have to blame my mother." She avoided looking at him as she removed the bulb from its protective cardboard. "She taught me never to climb on furniture with shoes on." Trying to change the subject, she asked, "Why did you come in the front?"

"Because your car was blocking the garage door," he answered dryly.

She flushed guiltily. "I'm sorry."

"So you would rather risk cutting a foot than getting a little dirt on the chair," mocked Jordan, reverting to the original subject without acknowledging her apology.

Kathleen walked back to the chair, stepping onto the seat with a hand on the wooden back for balance. She was aware by the direction of his low voice that he had moved closer. When she raised her arm to insert the new bulb, he was in front of her.

His hands gripped the sides of her waist. Automatically, she lowered her arms to his shoulders for support. He lifted her from the chair to the floor, holding her there for an instant while Kathleen's senses quivered with his nearness. His sexy smile was unnerving but maybe that had something to do with being in midair. "Put your shoes on so

I don't have to get out the first aid kit again," he ordered firmly. "I'll put the bulb in."

Her knees were weak as she bent to retrieve her shoes. Aware of his power to arouse her physically, Kathleen moved well away from the chair. With a few swift turns, Jordan had the new lightbulb in the socket and was stepping down from the chair.

"Where are the girls?" His hand brushed his black hair to one side, a gesture that seemed to emphasize his tiredness.

"In the kitchen playing Monopoly with Helen," Kathleen answered, picking up the dining room chair to return it.

"Helen?" Jordan frowned. "Do you mean my aunt?"

"Yes, we all went to church together, then I invited her out here for dinner with us," she explained, adding as an afterthought, "there's some cold roast beef left. Could I make you a sandwich?"

"Maybe later." He shrugged aside her offer and walked toward the kitchen.

Kathleen followed more slowly, taking her time in replacing the chair at the dining room table. Finally she entered the room where the excited girls were welcoming their father, the Monopoly game forgotten. She managed to stay pretty well in the background until Helen Long suggested it was time she went home.

"I'll take you," Kathleen volunteered.

Marsha was standing beside the kitchen chair where Jordan was sitting, her arm partially around his wide shoulders. He glanced up at her and smiled, a little wearily.

"Why don't you two girls ride along with Kathleen?'' he suggested. ''That way I can shower and change without interruptions while you're gone.''

Several minutes later, the four of them were in Kathleen's small car. They stayed for only a few minutes at Helen's home to make sure everything was all right, then drove straight back. This time Kathleen parked her car well clear of the garage door.

It was just as close for them to use the front door as it was to walk to the kitchen entrance through the garage. Jordan's luggage was still sitting inside the door along with his briefcase. Kathleen sent Annette to the kitchen to put away the Monopoly game and to start preparing a cold supper. She gave the briefcase to Marsha, assuming that Jordan would want it in his study.

She carried the luggage down the hall to the master bedroom. There was no sound of movement inside the room.

She knocked once on the door and it swung open. Jordan was lying in the center of the bed, his suit jacket thrown carelessly to one side. He was asleep.

Quietly, Kathleen walked in and set his luggage on the floor at the foot of the bed. She hesitated, glancing at the sleeping figure. The only thing he had removed was his jacket. He still had on his shoes and his shirt was buttoned all the way, with the tie still knotted at his throat.

Taking care not to waken him, she untied his shoes and eased them off his feet. Loosening his tie was a more difficult task. He was smack in the middle of the oversize bed, too far from the edge for Kathleen to lean over and reach him.

Lowering herself onto the bed, she carefully

began loosening the knot of his tie. He stirred once, and she waited, holding her breath. When he lay quietly again, her fingers resumed their work on the knot.

"Were you planning on strangling me in my sleep?" Jordan murmured unexpectedly, his voice thick with exhaustion.

Her gaze flew to his face, startled to see that his charcoal-gray eyes were open. For an instant, Kathleen was shaken by his discovery of what she was doing, then a professional calm took over.

"I was trying to loosen your tie so you could sleep more comfortably," she explained evenly, and continued her task.

His lashes closed, accompanied by a tired sigh. His right hand moved up as if to join hers. Instead it began unbuttoning his shirt, starting with the middle buttons so as not to interfere with her effort to loosen his tie.

"I didn't make it to the shower," Jordan stated the obvious. "I never got past the bed."

With the tie free of its knot, Kathleen undid the top buttons. "You were tired," she said softly. A smile curved her mouth. She had never expected to see the formidable Jordan Long look so vulnerable.

His hand fell away and she unbuttoned the rest of the buttons. With practiced ease, she turned him on his side and slipped off half of his shirt and turned him on the other side to free it completely.

There was a whimsical curve to his mouth when he was lying once again on his back, his eyes still closed. "It's been a long time since a woman has undressed me," he murmured. "You're very good at it."

"I'm a nurse, remember?" She stopped with the

shirt. But she was well aware that her professional detachment disappeared around Jordan.

One bronzed shoulder moved against the mattress in a stretching motion. "I haven't slept in thirty-six hours and I'm sore all over." One gray eye opened again. "I don't suppose your training as a nurse included rubdowns?"

Kathleen could see the corded tautness in his muscles and nodded. "I had a course in physiotherapy."

He rolled toward her onto his stomach, taking her statement as an agreement to massage his aching back.

The movement brought him closer to the edge of the bed, and Kathleen was able to stand on the floor while her hands kneaded his taut shoulders and upper back.

After several minutes his breathing became slow and steady, and she guessed he had drifted back to sleep.

Under her skilled fingertips, some of the tenseness had left, but not all. Annette appeared in the open doorway, and Kathleen held a finger to her lips to indicate silence. Annette nodded, smiling widely, and retreated to another part of the house.

When Jordan rolled away from her onto his back, Kathleen stopped, but he seemed about to waken, so she put a knee on the bed and began slowly rubbing his upper arms and the front of his shoulders. The position was awkward, and she began to tire.

As if he felt her firm touch faltering, Jordan reached up to lightly clasp her left hand in his right, sooty lashes lifting to gaze at her. Her leaning position had her balanced precariously above him.

"That's enough." The smoky light in his eyes thanked her. "Did anyone ever tell you that you have magic fingers?"

Her auburn hair had been tucked behind her ears. One side slid free, falling across her cheek and shimmering with a dark fire. For an instant she wanted to ignore his statement that she had done enough and let her hands continue their unrestricted exploration of his hard chest and arms. But it was simply too dangerous.

"No, never." She shook her head and began to straighten.

His right hand reached up and smoothed the hair behind her ear. The unexpected caress checked her movement away from him. His fingers remained along the side of her neck. The darkening light in his eyes made her heart leap suddenly.

Exerting the slightest pressure, Jordan pulled her head toward him. Caught in the magnetic pull of his animal attraction, it didn't even occur to Kathleen to resist.

Warm and languid, his mouth closed over hers, kindling a slow-burning flame in her that grew steadily hotter.

Her fingers spread themselves over the granite strength of his chest, encountering the curling dark hairs that tickled her palms. His hand over her pliant back, drawing her down to the nakedness of his torso. An avalanche of erotic desire coursed through her, stimulated by the seductive mastery of his expert lips.

There was no urgency to his caress. It was languorous and slow, as if they had all the time in the world. His left hand moved sensuously down her waist to the curve of her hip and along her thigh, entangling itself in the soft folds of her skirt. The musky male scent of him filled her senses. Primitive yearnings surfaced with a rush.

His hand pushed her skirt carelessly out of the way as it explored her silken-clad thigh. The arousing touch succeeded in awakening her to the danger of her actions. She turned her head away from the drugging ecstasy of his mouth, quivering with the fullness of her response.

"Please." But he focused his attention on the throbbing vein in her neck. "Don't!" She tried to push herself away. With a slight twist, Jordan forced her onto the bed beside him, her head resting on his shoulder.

"Stay with me." The order was issued in a low voice husky with passion.

"No." It was a protest against her own desire against how much he made her want to stay. She tried to recapture her sanity. "Jordan, don't do this."

Deliberately he tantalized her mouth, letting his lips play near one corner of it. "Say my name again."

"Jordan," Kathleen moaned softly, almost sinking again under his spell. Then his hand moved to rest lightly on the curve of her breast. With the last of her willpower, she slid free of his arms to the edge of the bed. On shaking legs, she took a step away. "Mr. Long"—her voice trembled traitorously—"you're tired and need sleep."

The smoldering light in his eyes faded a little, and there was a suggestion of labored breathing in the rise and fall of his tanned chest. Then he seemed to relax against the covers.

"Yes," he agreed simply.

Pivoting, Kathleen hurried through the doorway into the hall. There was no sensation of relief, only a lingering feeling of bitter disappointment, which did nothing to bolster her self-respect.

No man's touch had ever affected her so strongly. The possibility that it might be more than physical attraction, that she might be falling in love with Jordan, didn't exactly fill her with gladness. How could it when he had done nothing but insult and accuse her since they had first met?

A glimpse of her reflection in a hall mirror told her that she didn't dare rejoin the girls in her present state. Her auburn hair was tousled, there was a flush to her cheeks, and her lips were slightly swollen from Jordan's seductive kisses. Her appearance was a definite betrayal of her passionate romp on the bed only moments before.

Altering her direction, she walked toward the stairwell door. Her hand closed over the doorknob and started to turn it.

"Kathleen?"

She nearly jumped out of her shoes at the sound of Annette's voice. A deep blush spread over her face and neck as she turned to answer.

"Yes?" Her voice was brittle. The professional poise she usually could summon had deserted her.

The young girl's careful study of her was unnerving. "I have a cold supper all set out."

"Good." Kathleen couldn't even force a smile. "Why don't you girls go ahead and fix a sandwich? Your father is sleeping." A nervous hand ran lightly over the front of her skirt. "I was going upstairs to change. I . . . I'll be right down."

"Okay." Innocent gray eyes blinked agreement before Annette turned to reenter the living room.

* * *

Annette was sprawled crosswise over an armchair, watching a Nature Channel wildlife documentary with interest.

Marsha sat cross-legged on the floor in front of the television, equally engrossed in the program.

The sound of firm strides shifted Annette's attention to the hall, without changing her position. She smiled somewhat absently when her father appeared.

"Hi, Dad," she greeted him. "We were beginning to think you'd sleep until morning."

The lines of tiredness had left his strong features. His ebony hair gleamed wetly, a sure indication, along with his fresh appearance, that he had just showered. A pair of blue jeans hugged his muscular thighs and slim hips, complemented by a patterned silk shirt that molded the breadth of his chest.

An absent frown of disapproval drew his dark brows together as he glanced at his older daughter. "Chairs are for sitting, Annette, not lying." Grimacing, she swung her legs off the chair arm and sat up. His charcoal gaze swept the living room. "Where's Kathleen?"

A knowing sparkle entered Annette's lighter gray eyes, but it was Marsha who answered. "She's in the kitchen washing up the supper dishes."

A dark brow shot up. "Shouldn't you be helping?"

"Not on Sunday," Marsha explained, her attention not diverted from the television. "It's our day off. Kathleen says we're entitled to one, too."

"There's plenty of food left if you're hungry," Annette suggested. "We didn't know how long you'd sleep, so we put it all away, but Kathleen will fix you something if you ask her."

Jordan didn't reply, but walked through the living room to the dining room, obviously heading for the kitchen. Annette watched him from her chair, waiting until she heard the swinging of the kitchen door before she moved to follow. Marsha glanced at her curiously.

"You wait here." Annette waved a hand at her. "I'm just going to see what's happening."

Marsha shrugged and looked back at the television while Annette stole silently into the dining room, pausing beside the door to the kitchen and cocking her head to listen.

Kathleen rinsed a plate under the tap and set it in the dish drainer. At the opening of the door, she glanced absently over her shoulder, expecting to see one of the girls. For a startled instant, her hazel eyes met the piercing steel gray of Jordan's.

Her pulse raced, but she looked away quickly, and dipped another plate in the sudsy water.

"There's cold meat and salad in the refrigerator if you're hungry," she offered.

Jordan's gaze bored holes in her back for several seconds. "That isn't why I'm here," he stated cryptically.

He walked to the counter beside the sink where Kathleen was washing dishes. Although he was within her line of vision, she didn't glance at him, but her senses were raised to a fever pitch of awareness. Soap and aftershave lotion mingling with the musky scent of his maleness made an intoxicating combination. Her nerve ends vibrated at his nearness.

"What was it you wanted?" Did that cool and

calm voice belong to her? Kathleen marveled silently.

"I owe you an apology." His gaze compelled her to look at him. She did so, reluctantly. His aloof regard was almost freezing. "The only excuse I have for my behavior earlier this evening is that— well, I was tired."

"I understand."

Bitterness welled in her soul. She understood very well. He probably would have asked any woman to stay. Kathleen just happened to be the one who was there.

Jordan seemed to find her acknowledgment of his apology less than acceptable and his expression hardened. "I don't make amorous advances to female employees, Kathleen," he scowled.

It would have been much easier to withstand his piercing gaze if he had addressed her more formally. As it was, Kathleen had to look away. The sight of his mouth forming her name was just too much.

"I never thought you did, Mr. Long," she replied.

A muscle twitched along his jawline at her formal reference to him. Her hands were remarkably steady as she continued washing the dishes and rinsing them under the tap.

"I also wanted to assure you that I won't ever do that again," Jordan said tersely.

Kathleen paused, indignation rising within her. He didn't have to make it quite so plain that he wasn't interested in her.

"I'm an adult and a nurse." She spoke slowly and concisely, anger trembling on the edge of her voice. "I'm aware that physical urges are just that—

physical. So we kissed . . . no big deal. I've already put it out of my mind.'' It was a blatant lie, but there was little else she could say if she wanted to save her pride.

His gaze narrowed on her profile, measuring the amount of truth in her words. Kathleen tossed her head back, dark red fire gleaming from the silken curls of her hair, as she met his hard gaze without flinching.

''I'm glad we understand each another,'' he said finally. ''There's something else I wanted to discuss with you.''

She turned back to the sinkful of sudsy water, unconsciously squaring her shoulders. What was left to talk about? she asked herself.

Aloud, she merely said, ''Yes?''

''Under the circumstances, I think it's time to call it quits,'' Jordan declared. ''This isn't going to work out.''

Her heart sank. ''I couldn't agree with you more,'' she replied bravely. ''If you like, I'll pack and leave in the morning.''

''I didn't mean to end it that abruptly.'' There was a humorless twist to his mouth. ''What I had planned to suggest was that I begin interviewing for a replacement, if that meets with your approval. You may stay on until I find one or you may leave. The girls and I can make do.''

Kathleen moistened her lips, wishing her heart hadn't leaped so wildly at the brief reprieve. ''Oh. I got the impression that you wanted me to leave immediately.''

''That's not necessary,'' he qualified. ''Since we both know what can happen, we just have to avoid any, um, uncomfortable situations in the next few days.''

"Of course." There was a tight lump in her throat. "In that case, I'll stay." She stared down at her hands and the dishcloth that she was clutching in her fingers. "Will you tell the girls immediately?"

There was a second's hesitation, and she darted a quick glance at the grim set of his mouth.

They both knew how much the two girls liked her. His decision wouldn't be popular.

"Not immediately." There was a note of impatience in his voice. "Not until I've decided on a replacement. There's no need for them to get upset in advance. I'll contact the employment agency tomorrow and arrange for the interviews to be held in their offices."

"That would be best, I suppose," Kathleen agreed. A poignant smile touched her mouth. Whoever her replacement turned out to be, she would never have the wonderfully odd experience of being interviewed by Annette and Marsha.

"What's the matter?" Jordan questioned her brief smile.

"I was just remembering the first time I met your daughters." She shrugged, and began washing the rest of the dishes.

Jordan studied her silently, then walked to the refrigerator to investigate the leftovers. He found his cold supper waiting and lifted off the plastic wrap for a taste.

Annette straightened up and moved away from the door. "No, no, no," she muttered as she stalked back toward the living room. Draping herself over the armchair, she began thoughtfully nibbling at her lower lip. Somehow she had to think of a way to stop her father.

CHAPTER EIGHT

The two girls huddled together outside the study door, the blond head bent confidently toward her dark-haired younger sister.

"Now, remember," Annette whispered, "don't let anyone pick up the phone in the living room. And if it looks like Dad is heading for the study, you'll have to sidetrack him somehow."

"How?"

"I don't know how," Annette sighed impatiently. "Take him outside to see what's wrong with your bike."

"But there isn't anything wrong with my bike."

"Slip the chain off! *Pretend* there's something wrong with your bike!" Her hands waved the air at the sheer hopelessness of her sister.

"Okay," Marsha grumbled.

With a sideways glance to be sure no one was watching, Annette slipped into the study, quietly closing the door behind her. She walked hurriedly to the desk, looked up a phone number in the directory and dialed. Her fingers drummed the desktop as she waited for an answer.

"The business office, please," she requested in her oldest voice. There was another pause. "Yes, this is Mrs. Long. I would like to request that this number be temporarily disconnected for a month while we are on vacation . . . That's correct. I would like it done immediately—today—this morning . . . I realize it's very short notice, but surely you can arrange it . . . You can? By ten o'clock. Thank you very much."

A gleam of satisfaction lit her eyes as she replaced the receiver. She sighed, then smiled widely, rising from the desk chair.

"Well, we've postponed that for a couple of days anyway," Annette murmured to herself. "Now for Plan B."

At the door to the hall, she heard voices and one of them was Marsha's. Crossing her fingers, she waited silently beside the door. Then there was the sound of the front door opening and closing, and Annette exhaled the breath she had been holding with relief. She slipped quickly back into the hall and out the front door.

"There you are!" she called out, as if in surprise, when she saw her father wheeling Marsha's bike out of the garage. "What are you doing?"

"Marsha said there was something wrong with her bike," Jordan replied.

"Her chain was slipping the other day," Annette said, backing up her sister's little lie.

He studied the chain for a few minutes, testing it out. "It seems to be all right now."

"I did try to tighten it"—Annette spoke up again as Marsha shifted uncomfortably beside her father—"but I wasn't sure if I'd fixed it."

"I think you did." He straightened. "You can put it back in the garage, Marsha."

"Kathleen should have breakfast ready. I heard her out in the kitchen." Annette started walking toward the garage and the side entrance.

"I'll be right there," said Jordan. "There's a phone call I want to make first."

"It can wait until after breakfast," Annette argued, holding her breath. "You know how much you hate cold eggs, Dad. Besides, you're on vacation, remember? So your phone call can't be that important."

He hesitated, then smiled rather tightly. "No, I guess it can wait for another hour."

Annette glanced at Marsha, the flicker of her lashes indicating her relief.

Jordan walked out of the study into the living room and picked up the telephone extension there. He replaced the receiver after a minute and frowned.

"What's the matter, Dad?" Annette looked at him blankly.

"The phone's dead." He glanced at Kathleen. "I don't know why. Thunderstorms? Squirrels with the munchies?"

Annette giggled. "Well, it was working yesterday morning when I called Helen," she answered.

"It's out of order now," Jordan said, moving to the side door into the garage. "I'll have to drive to the service station on the highway and use their phone to report it. I stepped on my cell phone when I unpacked.''

''We'll ride along and keep you company, Dad,'' Annette said, following him and pushing Marsha in front of her.

He hesitated at the door. ''There's no need for you girls to come along.''

Annette gave him an adoring look. ''But we want to.''

Jordan's eyes sought Kathleen's over the top of the girls' heads. She knew the cause of his indecision. After reporting the trouble with their telephone, he had intended to call the employment agency, and with the girls along, there was a chance they would overhear. Yet he would seem mean if he refused to let them accompany him.

She tried to come to his rescue. ''I thought you girls were going to bake cookies this morning.''

''We can do that when we get back,'' Annette said offhandedly. ''We aren't going to be gone that long.'' She turned back to her father, a frown creasing her forehead. ''What's the matter? Don't you want us, Daddy?''

There was a brief tightening of his mouth before he smiled. ''Of course I do. Come on.''

Twenty minutes later they were back with the information that the telephone repairman would be out late that afternoon or Tuesday morning. He didn't show up at either time, so on Tuesday afternoon Jordan drove back to report the delay and find out why. The girls went with him.

They took considerably longer coming back this time, and one look at the forbidding set of Jordan's mouth when he walked through the door told Kathleen that someone at the telephone company had gotten an earful.

"Are they sending a repairman out?" she asked.

"They don't need to," he answered curtly.

"You'll never believe what happened!" Annette exclaimed.

"What?" Kathleen glanced curiously at Jordan, who had walked to the counter to pour himself a cup of coffee.

"The telephone company received a request to temporarily disconnect the service while we were on vacation," he explained.

"Can you believe that?" Annette shook her head and walked to the cookie jar.

"A request? From whom?" Kathleen frowned.

His dark gray eyes slid briefly to her, at once measuring and guarded. "From some woman claiming to be Mrs. Long," he answered.

Jordan didn't actually think she had done it, did he? Or did he actually believe she had done it to prevent him from contacting the employment agency? She had volunteered to leave immediately without waiting for him to hire a replacement.

"There must have been some mix-up," she said aloud. "The request could have been from another family in the area named Long."

"Possibly," he agreed.

"Or else it was some geek's idea of a great practical joke," Annette suggested, biting into a sugar cookie.

"Either way, the phones will be on this morning," Jordan announced.

Annette walked over to lean against the counter beside Marsha.

"What are we going to do today, Dad?"

"Nothing, until I make sure the phone is working again."

Out of the corner of her eye, Kathleen saw the sharp nudge Annette gave Marsha with her elbow. For a moment, Marsha looked at her sister blankly, then turned to her father.

"If we can't go anywhere today, then tomorrow can we go to Rehoboth Beach?" Marsha inquired hesitantly.

He seemed to consider the suggestion for a moment, then nodded. "I don't see why not," he agreed. "We can make a day of it and let Kathleen have tomorrow as her free time this week."

"Oh, no!" Annette's protest was immediate. "I meant for all four of us to go together," forgetting that it was Marsha who had made the initial suggestion, prompted by her elbow.

Jordan flashed another look at Kathleen. "I think not."

"But, Dad"—Annette wasn't giving up—"you know how you hate wandering through the shops along the boardwalk. It would be so much more fun for Marsha and me if Kathleen went along. Besides, she hasn't had her weekend off yet this month, so really her free time this week should be Saturday and Sunday. That was the agreement when she came to work here."

"Okay, okay." He made no attempt to disguise his displeasure even as he agreed to make the outing a foursome.

While she didn't like the idea of being the unwanted fourth as far as Jordan was concerned, Kathleen knew she needed the weekend to begin making arrangements for the day when she would no longer be working there. She had sublet her apartment and had to face the unwelcome task of finding another one . . . . and a new job.

Soon after midmorning the next day, they arrived at the resort town on the coast of Delaware. The day was warm, the sky brilliant blue. The car was parked in a lot near the beach, a picnic hamper in the back.

The girls decreed that the first order of the day was a stroll along the beach's boardwalk to investigate the shops. True to Annette's comment, Jordan waited for them outside, while Kathleen and the girls looked at trinkets and souvenirs to their hearts' content.

Before long, Kathleen's vague misgivings about the outing had vanished. The lighthearted spirit of the two girls was contagious. Soon even Jordan's aloofness was fading under the charm of their enthusiasm. With it, Kathleen's wariness whenever he was with them began to disappear, too. As if for the girls' benefit, they established a friendly rapport.

They had just stepped out of a shop and rejoined Jordan when Annette breathed in deeply. "What smells so good?" she asked.

Kathleen sniffed the yeasty aroma and sighed in instant recognition. "Hot pretzels!" She immediately looked around for the vendor. "Over there."

"Let's buy some," Annette suggested.

"Later," said Jordan. "You'll spoil your appetite for the picnic lunch Kathleen brought."

"Not if we have just one apiece," Kathleen protested, lifting her head to look at him.

As he gazed down at her upturned face, low

laughter broke from his throat. "I believe you want one more than the girls!"

A happy smile curved her mouth and brightened her eyes. "I do," she admitted with rueful amusement. "I can't resist a big, fat pretzel still warm from the oven, can you?"

"Come on, Dad," Annette coaxed. "We'll work up our appetite again just walking back to the car."

"How about you, Marsha? Do you want one, too?" Jordan smiled at his youngest daughter.

"Yes," she nodded with shy eagerness.

"I'm outnumbered, then." He gave in with a big grin. "Lead the way, ladies."

They joined the line at the vendor's window, waiting their turn as they inhaled the mouthwatering aroma emanating from the stand. Minutes later they were strolling down the boardwalk, each holding a warm, oversized pretzel, the brown crust frosted with yellow mustard.

Annette glanced over her shoulder, her gaze taking in Jordan and Kathleen walking behind her.

"Mmm, they're delicious," she declared appreciatively between mouthfuls.

"I could eat a dozen," Marsha agreed.

"Then you definitely wouldn't have any room for lunch." Jordan chuckled. "Considering the time Kathleen spent fixing it, she might not like it if we didn't eat." He slid Kathleen an amused sideways glance and clicked his tongue at her in mock reproof. "You're as bad as the girls," he accused.

"Why?" Kathleen blinked, her tongue darting out to lick the mustard from her lips.

"You have mustard from ear to ear." Kathleen stopped and quickly began wiping the edges of her mouth with a paper napkin. "Let me do it," Jordan insisted, almost affectionately.

He took the napkin from her hand. Her mouth opened to protest, but he was already rubbing the paper with rough gentleness over her cheek. A pink glow tinted her skin at the intimacy of his action, yet Jordan seemed unconcerned. Kathleen didn't dare breathe in case he noticed that even this casual gesture thrilled her.

But her emotional reaction must have been obvious, because he stopped. Unwillingly, she looked upward, focusing on the cleft in his strong chin, then the immobile line of his mouth, past his straight nose to his eyes. They smoldered for an intoxicating instant before they turned a bleak, stormy gray.

Simultaneously his hand left her cheek, and he turned away. "That should do it," was his gruff comment.

Her stomach was twisted in knots. Stupid of her to believe even for a minute that she could spend a day in his company without being aware of him in a physical way. Her attraction to him was too strong—not that it meant anything.

Miserably, Kathleen reminded herself that the kiss they'd shared didn't matter since he had so plainly regretted it. The pretzel had lost its flavor and it was only to be polite that she finished the rest of it.

The souvenir shops, the clothing stores with their window displays of beachwear, and the restaurants lining one side of the boardwalk all melted into a sameness in Kathleen's vision. The opposite view of ocean waves rolling onto the golden sand beach didn't seem any different. She kept walking along the planked boards, but without the inner gladness she had known a few minutes ago. Jordan had withdrawn again.

When they reached the car, Annette suggested they get the hamper and choose a place on the beach for their picnic. As Jordan took the picnic hamper from the rear seat of the car, the owners of the car parked next to them returned. The woman paused beside him, glancing warmly at the two girls and Kathleen waiting in front of the car.

"You have a lovely family," she commented with a beaming smile. "Your two daughters will be as beautiful as your wife when they grow up."

Jordan stiffened, then nodded with a trace of embarrassment. "Thank you."

Kathleen turned toward the ocean as he approached, hurt and kicking herself mentally for it. It would have been pointless for him to take the time to deny that she was his wife. The woman had been a total stranger who had been merely complimenting him on his daughters. Still, Kathleen wished that Jordan had told the woman the truth.

"Wow," Annette murmured. "That woman thought Kathleen was our mother, didn't she, Dad?"

"Yes," he said tersely, and Kathleen cringed inwardly at his harsh tone.

"I wish she was," Marsha added quietly.

Kathleen wished she could just disappear somehow. There was too much twisting pain inside for her to see any humor in the situation. Marsha's comment hovered in the air, deepening the silence.

"Actually," Annette began thoughtfully, "I think

we get most of our looks from you, Dad." Her clear gray eyes shifted to Kathleen, who was walking beside her on the sand. "He's handsome, don't you think?"

Swallowing the lump in her throat, Kathleen smiled nervously. "Yes, he is."

"Of course you're very pretty, too," Annette added quickly, as if she was afraid that she might have offended her. Just as quickly she changed the subject. "This looks like a good place for our picnic. Let's have it here."

Jordan obligingly set the hamper on the sand, while Annette and Marsha began spreading out the blanket. Kathleen made a pretense of checking the contents of the hamper to avoid looking at Jordan. With the blanket in place, Annette sat crosslegged on one corner.

Again her thoughtful gaze rested on Kathleen. "It would be nice if you were our stepmother." Then she sighed. "It's a pity that Dad is so much older, otherwise the two of you could get married."

"There isn't that much difference in our ages," Jordan snapped.

Annette tipped her head back to gaze up at him. "You don't think so?" she inquired innocently.

"No, I don't," he retorted, a little less abruptly than before. "And try to remember that I'm not going to get married just to provide you girls with a stepmother."

"Well, of course not!" Annette declared with an exasperated glance at her father. "People get married because they're in love, and you're not in love with Kathleen."

"Annette, please," Kathleen said with a brittle

laugh, "this kind of talk is embarrassing to your father and me."

"Is it?" She looked startled. "Geez, I'm sorry. Actually I was just trying to make conversation."

"Okay, then choose another topic." Jordan's voice was brusque. He flashed a look at Kathleen that was ominously harsh, and finally noticed Marsha's silence. "Let's walk down by the water, Marsha," he ordered. "Kathleen and Annette can call us when the lunch is ready."

It was a long, uncomfortable afternoon. By the time they returned to the house, Kathleen's nerves were so raw that she wanted to collapse. Of course, she couldn't, not until the picnic things were washed and put away, a light supper had been served and the dishes done. Only then could she retreat to the security of her room, letting Jordan have the responsibility of the girls for the rest of the evening.

"I wish I could understand what's going on in Dad's mind," Annette grumbled as she changed into her scarlet swimsuit.

"What do you mean?" Marsha sat on the bed, already dressed in her blue swimsuit and twirling a hair scrunchie on one finger.

"He's been so rude to Kathleen since we went to Rehoboth Beach. And he practically bit our heads off if we even mentioned her name over the weekend," Annette sighed.

"I think he hates her," Marsha declared grimly.

"He doesn't. I'm positive he doesn't." Annette began rummaging through the top drawer of her dresser. "Where's my scrunchie?"

"Here." Marsha picked up the white beaded thingy that was lying on the bed beside her.

"To tell you the truth"—Annette walked over to the bed and reached for the beach bag at Marsha's feet—"I was kind of afraid that Kathleen wouldn't come back Sunday night. I thought Dad might have fired her before he found someone to replace her."

"That's where he is now, isn't he, interviewing people?"

"I guess so," Annette sighed, and stuffed her cap in the beach bag. "I know he was interviewing someone on Friday. I heard him on the telephone. If only I could think of something—some way to get them together."

"Maybe it's time we told Daddy the truth," Marsha suggested, never having been in favor of the deception from the beginning.

Annette shook her head. "He'd just be as mad at us as he is at Kathleen. No, it will definitely have to be something else. Come on, we'd better go downstairs. Kathleen's waiting for us."

The isolated stretch of beach on Delaware Bay was deserted except for Kathleen and the two girls. Its location, a little over a mile from the house, made it one of their favorite haunts. The three of them often bicycled out to spend an hour or an afternoon or a day.

Today more than ever, Kathleen welcomed the chance to get away from the house. Even though Jordan was gone, his invisible presence dominated the rooms, filling her with the sensation that he was actually there. In the privacy of her heart, she could admit that she had fallen in love with him, even if she would never say the words out loud.

Her gaze searched the beach for the girls. Marsha was wandering along the tideline, looking for whatever odd treasure the waves might have washed ashore. Annette was floating on her air mattress, drifting closer to the beach.

Satisfied that they were safe, Kathleen lay back on her beach towel to bask in the warmth of the sun. Its glare was brilliant, reflected and intensified by the golden sand around her. Shielding her closed eyes with her forearm, Kathleen wished for the sunglasses in her beach bag, but she felt too relaxed to move.

The strain of maintaining a professional mask of calm unconcern in front of the girls and Jordan—and over the weekend, for Barry's benefit—had begun to take its toll. Nervous energy had drained her reserve strength down to nearly nothing.

A shadow fell across her. There was a gently indulgent curve to her mouth as she smiled and asked, "What did you find, Marsha?" She lifted her forearm away from her eyes, opening them slowly.

She didn't see a little girl's eager face. Instead she focused on muscular thighs, tanned a toasty brown and covered with fine, dark hair. She couldn't help noticing how his black swimming trunks clung to his lower body before her eyes moved up to his hard, golden-brown chest and broad shoulders.

Aggressive lines carved out the face. A jutting chin with a cleft in its center formed the point of the strong jaw. Lean cheeks rose to powerful cheekbones, and thick black hair was brushed carelessly across a wide forehead. A straight nose, slightly flared, focused attention on black, spiked lashes outlining charcoal-gray eyes. Their gaze had just completed an equally thorough study of Kathleen and the bare flesh exposed by her copper-gold bikini.

"I"—Jordan paused for emphasis—"found the note you left at the house."

Her stomach was somersaulting while her heart raced at an alarming rate, making her feel weak and giddy. The torment of seeing him again so unexpectedly almost closed her throat.

All she could squeeze out was a tiny "Oh," and she propped herself up in a reclining position on one elbow.

"Dad!" came Annette's squeal of delight, followed by two sets of racing footsteps in the sand as she and Marsha ran toward him. "How long have you been here?"

"About a minute," he answered when they stopped breathlessly at his side. "Is this a private party, or am I allowed to join?"

"Of course you are," Marsha insisted.

Annette grabbed hold of his hand. "I've learned to do the butterfly. Come on, I'll show you!" She had barely started to lead him toward the water when she stopped, glancing at Kathleen. "Aren't you coming in, too?"

"Not right now." A tense smile accompanied her refusal.

It was useless to pretend she could lie back and forget he was there. Jordan's tall figure was like a magnet, drawing her gaze with an irresistible force. She watched him with his two daughters, listening to their laughter and happy voices, wishing hopelessly that she could be a part of the family forever.

Tears scalded her eyes. It all seemed so unfair. She had gone through the various stages of infatuation with other men, genuinely liking some and almost loving others, and kept waiting for the real thing to come along—the right man to enter her life. At twenty-five, she had found him—and knew not the joy but the agony of loving.

Her blurring vision saw Marsha wading ashore and Annette moving to follow. Kathleen lay back, covering her eyes with her hand and blinking rapidly to rid herself of the tears.

"Water, water, everywhere, and not a drop to drink," Annette chanted as she caught the beach towel Marsha tossed her and began rubbing her wet skin. "I'm absolutely dying of thirst!" she declared with an exaggerated sigh. There was a gleam of childish intrigue in her gray eyes as she glanced at Kathleen lying silently in the sun. "Is it all right if Marsha and I go back to the house for some cold drinks?"

Marsha opened her mouth to protest that she didn't want to go, but Annette immediately sent her a glowering look to shut her up. Her lips closed together in a mutinous line.

"As long as you come straight back," was Kathleen's somewhat stiff reply.

"We will," Annette promised, tossing her towel over the beach bag and digging her fingers into her sister's resisting arm. "Come on, Marsha."

Marsha waited until they were out of Kathleen's hearing before she retorted angrily, "But I don't want to bike all the way back to the house and then all the way back here. If you're so thirsty, you can go by yourself."

"Being thirsty was just an excuse to leave so Dad and Kathleen can be alone for a while," Annette patiently explained her strategy. "Honestly, Marsha, sometimes I wonder how you can possibly be my sister. You can be so dense sometimes."

"No, I'm not," Marsha said defensively. "I just think all these plans of yours are going to get us into a lot of trouble."

"You worry too much," Annette replied indifferently as she climbed onto her bike.

CHAPTER NINE

As the girls rode out of sight, Kathleen let her gaze slide to the bay. Jordan was wading ashore, bronze skin and dark hair gleaming. Her heart constricted sharply. He looked sensational wet.

Scrambling to her feet, she wandered idly toward the water, but in the opposite direction. She walked to Annette's bright yellow air mattress, which the waves were tugging in the water. She pulled it back up onto the sand, then began wading into the surf, intending to swim until the girls returned.

"Where are Annette and Marsha?" Jordan paused in ankle-deep water, several yards from Kathleen.

She stopped to answer, but turned only a fraction so that she wouldn't have to meet his gaze. "They rode to the house to bring back a cold drink."

"Where are you going?"

The water was almost up to her thighs. "For a swim."

She began wading farther out. The sloshing sound of her awkward steps blocked her ears to the sound of Jordan's approach. Not until his sun-browned fingers closed over her forearm did she realize he had followed.

"The first rule of the water, Kathleen," he said as she pivoted around in alarm, "is never to swim alone. Let me take a breather and I'll join you."

Her widened gaze locked on the mouth that had said her name so softly. The sweet torment of his touch made her skin quiver in silent betrayal. She lifted her gaze to meet his, all the pent-up longing for his kiss revealed in the shimmering depths of her hazel eyes.

The sensually charged message was there for Jordan to read. His gray eyes darkened with a glittering fire, running over her delectable curves, dwelling for tantalizing seconds on the shadowy cleft between her breasts, then blazing again on her face. His fingers tightened on her arm, almost imperceptibly pulling her toward him.

"Jordan, no," Kathleen whispered achingly, trying to deny how much she wanted his kiss.

"Yes." His other arm snaked around her bare waist, easily overcoming her token resistance. "Yes, damn it," he groaned when she shuddered against him.

His mouth opened over hers, warm and moist, devouring her lips with a hungry, demanding kiss. Kathleen felt herself drowning in a sea of heady sensations. Sliding her arms around the hard muscles of his shoulders, she surrendered to the man who already owned her heart and soul. He seemed to be intent on possessing her body as well.

Glorying in the caress of his fingers on her back, she arched even closer to his male length, barely aware of the moment when he lowered her to the sand. His weight pressed her into the firm earth, gentle waves lapping and breaking over their legs and hips. They were both indifferent to all but the raging tide of their shared passion.

Instinctively, Kathleen's body moved sinuously beneath his in response to his hardness. Their driving need for gratification was bringing them both to the point of no return. Then, in a fleeting moment of sanity, Jordan broke free, rolling to his feet and drawing her with him.

His breathing was labored, his heart beating as rapidly as her own when he gathered her into his arms, holding her trembling body close to his own. He rained more kisses on her neck and throat.

"Jordan," Kathleen murmured, letting him know her need had not diminished.

"The girls will be back soon," he reminded her huskily, tangling his fingers in the damp tendrils of her fiery auburn hair and tipping her head back so he could gaze at her face. "I want to spend the afternoon making love to you, not a stolen moment."

Quickly she buried her face in the tanned column of his neck, sure she would never again know the sensual joy she felt at this moment. She couldn't speak, afraid that if she tried she would cry from sheer happiness.

"I'll find some excuse to drive them over to Helen's to spend the night," Jordan murmured into her hair. "We can either come back to the house or go to your apartment in town."

"I don't have one," she answered with a sobbing laugh. "I sublet my old one and hadn't found another that I could afford."

Now she wouldn't even need to look. Jordan wanted her.

His arms tightened almost cruelly around her. "You won't need to worry about that anymore," he assured her firmly. "I'll take care of it. I've hired a nanny to look after the girls. She starts on Wednesday. And on Thursday"—he smiled against her hair—"you and I will start looking for an apartment for you without any worries about whether *you* can afford it."

A cold knife was plunged into her heart, then twisted until the freezing pain was unendurable. Of all the romantic fools, Kathleen thought, she had to top the list! In her crazy, old-fashioned thinking, she had believed he would want to marry her. Instead, he was setting her up as his mistress.

Slowly her frozen arms unlocked and slid from around his shoulders. When her hands pressed against his bare chest in a mute request to be released, Jordan let her step away, smiling at her in that disturbing way that made her heart skyrocket even as it shattered.

Her eyes searched the beloved features of his ruggedly handsome face. Could she be satisfied if she were only his mistress and nothing more? Available whenever it suited him to see her? Willing to accept the crumbs of his attention left over after his work and his daughters? Never sharing the pain, the joy, the pleasurable everyday routine of life?

"No." The single word would have to be her only response.

"What?" Jordan frowned, his gaze narrowing on her wan expression.

Kathleen glanced at him, startled to discover she had spoken aloud. The sight of him didn't lessen the truth of her answer. If she couldn't have all of him, then the heartbreak of having nothing couldn't be worse.

"I said the answer was no," she repeated, turning away to walk toward her beach towel.

"No?" he repeated in disbelief, anger vibrating in his low voice. "No to what?"

She picked up the towel with a nonchalance that surprised her and began wiping away the sand clinging to her skin. "No, I don't want you to make love to me."

Towering beside her, he ripped the towel from her grasp. "A minute ago you were damned eager!" he reminded her savagely.

Summoning all the courage of her convictions, Kathleen met the piercing steel of his gaze. "That was a minute ago."

"What kind of a woman are you?" his harsh voice taunted. "How can you turn passion on and off like that?"

She fought a momentary impulse to tell him that passion could be turned off even if love couldn't, and she remained silent, holding out her hand for the towel. With a vicious flick of his wrist, he tossed it at her, long strides carrying him away from her to the spot where his own towel lay.

*   *   *

Annette braked her bike to a halt short of the stretch of sandy beach. Her gaze centered on the two figures beyond, separated by several yards of golden sand.

She tossed a disgruntled look at Marsha. "Would you look at that?" she grumbled. "I'll bet they haven't said one word to each other since we left. This is beginning to get exasperating!"

When the two girls returned, Jordan set off for the house, saying that he had paperwork to do. But his gaze had flicked sardonically to Kathleen, and she had known she was responsible for the suppressed fury in his eyes.

He didn't know or care how difficult her decision had been. It was just as well, Kathleen decided. It was better that he didn't realize she loved him, or at least that she loved him so deeply.

Dinner that evening did not go well. Jordan's brooding silence dominated the table as he barely touched the food. For once, not even Annette was her usual talkative self, aware perhaps, of the tense undercurrents in the air. Kathleen had forced herself to eat, although the food was utterly tasteless.

When the dessert had been served and Kathleen had eaten as much as her constricting throat would swallow, Annette rose from the table.

"Marsha and I will wash up, Kathleen," she announced, and began gathering the dessert plates. "You can go into the living room and relax with Dad."

"No, I'll help," Kathleen said quickly. She didn't trust herself to be alone with Jordan, not even for a few minutes.

"Marsha and I didn't help with dinner, so we'll clean up," Annette insisted.

"That doesn't matter. I—"

"Let them do it," Jordan interrupted curtly. "I want to speak to you, Kathleen."

Apprehension darkened her eyes as she met the pinning force of his. It was all she could do to remain in her chair and not race from the room.

"There, you see!" Annette declared brightly. "That's a direct order from your boss, Kathleen. You have to obey."

It wasn't his words that made her obey, it was the ruthless line of his mouth. Not for an instant did Kathleen doubt that Jordan would forcibly drag her into the living room if she attempted to refuse.

"Okay," she said warily, trying not to sound as trapped as she felt.

Awkwardly she rose from the table, all too aware of Jordan following her as she walked into the living room. Her pulse was hammering, increasing the throbbing pain in her temples. Her legs were just about able to carry her to an armchair, but only just.

Jordan didn't sit down. He stood beside her chair, his hands thrust deeply into his pockets. Bending her head slightly down, Kathleen stared at her clasped hands, aware of his eyes upon her and unable to meet them.

"What did you want to talk to me about?" she asked tightly.

There was a movement beside her, then his hand touched the auburn fire of her hair. Kathleen barely stopped herself from jerking her head away from his touch.

"You didn't really want me to accept your word

as final this afternoon, did you?'' The statement was issued roughly, accusing and faintly angry, as if she were playing games with him.

The touch of his fingers was unendurable. It intensified the desire to know again the rapture of his caress. Kathleen didn't care how Jordan interpreted her actions as she rose from the chair and took a hurried step away from him.

Did she want him to accept her answer? Probably not, she thought, but not for the reason Jordan assumed. With her, it was not simply lust.

"Yes, I did," she replied shortly.

The thick carpet muffled the sound of his footsteps. His hands lightly gripped the soft flesh of her upper arms, drawing her shoulders back against his chest. Her breath was stolen by his firm touch. A weakness raced through her body, making her almost incapable of movement.

"I want you, Kathleen," he declared with husky forcefulness.

She was nearly caught in the undertow of her own desire for him.

"I know you want me," she agreed, "as your mistress, your lover." She swallowed, trying to ease the tightness in her throat. "You're a hypocrite, Jordan. You don't want me to live in the same house with you for fear of what your daughters and others might think, but you're willing to set me up in an apartment so you can see me whenever you feel the urge."

Jordan stiffened, his fingers momentarily pressing hard into her flesh, then he released her and walked away. Her knees trembled, threatening to give way, but she managed to stand erectly.

His back was turned to her. "What did you want?" His voice vibrated harshly over her.

"A future," Kathleen admitted. "And children, and a home. I want to be involved in my husband's life and have him equally involved with mine."

"You could still have that. Later," he replied curtly.

"Not if I became emotionally involved with you," she answered, as if she wasn't already.

There was an abrupt movement of his head to the side. In a gesture of weariness, his hand rubbed the back of his neck, rumpling his dark hair.

"Being married to Rosalind, the girls' mother, taught me something—marriage wasn't for me," he said tautly. "We loved each other—I didn't mean to imply that we didn't—but that love had begun to disintegrate when she died. You see, she didn't like my job or the travel or the time away from home that it demanded. She had a congenital heart defect, which didn't prevent her from leading a normal life." He paused, struggling for control of his emotions. "One year she forgot to get a flu shot, and she contracted it. That was ultimately the cause of her death. She'd begged me to spend more time with her and our family, and it had become a source of conflict between us. A woman deserves her husband's time and attention, and I can't afford that. I don't ever want to go through that cycle of meaningless apologies and bitter arguments. I've had more than my share of tearful goodbyes and poignant reunions."

Kathleen brushed a hand across her face. Her unshed tears stung her eyes. "Then let's just say goodbye, Jordan," she said in a choked voice. "I can't offer you a casual affair, and you can't give me what I want. If we make the break now, it'll be easier for everybody."

"That's true." He took a deep breath but didn't turn around.

Proudly Kathleen lifted her chin, "I'll leave in the morning. You said you'd hired a replacement. There's no need for me to stay until Wednesday. It may take her a few days to get used to the routine, but I'm sure she'll manage."

"I'll tell the girls," Jordan stated flatly.

She had to press her lips tightly together to check an involuntary sob of pain. "I'll . . . I'll go and start packing."

Walking shakily, she started from the living room. By the time she reached the hall, she was practically running. The tears refused to be held back and streamed down her cheeks.

Marsha was slumped morosely in the kitchen chair. Annette was standing behind another, her white knuckles whitely gripping its back. Her resentful gray eyes were watching the violent swinging of the kitchen door, the result of her father's suppressed anger when he had left the room seconds before.

"I told you none of this would work," mumbled Marsha, tears brimming in her blue eyes.

"I don't want a bunch of I-told-you-sos!" Annette snapped.

Marsha's chin trembled. "Don't you start yelling at me. This was all your idea," she retorted in a quivering voice. "And now Kathleen's leaving."

Silently Annette had to admit that she was taking out her frustrations on her sister. None of her protests, pleas or accusations that her father was breaking his word had made the least impression on him. She hadn't been able to persuade him that Kathleen should stay even a day longer, much less permanently.

"She isn't leaving for good," Annette stated with a determined set of her jaw, the telltale gleam of battle in her eyes.

Marsha simply looked at her and said nothing. She had witnessed the bitter argument between her older sister and her father and shuddered at the thought that there might be another.

Telling Annette to be sensible would only start an argument between them, and she already felt miserable enough knowing that Kathleen was leaving in the morning. Marsha couldn't summon up much hope for Annette's next plan, whatever it was.

Saying goodbye to Annette and Marsha and knowing she would never see them again had been the second hardest thing Kathleen had ever done. The hardest had been walking away from Jordan.

She'd moved in with Maggie and Betty, gone through the motions of resuming her old life, reapplying at the employment agency and going out on job interviews, but she was a brittle shell of her former self. The only emotion she felt was an intense heartache.

In the three weeks since she had left Jordan's home, the impossible had happened: instead of gradually forgetting him, she was thinking of him more and more each day. Sometimes she was positive she had been right to leave and other times she was sure she'd been a fool not to settle for a few fleeting moments of sublime happiness in his embrace. Wrapping her arms around her waist, she tried to fight off the shiver of excruciating pain and huddled into a tighter ball in the armchair. Her watch indicated that it was time to get ready for another job interview, but she didn't move, not even when the phone rang.

She listened to its shrill demand, waiting for it to fall silent. It was probably Maggie or Barry. They phoned often whenever she was alone during the day. Her mouth twisted, wryly. Were they afraid that she would attempt suicide? Well, she hadn't sunk to that level of depression yet and doubted that she would, no matter how unbearable the pain became.

The phone stopped ringing, then started again. Sighing, Kathleen uncurled from the chair and walked to answer it. Tucking her hair behind her ear, she lifted the receiver.

"Hello," she said indifferently.

There was a crackle of interference, then an achingly familiar voice answered, "Kathleen?"

Her fingers clutched the receiver in a death grip. A giddiness buckled her knees as she sank onto the straight-backed chair beside the phone.

"Jordan?" she whispered after a panicked silence when she was certain she had imagined his voice on the other end.

"Yes." It was his voice, tense and strained, but it was his voice.

"How—why—" Tears spilled from her eyes. She should hang up the telephone, but she couldn't.

"I had to talk to you. The employment agency gave me your number," he explained tautly.

There was more interference and Kathleen asked, "Where are you?"

"In Saudi Arabia."

"But—" She glanced at her watch. "The time—"

"Yes," Jordan interrupted, "I know, but I couldn't sleep. I've been thinking about you—which shows you the state of my mind if I have to phone you at three o'clock in the morning here. Kathleen, I—"

The connection was broken up. "I didn't hear you. What did you say?" she asked frantically.

"Damn!" The muttered curse followed her question. "Kathleen, I'll be flying back this Friday. I have to see you."

"Jordan, no," Kathleen protested, her heart breaking all over again as she spoke. "There's no point."

"I can't leave things the way they are."

"I can't go through this again, please," she begged. "I haven't changed my mind."

"We can't really talk on the phone. I—"

Kathleen didn't dare to see him again. She ached so much for the sight of him she knew she would give in to whatever he asked. She loved him too much. The mere sound of his voice was making her regret her adamant stance.

Before she let him persuade her to reconsider, she very slowly replaced the telephone receiver on its cradle. She stared at it. Its blackness seemed to blur into the ebony color of his hair.

It started ringing again as she guessed that it would.

She rose from the chair and walked slowly into the small kitchen, turning on the radio as loud as it would go.

* * *

"Keep Mrs. Prentiss in the kitchen until I come in there," Annette ordered.

"What are you going to do?" Marsha looked at her doubtfully.

"I'm going to FedEx a letter to Mrs. Prentiss telling her that she's fired as of today," Annette announced, opening the study door.

"You can't do that!" her sister cried in astonishment. "She won't leave just because you say so."

Annette tossed her head airily. "The letter will be from Dad."

"You can't do that!" Marsha repeated. "He'll be home in three days! He'll be furious when he finds out—and you can bet he *will* find out! There isn't any way you can pretend that he sent the letter, because he's going to know he didn't!"

"Of course he's going to know, but let's hope if the rest of my plan works, he won't care."

"The rest of your plan? Annette," Marsha began hesitantly, "what's the rest of your plan?"

"Hey, go to the kitchen and keep Mrs. Prentiss occupied," Annette reminded her.

"I'm not going anywhere until I find out what you're doing," her sister refused.

Annette's mouth thinned into a grim line. "Oh, all right. I'm going to call Kathleen after Mrs. Prentiss leaves, and I'll ask her to come stay with us."

"She won't come," Marsha sighed.

"Yes, she will, *if*—" she strongly emphasized that if—"she believes that Mrs. Prentiss left of her own accord and you and I are here all alone."

"Kathleen will simply tell us to go and stay with Aunt Helen."

"If she does, I'll tell her that Aunt Helen is sick. She'll believe me. And she'll come out here, too. I know she cares about us, and she would never let us stay alone in the house."

"But what about when Dad comes home on Friday? What are you going to do then?"

Annette's eyes rounded with false innocence. "He'll find Kathleen here, won't he? I've told you what I'm going to do, now you'd better get into the kitchen and keep Mrs. Prentiss busy."

CHAPTER TEN

"How did the job interview go today?" Maggie gave Kathleen a searching look across the small table.

Her face was nearly colorless, faint blue shadows beneath eyes that had obviously been crying. Kathleen didn't meet her friend's gaze as she pushed the macaroni and cheese around on her plate.

"I forgot about it," was her indifferent answer. Jordan's phone call had blocked out everything in her mind but him.

Maggie darted a knowing glance at Betty, who shook her head with concern. The sad young woman at the table seemed like a different person, nothing at all like the calm and competent nurse with an ever-ready smile that they had always known.

The telephone rang and Kathleen nearly jumped out of her chair. Nervous apprehension replaced the troubled dullness of her eyes, and Maggie and Betty exchanged another look.

"I'll answer it," said Maggie, and rose from the table.

Frozen, her pulse fluctuating madly, Kathleen watched Maggie walk to the telephone and lift the receiver. Unconsciously she was holding her breath, afraid that it was Jordan and afraid that it was not.

"It's for you, Kathleen." Maggie held out the telephone to her.

"Who is it?" She released the breath she had been holding with a rush.

"A young girl," was all Maggie would say.

A shudder of disappointment raced through her. It was insane. She would have refused to talk to Jordan if he had called, so why did the news that it wasn't him hurt so much? Kathleen forced herself to walk to the telephone, saying hello like an automaton.

"Kathleen?" a frantically eager voice asked. "This is Annette."

Kathleen tensed, her nerves drawn taut. "Yes, Annette?" she replied in a brittle tone.

"I'm sorry to bother you, but I didn't know what else to do." Something resembling a sob of panic punctuated the explanation.

Her hand tightened on the receiver until her knuckles were white. "What's wrong? Your father? Has something happened to him? Is he hurt? Was there an accident?" Her fearful questions tumbled after each other, not allowing Annette time to answer any of them.

"No, no, he's all right. At least, I think he is," was the qualifying answer. "Oh, Kathleen, it's Mrs.

Prentiss, the lady that was hired when you left. She walked out. I mean, she's left! Marsha and I are here all alone, and I don't know what to do! I've tried to reach Dad, but I can't get through, and Aunt Helen is sick so she can't come. I didn't know who else to call. Marsha is terrified. Kathleen, can you come? Here? Tonight?"

"She just walked out without giving notice? Without making sure there was someone to stay with you girls?" Kathleen repeated in angry disbelief.

"Yes," Annette gulped. "She said we could fend for ourselves." A pause. "If you can't come, Kathleen, I don't know what we're going to do!"

"I'll be there within an hour," she promised.

"Will you stay?"

"Until your father comes home on Friday," Kathleen answered, suddenly feeling trapped. But there wasn't anything else she could do. She couldn't leave the girls alone in that big country house, and she certainly couldn't bring them here to Maggie's apartment. There was nowhere near enough room.

After she hung up, she explained the situation at the Long home without going into detail. She could see by Maggie and Betty's expressions that they thought she was wrong to involve herself with the family again, but they didn't say a word. Kathleen sent up a silent prayer of gratitude for being blessed with understanding friends.

"Did you see how happy Kathleen was to see us again?" Marsha sighed contentedly, her eyes bright and vivid blue. "She was practically crying."

"So were you," Annette returned, changing the CD in the boombox.

"I didn't realize how much I missed her." Self-consciously Marsha studied her fingers twisting in her lap. "It's going to be awful when she leaves again."

"Oh, stop it," Annette scolded her. "Maybe she won't leave again. I'm doing everything I can, you know."

"You're forgetting that Dad comes home tomorrow," Marsha reminded her.

"No, I'm not forgetting that. I'm counting on it." Then she spoke more thoughtfully, "I wonder how Kathleen knew Dad was coming home on Friday?"

Every sound had Kathleen tensing. Her nerves were raw and had been since she had awakened that morning. It was Friday, and Jordan was due home.

For two days she had ignored that fact, enjoying each moment in his house with his daughters as fully as possible. Now all hell was about to break loose, and heaven only knew what might happen.

Kathleen looked at the kitchen clock again—she didn't know why. She had no idea what time he would come. Logic said it would be late in the afternoon, and it was barely eleven o'clock now.

Her hand trembled as it spread the chocolate frosting over the yellow cake. The sound of a car pulling up immobilized her. It stopped, then a car door slammed. The knife dropped onto the counter as Kathleen's hand flew to her hair, a feminine gesture of insecurity.

With her stomach doing somersaults, she turned toward the door, trying not to devour Jordan with her eyes when he walked in. There was a haggard look to his face, his features strained to the point of tautness, gray eyes clouded with strong emotions.

His hand raised, passing in front of his eyes, then he stared at her again. "I saw your car." His expression hardened. "What are you doing here, Kathleen?" he demanded with a tinge of bitterness. She blanched and turned away, but instantly long strides carried him to her side. "I don't care why you're here," he muttered hoarsely, his fingers closing over her shoulders. "I've been through hell—wanting you—needing you, and you wouldn't even answer the damned phone!"

"Jordan." His touch was melting her resolve. She wanted to run into his arms and invite his caress, but she forced herself to remain rigidly unresponsive. "I'm here because of the girls. They weren't able to reach you, although they tried several times. The woman you hired walked out and left them. Helen is sick, so they called me. I told them I would stay until you came back."

The cruel pressure of his fingers forced her around. "What did you say?"

"I said I'm leaving." The words ripped at her heart like a sword. "I'll be gone within the hour."

"No!" Jordan snapped.

"Yes, I—" Kathleen stared at the loosened tie around his neck, unable to look into the face she loved so desperately.

"No, I mean about Mrs. Prentiss!"

Startled, she lifted her head, gazing into the piercing gray eyes.

"She walked out. She just quit and left the girls without anyone to stay with them," Kathleen explained again.

"The hell she did!" Abruptly he released her and walked with impatient strides to the swinging door leading to the dining room. "Annette! Marsha!" he barked.

They walked through the door a split second after he had called them. Stunned, Kathleen watched in confusion, rooted to the floor where Jordan had left her.

"Hi, Dad!" Annette greeted him with her usual bright smile. "You're home earlier than we thought."

Marsha's smile was much more hesitant, intimidated by the glowering look on his face. "Hi, Dad."

"Kathleen was just telling me that Mrs. Prentiss isn't here." His expression was grimly forbidding.

Annette rolled her eyes. "That's right. She just walked out on us, said she was fed up with taking care of a house and Marsha and me. You don't know what a panic we were in until we finally reached Kathleen," she declared with an exaggerated sigh.

"She quit, is that right?" Jordan repeated.

"Yes, just like that!" Annette snapped her fingers to indicate the abruptness of Mrs. Prentiss' departure.

"Then would you mind explaining why she left a message at the company's main office, saying that since I had *fired* her, she was entitled to two weeks' severance pay and demanded that she receive it?" His accusing gray eyes fixed on the girls.

Annette returned the look blankly while Marsha shifted uncomfortably from one foot to the other. "I don't know what you're talking about, Dad," Annette laughed nervously. "She quit."

"What about the FedEx letter *I* supposedly sent

her?'' Jordan asked, an arrogant arch to one dark brow. ''Would you know anything about that?''

''A letter?'' Annette breathed, and glanced hesitantly at Marsha.

''We'd better tell him the truth,'' Marsha murmured.

''Yes, I think you'd better,'' he agreed grimly.

''Well, you see, Dad,'' Annette began, wandering toward the kitchen table, as if she wanted to put distance between herself and her father, ''actually I'm the one who sent the letter telling Mrs. Prentiss she was fired. We—Marsha and I—wanted Kathleen back. And that seemed like a sure way to do it.''

''Did it ever occur to you that Kathleen might not want to come back?'' Jordan asked.

''No,'' Annette replied decisively.

''Annette''—Marsha glanced at her sister—''we'd better tell him the rest.''

''The rest of what?'' he demanded, eyeing both girls in an ominous way.

Kathleen's curiosity was thoroughly aroused, especially because Marsha looked so guilty. Annette, as always, seemed all too sure of herself.

''Well, there are a few things you don't know,'' Annette admitted, then paused.

''Such as?'' he prompted.

''Such as how Kathleen came to work for us in the first place,'' Marsha said in a small voice.

''Oh?''

There was a wealth of meaning in that one word, and his younger daughter quailed at the sound.

Kathleen assumed they were referring to the interview, although at this point she didn't see what relevance it had.

"Remember the mistake on her application?" Annette spoke up. "Actually, Kathleen didn't make a mistake. We, I mean, I forged another application, changing her age, so you would think she was older."

"And Aunt Helen really didn't recommend her," Marsha added. "We changed her letter, too."

"No!" Kathleen breathed, unable to believe that any of this could be true.

"I'm sorry, Kathleen," Marsha apologized. "I know how angry Dad was when he found out, but it was the only way we could think of for you to get the job."

"But why?" Kathleen frowned, moving to stand beside Jordan as he faced the two girls.

"Because"—Annette studied her father for a few long, seconds—"we thought it was time Daddy got married again. We liked you the minute we met you and hoped that he would, too."

"So you took it upon yourselves to find me a wife!" he said flabbergasted.

"You didn't seem to be able to find anyone even halfway nice. We didn't think we would do any worse than you," Annette shrugged and an impish light entered her gray eyes. "We didn't do too bad a job either. I mean, you fell in love with her and she fell in love with you. And that was the whole point of our plan."

"It was, was it?" Jordan released a slow breath.

"And," Annette said, tempting fate, considering her father's hooded look, "if I timed this confession correctly, Marsha and I should leave the room now so you and Kathleen can straighten things out. You don't have to be angry at her anymore. We're the ones who deceived you, not Kathleen."

The air was charged with tension. Covertly Kathleen glanced at Jordan, unable to decipher the enigmatic light in his gray eyes. Without another word, Annette moved away from the table with Marsha following more hesitantly. The silence crackled with electricity when they were gone.

"Do you love me?" Jordan asked at last.

Kathleen turned her head away. "Yes," she answered calmly, her heart beating so fast she could almost hear it. "But it doesn't change anything. I want to share more than just the physical side of love with you." His hand touched her cheek and she jerked away. "Please, I don't have much strength where you're concerned. Don't tempt me. I know now how much you want me, and I want you, too, but—"

"Want you!" The harsh exclamation indicated that Kathleen had understated his need.

Her movement away from him was roughly checked. His hand captured her face, lifting it to meet his descending mouth. Her resistance lasted only for an instant as his hard, demanding kiss aroused the response she had known it would.

Circling her arms around his waist, she allowed herself to be swept away by pure desire. His hands slid down, molding her pliant flesh against the hard contours of his male body. His mouth parted her willing lips, sending quicksilver fires of ecstasy through her veins.

When mere kisses could no longer satisfy their sensual hunger, Jordan drew his head away, burying his mouth along the side of her hair. He shuddered against her as he fought for self-control. "Now do you understand?" he muttered hoarsely. "I don't simply want you. I need you, Kathleen, I haven't been worth a damn since you left. I made such a mess of things in Saudi Arabia that the company had to send over another man to straighten it out."

"Jordan, darling," Kathleen whispered achingly, winding her arms more tightly around him.

"I couldn't open my eyes without seeing you somehow. I kept remembering the feel of your body in my arms and the taste of your lips. It was your voice I heard in my dreams." He held her more fiercely and shuddered again. "They all thought I was crazy, and I am. No woman has ever destroyed me the way you have. I love you, Kathleen, and I can't live without you. I don't have the strength to try."

"Neither do I," she sighed, lifting her head for him to see the shimmering glow of rapture in her eyes. "I love you, Jordan—I could say it a thousand times."

He smiled, and melted her heart all over again. "Say it a million times—that might be enough. Marry me, Kathleen. Nothing else will satisfy either of us."

A diamond tear slipped from the corner of her eye. "Yes."

Jordan kissed away the tear. Unable to stop, he went on kissing her, lingering on each feature until he finally reached her trembling lips. Then, shaken again by her scorching response, he held her away from him, his gray eyes drinking in her radiance.

"I should be furious with Annette and Marsha," he said in a husky voice that sent shivers down her spine. "But how can I be angry with them for getting you here, waiting for me when I came home? I thought I was going to have to batter down doors to see you."

Kathleen wanted to go back into his arms, but she let him keep her at arm's length. "I can't believe they pulled a trick like that to have me hired," she murmured.

"I have a hunch"—his mouth quirked with dry amusement—"that they arranged a few other things to keep you here so I would fall in love with you. I don't regret it. I'm just glad they love you as much as I do."

"I love them, too," Kathleen smiled. That was nothing new—and now they had brought her to the man she loved.

"Some day we'll find out the whole story and exactly how you and I were outsmarted. Right now"—the smile was crinkling his eyes—"I suppose we should let them know how successful they've been. That is, if they haven't been listening at the door." His gaze swung to the dining room door. "Have you been listening, Annette?"

There was a moment of silence, then the door was pushed open. Annette sauntered into the room, followed by Marsha, who smiled shyly at Kathleen. There was a complacent gleam in Annette's gray eyes as she looked at the two of them.

"Congratulations," Annette offered, trying not to grin too widely. "When's the wedding?"

"As soon as possible," Jordan answered.

"Can we be in it?" Marsha asked.

"Who else would I ask?" Kathleen laughed.

"Tomorrow we'll have to go and buy your wedding dress," Annette declared, "and gowns for Marsha and me. Then we—"

"Hold it!" Jordan interrupted. "There'll be no

more planning by you girls. You've done all you're going to do—and don't think that there won't be some punishment meted out before this is over. Whatever future plans that you have forming in your minds, you can forget."

An impish light glittered in Annette's eyes. "Actually, I was thinking that it might be nice to have a baby brother."

"I'll handle any future additions to this family," he said firmly, reaching for Kathleen's hand, "without any help from you or Marsha!"

A rush of delicious warmth surged through Kathleen as Jordan drew her to his side, fitting her into the crook of his arm. Annette shrugged her shoulders, but the silver light didn't leave her eyes. "If you say so, Dad," she sighed. "We'll let you handle things from now on. Since you probably have plans to make, is it all right if we go and call Aunt Helen and tell her the news?"

"Go on," he agreed. When the dining room door swung shut behind them, he glanced at Kathleen, his attention centering on her dimpling smile. "What's that smile all about?" he asked, touching a fingertip to the closest dimple.

"I was just pitying the first man that Annette sets her sights on when she's grown up. He won't stand a chance," she murmured, unconsciously moving her cheek against his caressing hand.

"If she picks the right man, she'll be the one who won't stand a chance," Jordan corrected, turning her into his arms and studying her upturned face. "Now, about our son . . ."

Here's a thrilling preview of
SHIFTING CALDER WIND by Janet Dailey.
A June 2004 paperback
from Kensington Publishing.

A blackness roared around him. He struggled to surface from it, somehow knowing that if he didn't, he would die. Sounds reached him as if coming from a great distance—a shout, the scrape of shoes on pavement, the metallic slam of a car door and the sharp clap of a gunshot.

Someone was trying to kill him.

He had to get out of there. The instant he tried to move, the blackness swept over him with dizzying force. He heard the revving rumble of a car engine starting up. Unable to rise, he rolled away from the sound as spinning tires burned rubber and another shot rang out.

Lights flashed in a bright glare. There was danger in them, he knew. He had to reach the shadows. Fighting the weakness that swam through his limbs, he crawled away from the light.

He felt dirt beneath his hand and dug his fingers into it. His strength sapped, he lay there a moment, trying to orient himself and to determine the location of the man trying to kill him. But the searing pain in his head made it hard to think logically. He reached up and felt the warm wetness on his face. That's when he knew he had been shot. Briefly his fingers touched the deep crease the bullet had ripped along the side of his head. Pain instantly washed over him in black waves.

Aware that he could lose consciousness at any second, either from the head wound or the blood loss, he summoned the last vestiges of his strength and threw himself deeper into the darkness. With blood blurring his vision, he made out the shadowy outlines of a post and railing. It looked to be a corral of some sort. He pushed himself toward it, wanting any kind of barrier, no matter how flimsy, between himself and his pursuer.

There was a whisper of movement just to his left. Alarm shot through him, but he couldn't seem to make his muscles react. He was too damned weak. He knew it even as he listed sideways and saw the low-crouching man in a cowboy hat with a pistol in his hand.

Instead of shooting, the cowboy grabbed for him with his free arm. "Come on. Let's get outa here, old man," the cowboy whispered with urgency. "He's up on the catwalk working himself into a better position."

He latched onto the cowboy's arm and staggered drunkenly to his feet, his mind still trying to wrap itself around that phrase "old man." Leaning heavily on his rescuer, he stumbled forward, battling the woodenness of his legs.

After an eternity of seconds, the cowboy pushed him into the cab of a pickup and closed the door.

He sagged against the seat back and closed his eyes, unable to summon another ounce of strength. Dimly, he was aware of the cowboy slipping behind the wheel and the engine starting up. It was followed by the vibrations of movement.

Through slitted eyes, he glanced in the side mirror but saw nothing to indicate they were being followed. They were out of danger now. Unbidden came the warning that it was only temporary; whoever had tried to kill him would try again.

And here is a preview of
CALDER PROMISE by Janet Dailey
A July 2004 hardcover release
from Kensington Publishing.

―――――――――――――――

"What happened, Laura? Did you forget to look where you were going?" The familiarity of Tara's affectionately chiding voice provided the right touch of normalcy.

Laura seized on it while she struggled to collect her composure. "I'm afraid I did. I was talking to Boone and—" She paused a beat to glance again at the stranger, stunned to discover how rattled she felt. It was a totally alien sensation. She couldn't remember a time when she hadn't felt in control of herself and a situation. "And I walked straight into you. I'm sorry."

"No apologies necessary," the man assured her while his gaze made a curious and vaguely puzzled study of her face. "The fault was equally mine." He cocked his head to one side, the puzzled look deepening in his expression. "I know this sounds awfully trite, but haven't we met before?"

Laura shook her head. "No. I'm certain I would have remembered if we had." She was positive of that.

"Obviously you remind me of someone else then," he said, easily shrugging off the thought. "In any case, I hope you are none the worse for the collision, Ms.—" He paused expectantly, waiting for Laura to supply her name.

The old ploy was almost a relief. "Laura Calder. And this is my aunt, Tara Calder," she said, rather than going into a lengthy explanation of their exact relationship.

"My pleasure, ma'am," he murmured to Tara, acknowledging her with the smallest of bows.

"And perhaps you already know Max Rutledge and his son, Boone." Laura belatedly included the two men.

"I know *of* them." He nodded to Max.

When he turned to the younger man, Boone extended a hand, giving him a look of hard challenge. "And you are?"

"Sebastian Dunshill," the man replied.

"Dunshill," Tara repeated with sudden and heightened interest. "Are you any relation to the earl of Crawford, by chance?"

"I do have a nodding acquaintance with him." His mouth curved in an easy smile as he switched his attention to Tara. "Do you know him?"

"Unfortunately no," Tara admitted, then drew in a breath and sent a glittering look at Laura, barely able to contain her excitement. "Although a century ago the Calder family was well acquainted with a certain Lady Crawford."

"Really. And how's that?" With freshened curiosity, Sebastian Dunshill turned to Laura for an explanation.

An awareness of him continued to tingle through her. Only now Laura was beginning to enjoy it.

"It's a long and rather involved story," Laura warned. "After all this time, it's difficult to know how much is fact, how much is myth, and how much is embellishment of either one."

"Since we have a fairly long walk ahead of us to the dining hall, why don't you start with the facts?" Sebastian suggested and deftly tucked her hand under his arm, turning her to follow the other guests.

Laura could feel Boone's anger over the way he had been supplanted, but she didn't really care. She had too much confidence in her ability to smooth any of Boone's ruffled feathers.

"The facts." She pretended to give them some thought while her sidelong glance traveled over Sebastian Dunshill's profile, noting the faint smattering of freckles on his fair skin and the hint of copper lights in his very light brown hair.

Despite the presence of freckles, there was nothing boyish about him. He was definitely a man fully grown, thirty-something she suspected, with a very definite continental air about him. He didn't exude virility the way Boone Rutledge did; his air of masculinity had a smooth and polished edge to it.

"I suppose I should begin by explaining that back in the latter part of the 1870s, my great-great-grandfather Benteen Calder established the family ranch in Montana."

"Your family owns a cattle ranch?" He glanced her way, interest and curiosity mixing in his look.

"A very large one."

"How many acres do you have? I don't mean to sound nosy, but those of us on this side of the Atlantic harbor a secret fascination with the scope and scale of your American West."

"So I've learned. But truthfully we don't usually measure in acres. We talk about sections," Laura explained. "The Triple C has more than one hundred and fifty sections within its boundary fence."

"You'll have to educate me," he said with a touch of amusement. "How large is a section?"

"One square mile, or six hundred and forty acres."

After a quick mental calculation, Sebastian gave her a suitably impressed look. "That's nearly a million acres. And I thought all the large western ranches were in Texas, not Montana."

"Not all." She smiled. "Anyway, according to early ranch records, there are numerous business transactions listed that indicate Lady Crawford was a party to them. Many of them involved government contracts for the purchase of beef. It appears that my great-great-grandfather paid her a finder's fee, I suppose you would call it—an arrangement that was clearly lucrative for both of them."

"The earl of Crawford wasn't named as a party in any of this, then," Sebastian surmised.

"No. In fact, the family stories that were passed down always said she was widowed."

"Interesting. As I recall," he began with a faint frown of concentration, "the seventh earl of Crawford was married to an American. They had no children, which meant the title passed to the son of his younger brother." He stopped abruptly and swung toward Laura, running a fast look over her face. "That's it! I know why you looked so familiar. You bear a striking resemblance to the portrait of Lady Elaine that hangs in the manor's upper hall."

"Did you hear that, Tara?" Laura turned in amazement to the older woman.

"I certainly did." With a look of triumph in her midnight dark eyes, Tara momentarily clutched at Laura's arm, an exuberant smile curving her red lips. "I knew it. I knew it all along."